misbehaving

ALSO BY ABBI GLINES

The Vincent Boys
The Vincent Brothers

The Sea Breeze Series
Breathe
Because of Low
While It Lasts
Just For Now
Sometimes it Lasts
Misbehaving

The Rosemary Beach Series
Fallen Too Far
Never Too Far
Forever Too Far
Rush Too Far
Twisted Perfection
Simple Perfection
Take a Chance

Abbi Glines

misbehaving

A Sea Breeze novel

www.simonandschuster.co.uk
www.simonandschuster.co.au

To learn more about her readers, for fun connect with her at:
Facebook: Abbi Glines (Official Author Page)
Twitter: @abbiglines
Website: www.abbiglines.com

SIMON AND SCHUSTER

First published in Great Britain in 2014 by Simon & Schuster UK Ltd
A CBS COMPANY

Published in the USA in 2014 by Simon Pulse,
an imprint of Simon & Schuster Children's Division

1 3 5 7 9 10 8 6 4 2

Simon & Schuster UK Ltd
1st Floor
222 Gray's Inn Road
London WC1X 8HB

Simon & Schuster Australia, Sydney
Simon & Schuster India, New Delhi

A CIP catalogue copy for this book is available
from the British Library.

ISBN: 978-1-47112-047-3
Ebook ISBN: 978-1-47112-046-6

Printed and bound by CPI Group (UK) Ltd, Croydon, CR0 4YY

Abbi l

To every reader out there who wanted me to write a "bad girl" heroine. This one is for you.

ACKNOWLEDGMENTS

I need to start by thanking my agent, Jane Dystel, who is beyond brilliant. The moment I signed with her was one of the smartest things I've ever done. Thank you, Jane, for helping me navigate through the waters of the publishing world. You are truly a badass.

My amazing editor, Bethany Buck. She makes my stories better with her insight and always seems as excited about the Sea Breeze stories as I am. That makes them so much easier to create. Anna McKean, Paul Crichton, Mara Anastas, Carolyn Swerdloff, and the rest of the Simon Pulse team for all your hard work in getting my books out there.

The friends that listen to me and understand me the way no one else in my life can: Colleen Hoover, Jamie McGuire, and

Tammara Webber. You three have listened to me and supported me more than anyone I know. Thanks for everything.

Natasha Tomic for always reading my books the moment I type "the end," even when it requires she stay up all night to do it. She always knows the scenes that need that extra something to make them a quality "peanut-butter sandwich scene."

Autumn Hull for always listening to me rant and worry. And she still beta reads my books for me. I can't figure out how she puts up with my moodiness. I'm just glad she does.

Last by certainly not least: my family. Without their support I wouldn't be here. My husband, Keith, makes sure I have my coffee and the kids are all taken care of when I need to lock myself away and meet a deadline. My three kids are so understanding, although once I walk out of that writing cave they expect my full attention and they get it. My parents, who have supported me all along. Even when I decided to write steamier stuff. My friends, who don't hate me because I can't spend time with them for weeks at a time because my writing is taking over. They are my ultimate support group and I love them dearly.

To my readers: I never expected to have so many of you. Thank you for reading my books. For loving them and telling others about them. Without you I wouldn't be here. It's that simple.

Chapter One

JESS

I should've known better. But I was an idiot. All it had ever taken from Hank was one pitiful bat of his eyelashes and a pout, and I came running. Well, not anymore. I'd forgiven him for becoming somcone's baby daddy. But there was only so much a girl could forgive.

Hank Granger had just screwed me over for the last time. I wasn't one to be a doormat. My momma had taught me better than that. It was time I stopped letting our history play on my emotions. He was nothing close to being a real man. The boy I'd grown up loving had become a low-down good-for-nothing. He'd never settle down, and I was done letting him trample all over my heart.

He thought parking his pimped-out truck behind the bar

was smart. The boy should know better than to think I wouldn't know where to look. Jackass. I'd found him, all right. We were supposed to have gone out tonight. He had promised me dinner. A real date. But then he'd called two hours ago and canceled, saying he wasn't feeling good. Being the dutiful girlfriend, I'd decided to make him some soup and take it over to him. Big surprise that he wasn't there. Not really. I think deep down I'd known he was lying.

I stepped out of the trees I'd walked through for over a mile, and into the darkness of the back of the local bar, Live Bay. I didn't want my truck to be seen here tonight, and it would be easier to run on foot into the darkness if I needed to make a fast getaway.

I gripped the baseball bat I'd borrowed from my cousin Rock two weeks ago when I'd had to go pick Momma up from work because her car wouldn't start. Three in the morning outside a strip club wasn't exactly safe. Momma kept a gun, but I didn't have a clue how to use it. When I had asked her to teach me, she'd laughed and said that I'd end up shooting Hank's balls off one night in a fit of rage and refused. Not because she cared for Hank, but because she didn't want me in jail.

Feeling the weight of the bat in my hands, I smiled. This bad boy would do some serious damage. Then there was the knife in my pocket. The paint job was also going to hell, and if I had time, all four tires were going down.

As I walked around the truck that Hank had pampered and treated like a damn baby for the past four years, a sense of power ran through me. He'd hurt me over and over again. This time *I* was going to hurt him. Me. Not Rock. Me.

I checked the dark area around me and made sure no one was out here. The busting of the glass was going to make some noise. I wasn't sure how much I could get away with before someone caught me. Hopefully, the local band, Jackdown, would keep everyone inside entertained enough that no one would leave anytime soon.

Biting back the roar of victory I could feel pumping through my veins, I held the bat back as I shifted my feet and focused on his driver's side door window. It was going to be the first to go. With all the anger and pain that had consumed me since the first moment I'd found out the boy I'd loved since I was ten years old had been sleeping around on me, I swung the bat. The ski mask I was wearing protected my face. The laughter bubbling up in my chest burst free, and I continued to shatter every window on his pretty little truck.

High on revenge, I reached into my pocket and pulled out my knife and flipped it open. I decided to write a few choice words in the paint job with my sharp blade, then bent down to jam it into the front tire.

"Hey!" a deep voice called out, and I froze. It wasn't Hank, but it was someone.

I picked my bat back up and pulled the knife out of the tire before breaking into a sprint back into the woods. He'd never catch me, but I still needed to get this stupid mask off so I could see. Running into a tree and knocking myself out wasn't exactly a great getaway plan.

The sound of feet hitting the pavement let me know I was being chased. Well, shit. Not what I needed. I was having so much fun. Hank deserved that. He did. He was a rat bastard. I did not want to go to jail over this. Plus my momma would be pissed.

"Hey!" the deep voice called out again. What did he expect me to do? Stop and let him catch me? Not likely.

Other voices came from the distance. Great. He was drawing a crowd. I turned off the path I'd followed earlier and headed deeper into the woods. I wouldn't have this cover for long. I'd be coming out onto a back road in a few more feet. I couldn't get my truck because it was outside my momma's house. I needed everyone to think that was where I was. I'd have to stay on foot and beat anyone there. Dang it.

I couldn't hear the sound of anyone else's feet hitting the ground, so either I'd lost them or they were talented in the art of stealth. Breaking out of the wooded area, I stopped on the side of the road. It was deserted.

Glancing back, I saw no one. Hank would know who to come looking for, but he would have no proof. Smiling, I took a deep breath. That would be the end of us. Finally. After what I'd done, Hank would never forgive me, so I wouldn't be tempted to go running back to him. He'd hate me now as much as I hated him.

"JESS!" Hank's familiar voice roared. Spinning around, I couldn't see him, but I could hear him running through the woods behind me. Shit. Shit. Shit. He'd come after me. How'd he find out so fast? Panicking, I looked around to see where I could run to hide from him. There was nothing but miles and miles of road. No houses, nothing.

Headlights came around the corner, and I did the only thing I could think of: I ran out into the middle of the road and started waving my arms in the air, still holding on to Rock's bat.

The car started slowing down and cut the bright lights. Thank God.

Wait . . . was that a Porsche? What the hell?

JASON

All I could see was a girl dressed in tight black clothing with lots of long blond hair, and she was standing in the middle of the road . . . holding a baseball bat. Only in Alabama did stuff like this happen. Stopping before I hit her, I watched as she ran over to the passenger-side door and knocked. The wild, panicked look in her eyes might have been disturbing if they weren't a bright, clear blue with thick black lashes. I pressed the unlock button, and she jerked the door open and climbed inside.

"Go! Go! Go!" she demanded. She didn't even look my way. Her eyes were focused on something outside. I turned my attention to the side of the road, where she was watching with such intensity. There was nothing. . . . Then a guy came bursting out of the woods with an angry snarl on his face and I understood. No wonder she was terrified. The guy was huge and looked ready to murder someone.

I shifted gears and took off before he got any closer.

"Ohmygod, thank you. That was so close." She let out a sigh of relief and leaned her head on the headrest.

"Should I take you to the police station?" I asked, glancing over at her. Had he attacked her before she'd gotten free?

"Definitely not. They'll probably be looking for me in about ten minutes. I need you to take me home. Momma will cover for me, but I gotta get there quick."

They'd be looking for her? Her mom would cover for her? What?

"It ain't like he's got any proof. The only thing I dropped was the ski mask, and it was a cheapo I bought at the Goodwill a couple of Halloweens ago. Not something he can trace back to me."

I slowed the Porsche down as her words started sinking in. I hadn't just saved a girl from being attacked. If I understood this babbling correctly, I had just become the getaway car driver.

"Why're you slowing down? I need to get to my momma,

like, now. She's just two miles from here. You go up to County Road Thirty-Four and turn right, and then you take it about three-fourths of a mile to Orange Street and take a left. It's the third house on the right."

Shaking my head, I pulled over to the side of the road. "I'm not going any farther until you tell me exactly what it is I'm helping you escape from." I glanced down at her baseball bat tucked between her legs, then up at her face. Even in the darkness I could tell she was one of those ridiculously gorgeous southern blondes. It was like the South had some special ingredient to raise them like that down here.

She let out a frustrated sigh and blinked rapidly, causing tears to fill her eyes. She was good. Real good. Those pretty tears were almost believable.

"It's a really long story. By the time I explain everything, we'll have been caught and I'll be spending the night in jail. Please, please, please just take me to my house. We're so close," she pleaded. Yeah, she was a major looker. Too bad she was also bad news.

"Tell me one thing: Why do you have a baseball bat?" I needed something. If she'd knocked someone unconscious back there, then I couldn't help her get away. They could be injured or dead.

She ran her hand through her hair and grumbled. "Okay, okay, fine. But understand that he deserved it."

Shit. She had knocked someone out.

"I smashed all the windows in my ex-boyfriend's truck."

"You did *what?*" I couldn't have heard her correctly. That did not happen in real life. Country songs, yes. Real life, no way.

"He's a cheating bastard. He deserved it. He hurt me, so I hurt him. Now please believe me and get me out of here."

I laughed. I couldn't help it. This was the funniest damn thing I'd ever heard.

"Why're you laughing?" she asked.

I shook my head and pulled back onto the road. "Because that's not what I was expecting to hear."

"What did you expect me to say? I'm carrying a bat."

Glancing over at her. I grinned. "I thought you'd taken someone out with the bat."

Her eyes went wide, and then she laughed. "I wouldn't have knocked someone out with a bat! That's crazy."

I wanted to point out that smashing your ex-boyfriend's truck windows and then running through the woods in escape at night was crazy. But I didn't. I was pretty sure she wouldn't agree.

"Right here, turn right." She pointed up ahead of us. I didn't bother putting on my blinker since no one was around us. "So, what's your name? You look familiar for some reason, but no one I know around here drives a Porsche."

Did I tell her who I was? I liked the privacy that Sea Breeze,

Alabama, afforded me. I had a lot to think about over the next month, and making friends with the locals wasn't on my agenda. Even if she was smoking hot.

"I'm not from around here. Just visiting," I explained. That was the truth. I was here staying at my brother's beach house while deciding on my next move.

"But I've seen you before. I know I have," she said, tilting her head and studying me.

She'd figure it out soon enough. My brother was Jax Stone. He had become a teen rock star, but now that he was twenty-two he was a rock god. We looked similar. And the media loved to follow me around when they couldn't get to Jax. While I loved my brother, I hated getting the attention. Everyone saw me as an extension of Jax. No one, not even my parents, cared about who I was as a person. They all wanted me to be who they expected.

"This is a Porsche, isn't it? I've never seen one in real life."

It was also one of my brother's toys. I didn't have a car here, so I just used the five he had in his garage. The house in Sea Breeze was where our parents used to make us spend our summers while Jax was juggling fame at a young age. But Jax was no longer a teenager and the house was his now. He'd turned twenty-two last month. And I'd turned twenty the month before that.

"Yes, it is a Porsche," I replied.

"Turn here." She pointed again toward the road ahead of

us. I took the left and then came to the third house on the left. "This is it. Thank *God* no one is here yet. I gotta go. You need to get out of here so no one comes questioning you. But thank you so much."

She opened the door and then glanced back at me one last time. "I'm Jess, by the way, and tonight you saved my ass." She winked and closed the door before running off toward her front door. Her ass in those tight black jeans was worth saving. It was the nicest ass I'd ever seen.

I shifted the car into reverse and pulled back out onto the road. It was time I headed back to the private island where my brother's house was. This night hadn't turned out quite like I'd planned, but it'd been pretty damn entertaining.

The sound of something sliding across the seat and hitting the door startled me, and I glanced over to see the baseball bat. She'd forgotten it. I looked back at her house and smiled to myself. I'd be sure she got it back. Not tonight, but soon.

Chapter Two

JESS

I let the screen door slam behind me before I thought about it, then turned to lock it. Just in case Hank decided to take the law into his own hands. Not that I thought he was that stupid. He knew better than to screw with my momma.

"That you, Jess?" Momma called from the kitchen.

I might as well go tell her what I'd done. If the cops showed up, she needed to have her game face on. "Yeah, it's me, and we might have some trouble," I replied, walking through the small living room and into the kitchen. The five-room house I'd grown up in was cinderblock and nothing special, but the rent was affordable. No man had to help us get the bills paid. Momma had always taken care of things.

"What the hell have you done now?" Momma asked as I

stepped into the kitchen. She was standing at the coffeepot with a cigarette between her red lips. Her favorite hot-pink satin robe was all she had on. She must have been getting ready for work and decided to stop and make some coffee.

I pulled out one of our vinyl-covered kitchen chairs and sat down. "I beat the shit out of Hank's truck."

Momma pulled the cigarette from her lips. "You did what?" she asked.

"He was at Live Bay with that whore he's messing around with. He lied to me again. I'm done with him, and I wanted to make him hurt."

Momma got rid of her ashes in the sink and, shaking her head, reached for a coffee cup. Her long blond hair was still pretty, but the face that had once been strikingly beautiful now showed hard lines from life. I was sure her smoking didn't help things either. "Shit, girl. I need to go to work in an hour. What if the cops show up?"

I hadn't thought of that. No alibi. I shrugged. "If they're coming, maybe they'll come before you leave."

Momma took her coffee black and walked over to sit down across from me. "Did you at least get it good? If we have to deal with the poe poe, then you better have made it worth it. I ain't in the mood for those bored shits tonight."

I smiled, thinking about how good it had felt to see his pretty truck's windows shatter. "Yeah, I think I got it good."

Momma nodded and put her cigarette out, then took a sip of her coffee. "He's a stupid, sorry-ass fucker who you need to stay away from. You've got a life ahead of you, and I'll be damned if you end up like me. Hank's already knocked up one girl he ain't gonna marry. I sure don't want you to be his next victim. This life ain't easy, and you know it. You got the looks to buy you a life outta this. I intend for you to do it," Momma said, leaning back in her chair and crossing her long legs.

This was a conversation we had been having since I was old enough to understand things. Which was since I was about nine. When your momma is a stripper in town, you learn things a lot sooner than other kids. There is no time for innocence.

"I'm done with Hank for good this time. I promise," I assured her.

Momma didn't look like she believed me. I couldn't blame her. This thing with Hank had been going on for years. I really needed to let him go. He was a one-way ticket to the life I'd watched my mother live. As much as I respected her for not leaning on a man to take care of us, I didn't want that life. I knew how much she hated it.

"My escape car was a Porsche," I told her with a grin. I still couldn't get over that car . . . and the guy in it. Way out of my league. Way, way out of my league. He was so wealthy he reeked of it. He also looked at me like I was a strange bird he didn't know what to do with. I had probably scared the guy to death.

He wasn't from here. He was just visiting and would have gone back to whatever mansion he hailed from.

"Don't see many Porsches around here," Momma replied with a skeptical look on her face.

"He wasn't a local. I imagine he's vacationing on the island. He looked like one of those."

Momma nodded. She knew all about those kind. I had been warned off two kinds of boys my whole life: the ones like Hank, who were "nothing but sorry shits," and then guys from the island, who Momma said were "only after you for the sex and then they split."

"Don't worry about him, though. I'm pretty sure he thinks I'm a crazy person," I assured her.

Momma raised her eyebrows and leaned on the table to look at me. "You really think that? I didn't raise you to be so damn naive. He's a man, baby. That's all that matters. One look at you, and he'll be back. You just be careful."

I had tried to land more than one wealthy local in Sea Breeze, but that had never happened. Marcus Hardy had been in my sights from the time I was a little girl. He was my cousin Rock's friend, but he was different than us. He lived in a big pretty house on the beach. But Marcus never saw me as anything but a fun time. When he laid eyes on Willow, no one else stood a chance. Now he was married with a kid and completely off-limits.

"I should've pushed you to go off to college. You could have met someone there and gotten out of this place." She said it like Sea Breeze was a bad place. I didn't see it the same way she did. I loved the coastal town I had grown up in.

"I didn't want to leave," I reminded her. I had chosen to go to the local community college instead. I didn't want to leave this town or my momma. We had been a team all my life.

Momma sighed and pushed her chair back and stood up. "I know, sugar. I let you stay because I like having you here. Still don't make it right. Finding a man to get you out of this life is gonna be hard, and I'll be damned if you fall into the life I've lived."

I was starting to argue when someone banged on the door. Momma looked toward the front door, fluffed her hair, and pulled the neckline of her silk robe low enough to show her very impressive cleavage. "Go on and get in the shower. I got this, baby girl. Don't worry 'bout a thing," she said, slipping into a pair of red heels that only made her long legs longer. Smiling, I hurried to the bathroom and turned on the shower but kept my ear to the door.

"Well, hello, Officer Ben. You know I'm not the kind of girl who takes house calls," she said in a low, sultry voice I had heard her use a million times.

"Good evening, Starla. I hate to bother you before you, uh . . . ,"
He cleared his throat and I rolled my eyes. I already knew good old

15

Officer Ben was a regular at Jugs, the strip club just on the outskirts of Sea Breeze. ". . . go to work. But I got a call about Jess, and I need to check into that. She here?"

"Not sure who called you, Ben," Momma said, letting his name roll off her tongue as if she were about to strip just for him, "but my baby girl has been here with me all evening. She's getting a shower now after helping me clean today. You can even check her truck hood—it's cold. Hasn't driven it all day long." Momma paused, and I heard her heels click on the wooden floor as she stepped toward him. "And as much as I like the idea of you walking in on my showers, I don't feel the same about you interrupting my little girl's shower," she said in a suggestive tone.

My momma was good at this.

"Uh, um, yes, I can, uh, understand that. Sorry I bothered you, Starla. Just had to check it out. There was only one person who saw her, and I'll be sure to check out her truck before I leave, to let them know her alibi is airtight." He stammered all over himself, and I covered my mouth to keep from laughing. He probably had a really good view of Momma's boobs at the moment. She used them to get her way with the opposite sex, and it always worked.

He needed to see me so that he could verify I was at home. I jerked my shirt off, grabbed a towel, and wrapped it around me before opening the bathroom door a crack. Ben's eyes moved from their lustful gaze on my momma to me as I stuck my head out.

"Everything okay out there, Momma? I heard voices," I called out, sounding as innocent as I could.

"Yeah, baby girl. It's just fine. Just visiting with Officer Ben," she replied flashing me a smile as she turned to look at me.

I closed the bathroom door just as Officer Ben apologized for bothering Momma again.

"That's all right, Officer. You're just doing your job and keeping our little town safe. Makes me sleep easier at night knowing we have brave, dedicated men like you taking care of us. That Martha sure is a lucky woman to have such a hardworking man like you coming home to her at night."

I had to roll my eyes. The fact that men believed this stuff never ceased to amaze me. Ben had a beer gut and a balding head. Nothing about him was brave, and since I knew how much of his hard-earned money he spent at Jugs several nights a week, seeing my momma and the other women there dancing in nothing but tiny thongs, I didn't believe Martha was lucky at all. Neither did my momma.

"Yeah, well . . ." He paused, swallowing so hard I could hear it from in here. "I'm glad it helps you rest easy. I do what I can. You, uh, gonna be at work tonight?"

"I'm getting all prettied up right now. You coming to see

me? I hope you do. I might just have a special lap dance just for you," Momma replied.

That made me want to gag. The idea that she could do that without throwing up in their faces blew my mind. She said she had learned a long time ago to turn off that switch in her head and remember that the better she performed, the more money she made.

"I'll be there," Officer Ben said. "Missed you last week due to an incident down at the station. Been thinking about that all week."

"Glad to know I was in that head of yours," she said sweetly.

"Always are," Ben replied, and cleared his throat when he realized he was openly flirting with my almost naked momma on the front doorstep. "I need to be going now and let them know Jess wasn't involved."

"You do that, and I'll see you later," Momma said, and her heels clicked as she stepped back from the doorway.

"Later," Ben called out, and the door closed. I heard the latch click into place, and I turned off the shower and opened the door. All the doors in this house opened to the living room.

"Thank you," I said simply.

Momma shrugged and waved her hand. "Just be glad it was Ben. He's easy to work. If it had been David or Rooster, I'd have had to show them a lot more than some cleavage and leg to get them off your scent."

I nodded, and the guilt from forcing my momma to flirt with a married cop to get me out of trouble settled in my stomach. "I'm sorry," I told her.

Momma stopped before walking into her room. "Don't be. Someone needed to beat that shit's truck up. I'm glad you did it." Then she closed her bedroom door.

I stood there, and a smile tugged at my lips. I had never had many girlfriends in my life because no one understood me or wanted to get close to me. But my momma, she really was my best friend.

JASON

Two days later, I was still thinking about the truck-bashing blonde. She was something else. Hard to forget. I had her baseball bat standing in the corner of my room, and I was trying to decide what to do with it. I figured right now she didn't need the evidence on her.

Chuckling, I shook my head. I was helping a girl get away with vandalism. That so wasn't me. But it made me smile. Guess I needed a little action in my life. I intended to give it a few more days, then go see if I could catch her at home. I needed to give her back that bat, and I wanted to see her again. It was a good excuse.

I walked down the stairs in my brother's summer house just as the front door opened and Jax and his girlfriend, Sadie, walked in. I had known they were coming down for the week-end, and I'd been expecting them.

Jax looked up at me and grinned. "Crashing your party."

"You know me, it's a wild one. Hope you can handle it," I replied.

Jax shook his head and laughed. "Yeah, is it sad that I wish there was some truth to that."

Sadie pinched Jax's arm playfully before walking over to give me a hug. "Ignore him. I think you're perfect just like you are. No need for wild parties."

My brother's girlfriend was beautiful in the head-turning kind of way. She had the kind of body and face you saw plastered on magazine covers. But Sadie was a small-town Sea Breeze girl and wanted nothing to do with the spotlight. She loved Jax and had learned to get over people splashing her face everywhere in the media, but before Jax she didn't like drawing attention to herself. Which was impossible to avoid. The girl drew attention everywhere she went.

"Thanks, Sadie. You can drop the rock-star life anytime you want and come live the simple, ordinary one with me," I told her, and winked at Jax, who was now scowling.

"Hands off, bro," he said, reaching for Sadie's arm. "Not funny."

That never ceased to entertain me. Jax had never had inse-curities. Even before he became famous, he was the most confident kid I knew. But let a guy look at Sadie, and he went all territorial. It cracked me up.

"Stop it, Jax. You're being silly," Sadie said, frowning at him and making him immediately look regretful. That was even funnier.

"Don't be mad," he said.

Sadie looked back at me. "You up for some company? I thought we'd have a little get-together tonight. I want to see everyone, and since we're only here two days, it would be easier if we just had the gang here." She beamed up at me.

Hell, Sadie wasn't mine, but she was hard to say no to. I was pretty sure if she smiled at anyone, they'd do whatever it was she was asking. "Sure," I replied.

Jax rolled his eyes at me, like he wasn't a complete sucker when it came to her. What did he expect? I was a man. "I'll go make sure the kitchen staff is prepared for the extra guests," Jax told Sadie as he pressed a kiss to her cheek and started toward the kitchen.

"I already called and talked to Ms. Mary. She's prepared," Sadie called after him. Ms. Mary ran the staff and the kitchen here. Once, Sadie had worked for Ms. Mary, so she knew her well. That was how Jax had met Sadie. She served him dinner one night, and I'm pretty sure he was sunk then. Even though he fought it hard.

Jax stopped and turned around to give her the smile that

magazines everywhere labeled as lethally sexy. "Then why don't you help me to my room to unpack?"

I saw Sadie's cheeks turn red, and she pressed her lips together to keep from smiling. "Okay, if you need help."

Jax walked back over to her. "Lots of help. You have no idea how much help I need."

"Either you two go to your room, or I'm going to throw ice water on you both," I told them.

Sadie ducked her head, and Jax just grinned at me. "See you later," he said as he held Sadie's hand and led her up the stairs.

I decided going out to the beach and out of this house for a while was the best idea. Not sure how much "unpacking" those two planned on doing.

Five hours later, voices were getting louder downstairs as I stood in my bedroom, looking out over the front yard. I knew I needed to go downstairs. Jax would want me there. But those weren't my friends. It wasn't that I didn't like them—I did. I just didn't really know them. Then there was the matter of Preston Drake.

The dude was not a fan of mine. I had tried my hardest to get Amanda Hardy's attention, only to lose her to Preston in the end. It's hard to compete with bad boys with blond surfer hair. It wasn't like I was in love with Amanda. Love wasn't something I was looking for. Ever. She was just pretty and sweet. I liked that. It was easy with her.

A knock on my door brought me out of my thoughts, and I turned to see my brother standing there with his hands in the front pockets of his jeans. "You planning on hiding up here all night?"

I had considered it. I wasn't great with people I didn't know. I was on the quieter side. Jax was the personality in the family. "I was coming down in a minute."

Jax cocked an eyebrow. "You look like you'd rather be anywhere else."

I shrugged. "Not crazy about hanging out with people I don't know that well. But I'm going to do it for Sadie."

Jax walked into the room. "If you're worried about Preston, don't be. He's really an easygoing guy."

I chuckled. He hadn't seen the side of Preston I had. "Trust me, he isn't very easygoing when it comes to Amanda."

"Maybe not. But he's got her. They've been together long enough now that he feels secure. You were dating the woman he was in love with. I can understand his moment of insanity."

Jax would. He had dealt with the same thing with Marcus Hardy. They were friends now. Because Marcus was married and had a kid, he no longer posed a threat to Jax. Amanda and Marcus are brother and sister, and Marcus worked at the house the same summer Sadie did.

"I'm coming down there," I told him. "I swear. Besides, I'm hungry."

"Good, because I suspect Sadie will be up here in the next five minutes if you don't get down there. She's worried about you feeling left out."

I reminded myself that I was doing this for Sadie. "Let's go," I told him.

I followed Jax to the stairs and took in the crowd gathering in the foyer as Sadie opened the door again to let in more of her friends.

When I had been with Amanda at Marcus and Willow's wedding, I had met several of them. They all seemed really nice, but Preston was one of theirs. I wasn't sure just how well they would accept me. I left Sea Breeze on good terms with everyone after the wedding. It was easy to see who it was Amanda wanted. I didn't even try to win her over. The girl's heart was obviously owned by Preston.

Marcus Hardy walked in, holding a baby in a red-and-white blanket that looked like it had an elephant on it. Sadie squealed in delight and hugged Marcus's wife, Willow, and then reached out to take the baby from Marcus. Two years ago that scene wasn't something any of them would have imagined. Marcus had been determined to get Sadie's attention, but he couldn't compete with Jax. But then, no one ever could compete with my brother. I never dared to.

"I get him after Sadie," Amanda's voice called out just as I saw her walking into the room.

"You get him all the time," Sadie told her, smiling down at the baby.

"He loves his aunt Manda," Amanda cooed over the baby. I hadn't seen Amanda since Marcus and Willow's wedding. Her long blond hair was hanging loose down her back, and she was wearing a skirt that showed off her tanned legs. Preston walked up behind her and placed his hand possessively on her hip, and I froze. This might be a bad idea.

"I swear to you he's over it," Jax whispered beside me.

I nodded and started down the stairs toward the group. It wasn't that I was scared of Preston—I just didn't want to spend my night feeling like the unwanted guest. I was fine with not showing up to this thing.

"Cage and Eva are coming. They're still getting used to life with a baby," Willow told Sadie.

"I can't wait to see Bliss," Sadie said with a happy sigh.

Another baby? Damn, this group was multiplying like rabbits.

"She's gorgeous," Willow said. "I'm not kidding you. Like, stop-in-your-tracks gorgeous. Her little cheeks are so chubby, and her eyes are Cage's. Eva can't take her anywhere without being stopped by a million people to ooh and aah over her." She smiled happily.

We reached the bottom step, and Sadie noticed us. She

beamed brightly. I didn't make eye contact with Amanda or even look in Preston's direction. Instead I walked over to shake Marcus's hand and congratulate him on the kid.

"Good to see you," Marcus said, grinning at me.

"You too. Looks like you added another member to the family," I replied. "Congrats."

"Thanks. He's keeping me up at night, but I'm okay with it. It's a good time to talk football. Teaching him early."

I laughed and turned to Sadie, who was holding the little guy out for me to see him. "Jason, meet Eli Hardy," she said in a soft voice reserved for babies.

"Nice to meet you, Eli," I replied. The kid smiled and stuck his hand in his mouth. The little fluff of hair on his head was as red as his mother's, but the kid reminded me of Marcus. Maybe it was his eyes.

"I'm hungry. We gonna stand around and look at babies all night, or is there food here?" a new voice said, drawing my attention from the baby. I recognized him, but I couldn't remember his name. He had his dreadlocks pulled back in a ponytail. Tattoos decorated most of his arms, and he even had one coming up his neck. I didn't stare long enough to figure out what it was. His lip was pierced, and when he talked you could see the metal in his mouth.

"We have plenty of food, Dewayne," Sadie replied, smiling at him like he wasn't a scary-ass dude.

"Good," he said, walking over and stopping to kiss Eli's head, which was not what I was expecting him to do. "Damn, that kid's cute. But then, he looks like his momma."

Marcus just chuckled.

Dewayne looked over at me and stopped. His gaze shifted from me to where I knew Amanda and Preston stood behind me. A slow grin stretched across his face. "Hell yeah. This should be a shit ton of fun. Preston, you gonna play nice with Jason?"

Sadie's eyes went wide, and everyone went quiet. I decided now was a good time to turn and address them and get this over with.

Amanda was glaring at Dewayne like she was about to take a swing at him, but Preston had an amused grin on his face. "I always play nice," Preston said with a lazy drawl that went well with his surfer-boy appearance. "I got no problem with Jason. At least not anymore." He dropped his arm from around Amanda's waist, stepped forward, and held out his hand to me. "No hard feelings," he said.

The guy was hard to dislike. I shook his hand. "Not at all," I replied.

"Good," he said, stepping back to put his hand back on Amanda. "See, dickhead? We're all good," Preston said to Dewayne.

Dewayne just chuckled and shook his head. "Sure you are."

"Okay, Dewayne, don't go getting everyone all stirred up.

We're at the Stones' house," Marcus said, trying to sound diplomatic.

Dewayne shrugged and glanced back at Marcus. "Just having some fun."

The doorway was filled again, this time with the massive brick wall that was Rock. A little girl with a head full of curls ran around his legs, squealing Preston's name. I turned to see Preston reach down and grab her just as she flung herself into his arms. Rock and his wife, Trisha, had adopted Preston's little sister and brothers when their mother passed away, making this group of friends even tighter.

"I missed you," the little girl said, planting a loud, smacking kiss on Preston's cheek.

"I missed you, too," he said.

"Sorry we're late," Rock said. "Trisha is bringing the boys after football practice. I had to go get Daisy. Jess was watching her at the house while we were at the boys' practice."

My head snapped around at the name Jess. The name of the girl I'd rescued the other night.

"You're letting Jess watch Daisy?" Willow asked, sounding surprised.

Rock looked over at her and frowned. "She's my cousin. I know you aren't a fan of Jess's, but she's good with Daisy."

"She's really not so bad, Low," Amanda piped up. "I know you had a bad experience with her, but Jess is loyal to a fault and

28

she loves those kids." That made me even more curious. If this was the same Jess who beat the hell out of her boyfriend's truck, then I could understand Low's concern. She didn't seem like the babysitter type.

"She seems so flighty," Willow said, frowning.

Dewayne walked back into the room with a handful of chips. "You're just worried because Jess had her sexy ass set on Marcus. Don't mean she's a bad girl. Just a little misguided at times."

Amanda shot an annoyed glare Dewayne's way. "Don't bring that up. It's old news."

"Don't, dude." Marcus's voice sounded pleading.

"Jess does some things that are not well thought out, and she's impulsive, but she's still good with Daisy," Rock said defensively.

"She bashed in Hank's truck the other night," Marcus pointed out.

This group had just won my complete and total attention. I couldn't keep from grinning. I had to rub my hand over my mouth so no one noticed. They were talking about the hot blonde I'd helped escape.

"She did what?" Sadie asked in shocked horror.

Willow sighed and shook her head. "Her on-again, off-again boyfriend was cheating on her, and she took a bat or something and shattered his truck's windows and apparently got a few dents in the side before she took off running."

Preston let out an amused laugh. "Sorry. But it's funny as hell. Every time I hear it, I can't stop myself from laughing."

Rock shook his head. "Crazy girl. Hank had it coming, but I still can't believe she did it. Although, she's claiming she didn't, and the only proof is Hank saying he saw her running and chased her down. Then he says she jumped into a Porsche and took off. That right there is a lie. Ain't no one in town with a Porsche. Then, when the cops got to her house, her momma said Jess had been with her all day and was in the shower. Cop said the hood of her truck was cool, so he couldn't argue with Starla."

I felt Jax's eyes on me, but I didn't turn around. I could almost hear his thoughts. He knew who owned a Porsche in Sea Breeze—he did.

"Knowing Hank, he was drunk or high. But it sure sounds like something Jess would do. No one else had motive. And we all know Starla probably entertains more than one of the cops in Sea Breeze at Jugs," Preston said, still amused and grinning.

Jugs? What's Jugs? I didn't ask. Instead I stayed quiet. Luckily, Jax never mentioned the Porsche that he left parked in the garage here.

Chapter Three

JESS

I had lain low for a week. I was tired of staying at home. Keeping Rock's little girl, Daisy May, earlier this week had been a fun distraction, but I needed some action. Thinking about Hank and all that wasted time just drove me crazy. It was almost as if I was begging to end up like my momma. Not that I didn't love my momma—I just knew her life was hard.

Besides, as much as I liked dressing to draw a guy's attention, I did not ever want to think I had to strip for men to make ends meet. My momma seemed to take it in stride. I just didn't think I ever could. I liked my body just fine. I just preferred to choose who I took my clothes off for. Balding, fat policemen were not gonna get to pay to see me naked. So help me God.

I slid my feet into my red cowboy boots and tugged my

short black leather skirt down until it covered my butt cheeks. Apparently, leather was back in this season. I loved leather, so that made me happy. I reached for one of my Jackdown T-shirts. I was going to go listen to Krit and his band tonight at Live Bay. Krit loved it when I wore one of the band's shirts.

Krit had also loved it when I took it off for him. But those days were over. His sister, Trisha, married my cousin. We were family now, even if he preferred to say that didn't count. Besides, Krit was not gonna be the guy to save me from my momma's life. He was just like me: born into a low-class situation and trying to find a way out. We also enjoyed trouble just a little too much. The two of us together had proved to be dangerous.

Momma had already left for work tonight, so I went to her room to spray a little of her Chanel on my cleavage. She used it sparingly, and I wasn't supposed to touch it.

When I was sure I was ready, I grabbed my truck keys and opened the front door. In my driveway sat a completely loaded black Hummer with dark-tinted windows. Who the hell was that? That wasn't your average Hummer. It was the kind that was special-ordered. I closed the door behind me and walked down the two cinder block steps.

The driver's door opened, and out stepped Mr. Porsche. In his hand was a baseball bat. Rock's baseball bat. Oh damn, I'd forgotten it. Smiling in relief because Rock would've killed me had I lost it, I walked over to meet him halfway.

"You forgot something," he said by way of greeting.

"Thank you," I replied, taking it from him and sticking it behind my back in case someone drove by and caught me with a baseball bat. That was the last thing I needed after this week.

"Can I trust you with it? Or should I be available for any escape plans?"

Mr. Porsche had a dimple in his right cheek. I hadn't noticed it before. "I think I'm hanging up my bat. Too much trouble," I told him.

"Good to hear. Stories of your truck bashing made it all around town this week," he said with an amused look. "Since the talk is that your escape vehicle was a Porsche, and no one believes Hank because they're saying no one has a Porsche around here, I decided I'd better drive something else if I was coming over here."

How did he know that? Sea Breeze was a small town, but it wasn't that small. Locals didn't share that kind of stuff with the summer people. He had to know someone with an in. "Who are you?" I asked.

"My name's Jason," he replied.

Jason. I didn't know any Jasons. Other than Jason Condoy, who overdosed last year. I tilted my head and studied him a minute. "So, Jason, who do you know in Sea Breeze? I could have sworn you were right off the island. The Porsche and all gave that away."

His grin grew and his dimple got deeper. I liked that dimple a lot. "My secret," he said simply.

I glanced down at his designer clothing and reminded myself that guys like him were so out of my league. I was looking for a local with some potential. That was as good as I was going to get. This guy looked like he would fit in perfectly in Beverly Hills. "Yeah, well, thanks for this and for the other night. I appreciate it," I said, deciding that prolonging this conversation was pointless.

"You headed somewhere?" he asked.

"Yeah, I'm going out. A friend of mine is in a band," I explained.

Jason didn't make a move to leave. What was he doing?

"They're playing at a bar," I continued.

"You meeting someone there?"

Um . . . what? Was he actually about to ask to go too? No. I had to be reading this wrong. "Uh, friends will be there, I'm sure."

"But no guy? Or is the friend in the band the guy?"

He was asking me if I had a date. Wow. For the first time in my life I felt at a loss for words. I just stood there, awkwardly staring at him.

"It's okay. Really. Don't look so panicked. I'll see you around," he said, then turned and started back toward his Hummer.

He was leaving. I had to say something. "No, wait. I'm not . . . There isn't a guy. I'm just going to listen to the band and see some friends. If you want to come . . ." I trailed off, still having a hard time believing he wanted to be seen with me.

He stopped and glanced back at me. "You sure?"

Yes! I managed to nod and not act like an idiot.

His grin was back. "I'll drive."

Taking a steadying breath, I walked toward him and realized I still had the baseball bat in my hand. "Oh." I stopped and held it up. "I need to put this away."

"You can put it in the Hummer until we get back," he said, walking over to open my door for me.

This was a first. No one had ever opened a car door for me. Ever.

"Thank you," I said, looking up at him and deciding that I could get used to this.

"For what?" he asked with a confused look on his face.

"For opening my door," I replied.

His eyes went wide and he stared at me a second, then leaned forward. "Jess, if guys don't open doors for you, then they aren't worth your time. No need to thank me." Then he leaned back and held out his hand to help me up into the Hummer.

I was pretty sure I understood the word "swoon" finally. I slipped my hand into his, and he closed his larger one around mine and then helped me up. It was higher than my truck, but my legs were as long as my momma's. Still, I liked having him help me.

When I sat down, I noticed his eyes on my legs before he lifted his gaze to meet mine. "Sorry," he said with a slight blush on his face. Then he closed the door and I had a moment to compose myself.

Had I ever seen a guy blush? Other than my high school history teacher who I'd had a crush on and had made sure to let him know it. I felt very underdressed. My sexy little outfit now seemed . . . kind of cheap. Jason opened the driver's door and climbed in. His biceps flexed, capturing my complete attention. I wondered what his abs looked like.

"Where are we going?" he asked as he cranked the engine.

"It's called Live Bay," I told him. "Ever heard of it?"

Jason smirked. "Of course."

JASON

This was probably a bad idea. I wasn't ready to tell Jess who I was. From the stories I had heard about Jess, I knew she was a trouble-maker. I had intended to return the bat and leave. Although the things the group had said about her were amusing as hell, I got the impression that once she knew my brother was Jax Stone, that would be the only thing she'd care about. I'd be on her radar but for all the wrong reasons. And I was only here for a month to get some alone time before school started back up.

Seeing her walk out of the house in that tiny skirt that hardly covered her ass and that tight T-shirt had made me forget exactly why I hadn't been planning to pursue getting to know her better. And those legs had made me weak. Rock had acted so protective of her when everyone was talking about Jess, and I could see the concern in his eyes when he explained her actions. He knew a Jess none of them had been given a chance to get to know.

I wanted to know that Jess. Because the sexy, half-dressed one who liked to use her body to make men buckle at the knees was pretty damn hot. I needed more, though. I was curious. That was it.

"You've been to Live Bay before?" she asked.

I glanced over at her. "Yeah, once," I admitted.

"Surprising. Normally, the island people don't make it over to our hangouts."

The way she said "island people" didn't sound appealing. "You got something against the island?" I asked, amused.

She shrugged. "Not really. Just a fact."

She was right. Jax, however, had blown that out of the water. He had not only come off the island, he had chased a girl down and made her his. "You ever been on the island?" I asked. I turned into Live Bay, then glanced over at her.

She shook her head. "Nope." She cut her eyes at me, and her long lashes fanned her high cheekbones. "Guys from the island don't normally invite girls like me over for dinner."

That was a shame. Guys from the island didn't know just

how entertaining Jess was. "Their loss," I said, opening my door. I had to jog around the front of the Hummer to get to Jess before she jumped out all on her own with those boots on.

She raised her eyebrows. "You help girls out of cars too?" she asked.

Damn, what kind of guys had she been dating?

I held out my hand, and she grabbed it before stepping down. Her chest pressed against mine, and I sucked in a breath. Her tits were not only on the generous side, but they were soft.

"Thanks," she said, smiling up at me with a knowing look in her eyes. I let her have her fun. She knew I liked feeling her chest, and she was keeping it right there for me to look down and see up close and personal.

I wasn't going to look, though. She expected me to. She had already caught me checking out those legs of hers. I wasn't going to ogle her tits, too. Instead I winked at her and stepped back.

"Ready?" I asked her.

The flash of disappointment in her eyes made me wish I had taken a look. I didn't want her to think I wasn't attracted to her. She may be flirty, but she was a female and she had feelings.

"Sure," she said, forcing a smile and turning to head inside. I started to grab her arm and assure her that her body was perfect. But I didn't. I had a feeling she was used to that. I didn't want to be what she was used to. She viewed me as different, and I wanted to be. I wanted to stand out.

Why? I wasn't sure.

I took several long strides to keep up with her and get to the door before her so I could open it. She stopped and watched me as I stood back and waited for her to walk in. A small smile touched her lips, and the flirty Jess was back.

I followed her inside. The music was already loud and the bodies were packing in closer to the stage. The band wasn't playing yet, but it must have been getting close to time.

Several guys called out greetings to Jess, who waved at them in return. They all knew her. Even the bartender, who winked at her. This was not something I'd be able to deal with. Glad I was getting to witness it tonight.

I saw several male eyes shift from her to me. They were all wondering if I was with her. I could feel it. I didn't move to touch her because she wasn't mine. We had just come here together.

"Where'd you find this one, Jess?" a girl with dark brown curls and bright pink lipstick asked as she stared at me with open curiosity. Her eyes scanned my body slowly.

"He's with me, Tiff. Pour ice water on yourself and move on," Jess said, reaching back to grab my arm and tug me closer to her.

I was trying real hard not to grin.

"When you get tired of her claws, come see me. I'm sweet as a kitten," the other girl called out as Jess pulled me through the crowd.

"Friend of yours?" I asked, amused by the stiffness of Jess's shoulders.

She stopped walking and looked back at me. "Uh, no," she snapped. "You stand out, island boy. It's all over you. It's gonna draw the gold diggers."

"What, it's not my good looks?" I asked, teasing her.

She started to say something and noticed the amused look on my face, and her shoulders relaxed. "You're hot, island boy. I'll give you that. So it's the whole package. Just stick close to me because Tiff is only one of many."

I nodded and she flashed me a real smile. The kind that made her eyes dance with amusement. "Come on. My friends are right over here," she said.

I followed her through the crowd. I noticed Rock first. He was sitting at a table facing the stage. Beside him was Dewayne. No sign of Preston or Amanda. I took an easy breath. I could deal with Rock and Dewayne.

Although, I was a little nervous as to how Rock would react to this. I didn't want to piss that dude off.

My secret would be out after Rock told Jess who I was. She already saw me as a rich boy who was out slumming it. I wasn't sure her knowing that my brother was Jax Stone would change her view that much. Her not knowing had seemed important to me at first, but now I wasn't sure she'd change like most girls did once they knew. I was used to girls going from interested in me to obsessed with me the moment they found out who my brother was. Having Jax as a brother normally got me any female I wanted for all the wrong reasons.

I'd know soon enough. If Jess began acting like one of Jax's crazy fans and getting clingy, I was out of here. This would be our test. I really didn't want this night to end. I had hopes Jess wasn't a Jax Stone fan.

Chapter Four

JESS

How did he do it? One sexy, amused grin from Jason and I was completely over being ready to bitch slap Tiff. I wanted to thread my fingers through his, but I didn't want to scare him off. He seemed to be waiting on me to do something stupid. Or mess up. He didn't have to say anything—I could see it in his eyes.

"That's my cousin Rock and one of his best friends, Dewayne," I told him, not wanting him to think I only had guy friends. Even if that was true, it didn't sound good. In reality they were Rock's friends. I had flirted with most of them and pissed off all their women. Except for Rock's wife, Trisha. She loved me. And then, of course, Amanda. She had never judged me or looked down on me. At school she had always gone out of her way to speak to me and act as if we were good friends. Then a little over a year ago she had decided to take a trip on the wild side and came to me for guidance. Our friendship had been cemented then.

Rock's eyes met mine and he smiled, and then they shifted to Jason and his smile faded. Was it because he was so obviously not from around here? I would have thought he'd be happy to see me with someone so clean-cut. Actually, anyone other than Hank should have made him smile.

Rock stood up, and I wondered if I should step in front of Jason. Before I could decide what to do, Jason stepped up beside me. "Rock, Dewayne, good to see you both again," Jason said with a familiar ease. I froze.

This didn't make sense.

"Well, I'll be damned," Dewayne said with a loud laugh.

Rock's frown turned to a scowl. "Want to explain this?" he asked Jason.

"I'm the Porsche," he replied simply.

Rock's eyebrows shot up, and he looked at me, then back at Jason. He ran a hand over his shaved head. "Why didn't I think of that?" he muttered.

I opened my mouth and was about to ask what the hell was going on, when Dewayne let out another hoot of laughter. "Motherfucker! That's priceless. And you didn't say a word about it the other night."

The other night? I turned to Jason, and he gave me an

apologetic smile. He knew who I was? He was with Rock the other night? How?

"I should be pissed that you didn't say anything, but I'm kinda glad you didn't," Rock said. "The Porsche has been the only thing in that story that makes Jess look innocent." He sat back down on his stool.

Finally I found my voice. "What are y'all talking about?" I asked, slamming my hand down on the table to get their attention.

Rock stared at me like I was crazy, then looked back at Jason. The question in his eyes only confused me more.

"She left the bat in my car. I took it back to her tonight. We ended up here. We haven't really talked about much else. We haven't even gotten as far as last names yet," Jason explained to Rock, then glanced back at me as if he was waiting on something to click with me.

"So you didn't know she was my cousin until the other night?" Rock asked.

"Didn't have a clue," Jason replied.

Rock sighed and nodded at me. "Dude, she's not gonna take this well. You should have told her before she waltzed in here with you."

I was done trying to read between the lines. "Who are you?" I demanded.

Jason opened his mouth, then closed it. How hard was it for him to tell me how he knew Rock?

"Meet Jason Stone, the only brother of Jax Stone, sweetheart," Dewayne announced loudly.

"Seriously?" Rock said, glaring over at Dewayne.

"What? He was taking for-fucking-ever to say it. The suspense was killing me," Dewayne replied.

Me, on the other hand—I just stood there and stared at Jason. How had I not seen it? He looked so much like Jax. I had seen Jason in tabloids and on television with Jax. He'd been seen with Star at the music awards. Everyone had talked about Star moving from one Stone brother to the next. Before that, I'd seen him in some tabloids with a girl from one of Jax's newest music videos. They had been pretty hot and heavy at a club. I couldn't believe this.

"I should've recognized you," I said.

Jason shrugged. "I'm not Jax."

Although his tone was void of any emotion, I could see it in his eyes. He was testing me. He hadn't told me who he was because he assumed I would treat him differently. Truth was . . . he was probably right.

My momma didn't raise an idiot. Sure, there were a lot of things in life I didn't know. Like algebra, for instance. I sucked at it. But men—I knew men. I had been watching my mother manipulate them for years. Jason wanted to be normal. Fine. I'd treat him like any other guy.

"No, you're not Jax," I replied. I glanced over at Dewayne. "Get me a beer, please."

I didn't miss the way Dewayne's pierced eyebrow lifted in surprise. I never said please. At least, not to him. That had been for Jason's sake.

"Time to dance, island boy," I said, shooting Jason a wink and walking toward the crowd, not waiting to see if he followed me. I had no doubt he would.

Suddenly a guy stepped in front of me and grabbed my hips. It was Will Fort, Hank's best friend. "Hey, sugar, coming to see me?" he asked. I had only used Will once to make Hank mad. Wasn't worth it. Will had one too many screws loose.

"Keep dreaming, Fort," I replied, taking his hands off my hips with a shove. He stumbled backward and bumped into another couple. It wasn't that I was that strong, it was that he was already that drunk.

He just cackled with laughter. The amusement on his face made me want to slap him. "I can play rough, sugar. Hank said that's how you like it," Will slurred.

I opened my mouth to tell him where I was going to kick his balls when a new hand settled on my hip. Startled, I turned to see Jason glaring at Will. This hadn't been expected, but it sure was a nice turn of events. I was surprised he even cared.

"It's probably best you step back and leave her alone. From the look in her eyes, the rough she's planning on sticking you with is gonna leave you crumpled on the ground."

Will shifted his gaze to Jason, and I could see the surprise in his eyes. It was obvious Jason wasn't one of us. I mentally cringed. I needed to get Jason away from Will before he said anything humiliating. Normally, he went for jokes about my momma.

"Let's go," I said to Jason, turning to face him and move him back into the crowd.

Jason went willingly, but his eyes never left Will as he backed away. I liked the protective streak, but the truth was, even drunk Will could have beat his ass. Guys like Jason didn't have the skills to take on a guy who had grown up being beaten by his father until he was old enough to start hitting back.

"Friend of yours?" Jason finally asked when we were deep enough into the crowd that Will was no longer in sight.

"Small town. The locals all know each other," I replied, which wasn't exactly true. But I didn't want to give Jason a history lesson on my life.

There was a good chance Will would alert Hank to my being here with a guy. Hank still hadn't paid me back for bashing his truck, and I wasn't in the mood to face him. Especially with Jason here to see it.

"This was a bad idea," I told him. "I have a better one."

Jason didn't reply, but he was curious.

"Can you swim, island boy?"

A crooked grin tugged at his lips. "Yeah."

"Good," I replied, grabbing his hand and pulling him through the bodies until we were at the door. "I know a place a lot less crowded."

JASON

When Jess had asked me if I could swim, I hadn't anticipated this. I wasn't one for breaking the law.

I watched as Jess climbed a tall iron gate, and I considered the stupidity of what I was about to do. She knew I had a direct line of sight up her skirt, and she was using that to her advantage. Glancing back at the empty beach house, I wondered if this was a common thing with locals. This obviously wasn't her first time doing something like this.

"You coming?" Jess asked as she threw a leg over the fence and grinned down at me. I wasn't one to back down from a dare, but then I'd never been dared to scale the fence of a house that wasn't mine. "Don't let me down," Jess said, and began her downward climb on the other side of the gate.

I glanced around to make sure we weren't drawing attention before I reached up and grabbed ahold of the cool metal. The trip up was much easier than Jess had made it look, but she'd been wearing a short skirt and boots. Which, to be honest, was the selling point to this whole thing. It was hard to tell those legs no.

When my feet hit the ground on the other side, I turned to

see Jess standing by the pool, dipping her toes into the water, wearing a pair of hot-pink panties that did little for coverage and a matching bra. She lifted her eyes and shot me a teasing grin. "Come and get me," she taunted before diving into the water.

Knowing those pink strips of satin that did so little to cover up her centerfold body were nice and wet was all the incentive I needed to strip. Glancing up at the house in front of us, I really hoped she was right and this place was actually a rental that was currently empty.

I dropped my jeans and shirt over the closest lounge chair before turning back to see Jess watching me. The tip of her tongue peeked out as she licked the water off her bottom lip.

Hell. This might be worth the possible trouble we could get into. I saw her shiver and decided it was probably best that I dove on in. I needed some cold water at the moment.

When my head broke the surface, Jess was treading water and grinning. "I have to admit, I didn't think you were gonna do it. I was afraid I might be swimming alone," she said, then moved closer to me.

"I almost didn't," I told her honestly.

She tilted her head and a long lock of hair fell over her shoulder. "What changed your mind?"

I glanced down at the water. The pool lights illuminated her body. I could be a gentleman and lie, but I decided Jess wasn't the kind of girl who wanted the proper response. She wanted the truth. "Those panties," I replied.

Jess's eyes went wide, and then she threw back her head and laughed. There was no teasing, coy act. It was refreshing. The girl knew she was sexy as hell and she liked it. She used it.

When she looked back at me, there was a wicked gleam in her eyes as she moved closer to me. The water was only six feet deep, so my feet were still touching the bottom with ease. I let her do this. She seemed to be sure of what she was doing, and I liked the show.

"Normally, I do this naked," she said in a whisper.

"I wouldn't have complained."

She put her hands on my shoulders to hold her up. "You want me naked? Then finish undressing me."

As tempting as that was, I wasn't taking the bait. I had done the meaningless sex thing. One-night stands with groupies weren't something new to me. I just didn't want that with Jess. Something was off in her eyes. Sure, she was throwing herself at me with an open invitation, but there was this silent pleading there, almost as if she was begging me not to.

I reached up and touched her full bottom lip. "Not tonight."

A small frown touched her lips as insecurity flashed in her eyes. She hadn't been expecting that. "Changed your mind on slumming it?" she asked as she shoved away from me and swam back out to where she couldn't touch the bottom.

I didn't like the term "slumming it" or the way it had sounded coming out of her mouth. "Don't sell yourself short, Jess," I replied. The urge to go after her and jerk her into my arms so I could kiss that hurt look off her face was hard to resist.

She let out a hard laugh. "I don't play games."

Yeah, she did. Her life was one big playbook. "I don't get a girl naked if I don't intend to fuck her."

Jess stopped treading water a second and filled her mouth up with water before spitting it out. "I can't believe you just said that."

"What? The truth?"

She shook her head. "No. I just . . . You seem so clean-cut and polite. I didn't expect you to actually get me naked, so that wasn't a big surprise, but you said 'fuck.'"

This time I laughed. She really had no idea. "Don't forget who I am. Jax may be taken, but I never have been. I enjoy his life even more than he does."

Jess was starting to say something when flashing red-and-blue lights lit up the darkness. She looked out toward the gate we had climbed to get in here, then back at me. "Time to run," she said, before swimming to the edge of the pool and climbing out.

We only had time to grab our clothes before the cop at the gate pointed his flashlight on both our faces. "Jess, I thought we went over this," the cop said in an annoyed tone before pulling out a set of keys and unlocking the gate.

I watched as Jess's body language instantly changed. She dropped her clothes to her side and sauntered over to the cop as he stepped inside. "But I got hot, Walt, and I needed to cool down."

The cop sighed and glanced over at me. "I bet you got hot. I told you that the next time you did this shit I was taking you in."

Jess moved closer to him and tugged on the front of his shirt. "But then that wouldn't be any fun. Momma's working tonight, and I'll be stuck there all wet until she comes to bail me out."

It was working. The cop had forgotten my existence as he stared down at Jess in her wet undies. "You shouldn't have been . . ."

"Swimming, I know. I'm sorry. I really am. But I got all sweaty dancing, and a nighttime swim sounded so good. I was a bad girl. You know I have weak moments."

Her hand was now lying flat on his chest as he tugged on his collar.

"Who have you got with you?" he asked, still not looking away from her.

"He's innocent. I begged him to come with me." She patted his chest. "Why don't you let him go, and then you can take me in if that's what you want."

I wasn't letting the perverted cop take her in without me. I appreciated the fact that she was trying to get me out of this, but the guy was old enough to be her dad.

"I need to do something to make you stop this," he said, his eyes looking down at her chest.

"Just let him go. If you promise to give me a blanket so I don't freeze, I'll wait in your office until Momma gets off work."

He was going to take the bait. "You go in and I'm going with you," I said, jerking my shirt on and walking over to stand behind her.

The cop's head snapped up and his gaze found mine. The lustful gleam in his eyes turned to annoyance real fast.

"This was my idea. You stay out of it," Jess said, reaching out to squeeze my arm in an attempt to shut me up.

I looked down at her. "I climbed that gate and got in that pool with you of my own free will." Her eyes went wide, but she didn't say anything else.

"You don't look familiar," the cop snarled.

I had foiled his plans and made an enemy. Grinning, I lifted my eyes to meet his angry ones. "Jason Stone. I'm staying on the island in my brother's vacation house."

Normally, I didn't use my brother's name as a way to influence people. But right now I was pretty damn sure that was the only way I was keeping Jess from getting hauled in by the creep.

Understanding lit the cop's eyes, and he looked back at Jess, who was still staring at me as if she couldn't believe I was doing this. "You telling me you're Jax Stone's brother?"

"You want ID?" I asked, mimicking his annoyed tone from earlier.

He shook his head and stepped back from Jess. "No, that won't be necessary. I'll, uh, let the two of you go, but be wise and stay clear of this one. She's full of trouble."

My blood heated and I clenched my fist at my side. The son of a bitch had been molesting her with his eyes only seconds before. Now he was warning me off her. "I'm a big boy," I replied, disgusted.

The cop turned to leave, then stopped. "Go ahead and get your clothes on. Then get out of here. I need to lock this back up."

I tried hard not to watch Jess as she wiggled her wet body back into that little leather skirt, but damn, it was hard. She pulled her shirt back on and grinned at me. The amusement in her eyes made it hard not to return her smile.

"So you do this a lot," I said, once I had my shirt back on.

Jess shrugged. "I do a lot of things."

I didn't miss the tone in her voice. She was doing it again. Throwing bait out there for me to snatch up. Normally, when a girl looked like Jess I didn't turn her down. But the emptiness in her eyes bothered me too much. I liked it when her eyes were sparkling with excitement.

"I bet you do" was all I said in reply. Then I turned and headed out the private gate. The cop was sitting in his car, watching us, and I nodded to him as I passed. Once I got to the road, I glanced back at Jess, who was walking behind me. Her gaze was fixed on my back. She was thinking. I had confused her. It was all over her face.

I held my hand out. "Come on."

She glanced at my hand, then at me, and frowned.

"Take my hand," I said.

She raised her eyebrows. "You think I can't cross a street by myself?" she asked. The edginess in her voice was hard to miss. She was ready to go off on me.

"I'm sure you can. But maybe I don't want you to. Hold my hand, please." I wasn't sure why I was pushing this. It wasn't like I thought she was going to get hit by a car. I just wanted to hold her hand. The lost, unsure look in her eyes got to me. I didn't want it there.

"Why?" she asked, stepping up beside me. Her skeptical expression told me more than I needed to know. Jess wasn't used to guys making small gestures. She was used to being used. It pissed me off more than I wanted to admit.

"Because I like having you close," I replied, wishing I hadn't said it quite like that. She didn't need to get the wrong idea. Hurting her was something I wasn't going to do, but I sure as hell wanted to teach her what to expect from a man.

"Oh," she said, then dropped her eyes to stare at my outstretched hand. I watched her as she slowly lifted her hand and slipped it in mine.

"That wasn't so hard, was it?" I asked with a grin, to ease her tense expression. Jess could easily offer up her body to drive me crazy, but this simple touch made her nervous and unsure.

"No, it's . . . nice," she replied.

I wanted to say more but I decided against it. Instead I squeezed her hand gently, then led us back over to the parking lot of Live Bay and to the Hummer. It was enough for tonight. I needed to take her home.

We didn't say much on the way back to her house. When we pulled into her driveway, I finally looked over at her. She had been sneaking peeks at me during the short ride here. "I'll get your door," I told her, then got out and went around to open her door and help her out. The T-shirt she was wearing was still damp from her body, but I didn't let myself enjoy the way it clung to her very generous curves.

"Thanks," she whispered softly.

I didn't reply. I just walked her to the door. When we got there, I waited while she reached for the key hidden above the door, then unlocked it. She was going to ask me to come inside. I needed to say something before she did, because declining her was much harder now that we stood outside her house. So very close to her bed.

"Put your number in my phone," I said, handing her my iPhone.

The startled expression on her face was brief, and the fake, flirty look was back. "You're not coming inside?"

"Not tonight," I replied.

The small glimmer of hurt in her eyes surprised me. What had I said to hurt her? I was using all my willpower not to hurt her. She reached for my phone and quickly entered her number, then handed it back to me. "I won't hold my breath," she replied with an annoyed smile before opening her door.

I started to reach out and grab her arm to stop her, but I knew I would have her back up against the same door with my hands on her tempting body if I did that. So I let her go. She didn't look back at me when she closed the door in my face.

The girl had a temper. It only made her sexier. Grinning, I walked back to the Hummer, knowing that her bat was still tucked safely inside. She'd need to get that from me.

Chapter Five

JESS

A knocking at the door woke me. I glanced at the clock beside my bed. It was a little after one in the morning. Momma wouldn't be home for another two hours. I thought about ignoring it, but the fear that something could have happened to Momma had me jumping up and heading for the door.

I opened it up only to realize too late that looking out the window first would have been a smarter decision.

There wasn't much about Hank I didn't know. I could read him so easily. Without him opening his mouth, I knew he was drunk. I counted myself lucky. I could beat him easier with my bat if need be.

"Hey, baby," he drawled, and leaned against the door frame as his eyes took a lazy stroll down my body. His dark hair had been cut shorter recently, and I had to admit I liked it better than the long shaggy thing he had been doing. Closing the door in his face was the smart thing to do. Unfortunately, when it came to Hank I lost every bit of my good sense.

"What do you want?" I asked.

His green eyes finally met mine, and he smiled. "You're wearing my shirt."

I glanced down at the T-shirt I had grabbed to sleep in. It was his. But then, most of my oversize T-shirts were his. We had been a couple since we were fifteen. I shrugged. "Didn't notice," I replied honestly.

Hank's pleased grin turned into a frown. He almost looked pained. "Don't say that, Jess. It hurts."

"It hurts"? Really? That was what he was going with? He had knocked up another girl while we were together. I rolled my eyes and crossed my arms over my chest. "You know nothing about what hurts. Don't go there," I warned him.

He took a step inside and I moved back. I didn't want him getting close. "I never loved her. I told you that. We were fighting and I cracked. She means nothing to me. It's just you, Jess." These were familiar words. Words I had fallen for after the birth of his child.

I held up my hand. "Don't. You've had too much to drink. This is pointless and you know it. I forgave you over and over again. Even after you had a kid, I forgave you. We tried, and you still couldn't keep it in your damn pants. You canceled on me with a lie that you were sick. But you were out with another slut. I'm finished. Over it. Over you. Now go on home."

Hank growled and ran his hand through his hair before slamming it against the wall. "No! Don't say that shit. It ain't over. It won't ever be over. I adore you, Jess. You know that. Hell, baby, I've worshipped you since we were kids. I made a mistake, and I'm sorry. I even understand why you beat the shit outta my truck."

"A mistake? You made thousands of fucking mistakes. I'm done. Go worship someone else. And I didn't touch your damn truck," I yelled, and I shoved him back but not hard enough. He was still inside my house.

Tears glistened in his bloodshot eyes. "I wanted you to marry me. You wouldn't marry me. I got mad and I acted out. You know I do that, but you push me anyway. Why wouldn't you marry me, Jess? I love you. You're mine. Always been mine."

I was his once. And when he had begged me to forgive him I had crumbled. Those days were over. This last time something inside me had shattered. I didn't love him anymore. He'd made sure of that.

"Hank," I said, stepping closer and grabbing his face with my hands. "It's over. We're over. I deserve more than you're willing to give me. I want more."

Hank reached up and grabbed my wrist and squeezed. "I won't fucking let you go. This ain't over, and it won't ever be."

The rage in his eyes warned me I had pushed too far. I was normally more careful with Hank's temper. I knew he was still pissed about his truck, but Hank wasn't exactly stable at times, and when it came to getting me back he could forget easily.

"Easy, I'm just reminding you of how things are now," I said in a soothing tone. I really didn't relish the idea of having to explain a black eye for a week.

Hank eased his grip and pulled me against his chest. I let him. "Let me stay with you tonight. I need you, baby," he whispered into my hair.

"Momma would use you as target practice and you know it. Go home, Hank." I left out reminding him that us sleeping together would never happen again.

"No one gets me like you do. I feel so alone. Only you understand me," he said as he ran his hand down my hair as if it were me he was consoling and not himself.

Once, words like that had made my heart melt. The chain-link tattoo around his arm was ripped in two with the name Jess holding it together. I had cried the day he got it because I'd thought that his permanently putting me on his body meant we'd be forever. I'd been so stupid. He had cheated on me two weeks later with the girl who now was the mother of his child.

"It's not my job to hold you together anymore," I told him, and his arms only tightened around me.

"I'm fucked up, baby. You know that. You know why. But

you always understood and forgave me. Why did you stop for-giving me?" The emotion in his voice tugged at my heart. I did remember the young boy who was beaten by his mother's count-less boyfriends and stayed in trouble because he was begging for someone to care. But that boy was gone now. The man he had become was someone who didn't know how to cherish anything or anyone.

"You broke my heart one too many times," I replied honestly.

"NO! Dammit, NO! I won't accept that. You and me, we're forever. You and me," he ended with a sob.

Seeing big six foot four, muscular, tough Hank cry was always my undoing. I couldn't stand it when the little boy under-neath made his appearance. I patted his back. "Let me go and I'll let you sleep on the sofa."

"I want to sleep with you," he said, sounding so defeated.

"No. You sleep on the sofa or you leave." I was playing with fire here. If I hadn't eased his temper enough, it could come back in full force.

"Just want to be close to you. Holding you feels so good." Again, those were words that had once been my weakness.

I stepped back and he lifted his head. Tears swam in his eyes, and he didn't look like the angry, brutal man I knew he could be. He didn't look like the heartless player who had thrown my love back in my face while he'd slept with other women. He was a lost, hurt little boy who needed someone to care. I had cared once. Deep down I always would, but the love was gone. There was no getting that back.

"I love you," he said with sincerity in his voice. I believed him—I knew that he loved that I cared about him. But Hank did not understand real love. Maybe I didn't either.

JASON

Jax sat across the table with a cup of coffee, staring at me like I had lost my mind. News in this town traveled fast.

"You could've used my pool," Jax said, a grin tugging at his lips. "Unless you actually got naked. You didn't get naked, did you?"

I leaned back in my chair and glared at him. "How the hell do you even know about that? After the cop ran us off, I took her home. We didn't see anyone."

"It's a small town. Sadie's connected. You should just be glad you're in Sea Breeze. That shit would've made it on TV had this happened in LA."

I didn't respond. Jax was just going to keep this up as long as it entertained him. Not to mention, I wasn't sure if I wanted to talk about Jess with him—or anyone—yet. Although, I did plan on seeing her again. Probably wasn't the best idea, but I didn't seem to care. She was different.

"Amanda thinks you should be careful. Jess has issues you don't want to get involved in," Jax said, studying me closely.

What did he think I was going to do? I'd spent one evening with the girl. It was not like I planned on anything serious. "I don't recall asking for Amanda's advice," I replied, more than a little annoyed. She was one to talk. I was pretty damn sure Jess's issues didn't hold a candle to Preston's. Besides, I'd been under the impression the other night that Amanda was one of Jess's only supporters on the female side of the group.

"Her ex is mentally off, I hear. She always goes back to him," Jax informed me.

"Good. Whatever. I don't care. I'm here to get away, not meet anyone. So lay off with the warnings."

Sadie cleared her throat, and we both glanced up to see her standing in the doorway with her arms crossed over her chest, watching us. Her long blond hair curled naturally and fell over her shoulder. Her blue eyes, framed by thick black lashes, were focused on my brother. "Thought we weren't going to say anything to him about it," she said.

Jax jumped up and walked over to her. "Sorry. I know you said not to, but I thought he needed to know what she was like," he told her, tugging one of her arms loose and pulling her toward him.

"Why don't we let him make his own decisions?" she replied, going into his arms easily.

"If you two are about to make out, please give me time to get the hell out of here," I snapped before standing up.

One weekend with these two and I was tired of their constant affection.

Jax frowned and glanced back at me. "You're in a bad mood. Maybe you should try going back to bed."

Or I could leave. Get away from the lovebirds so I could think about my life some without having Jax's life forced down my throat. "I'm leaving," I replied.

"No need to. We've got a plane to catch in an hour. You'll have the place to yourself. Maybe then you can figure out what the hell is eating at you and get over it."

I could see the concern on Sadie's face. She didn't like seeing us like this. Normally, Jax and I got along well. I loved him. But right now everything in my life revolved around Jax and his fame. I was tired of it. I needed to figure out what I wanted for my life. My mother was convinced I was going to be a damn politician, and I was unhappy with life at school. Going back for the fall semester was gonna suck. Even at Harvard, everyone still seemed to care more about Jax than actually getting to know me.

"I'm sorry I'm being an ass. I just need some time alone to think," I tried explaining.

Jax nodded. "I know. Figure it out. Then come home. I'm used to having you around in the summers. I miss you."

Chapter Six

JESS

Momma was pacing back and forth in front of me while she smoked her third cigarette in a row. "I can't believe you let that boy stay the night. Seeing his truck parked outside when I got home . . ." She shook her head, then took another long drag.

"Momma, he was passed out on the sofa. It ain't like I had him snuggled up in my bed," I replied, wishing she would sit down. It was never a good thing when Momma was pacing. It's a miracle she didn't put a bullet in Hank last night.

"He's trash, Jess. You know this. What is wrong with you? I thought you'd finally got that out of your system. He's got a kid, for God's sake. What more does he have to do to you before you wake the hell up?"

I ran my hand through my tangled hair and sighed. She

wasn't listening to me. She didn't believe that I had let Hank sleep over because he'd been drunk. She thought it meant something more. "I don't want Hank. It's over. But he needed to sleep it off. I didn't see any harm in it."

"Any harm in it? Really, baby girl? That's what you're gonna say? Do I need to remind you that when that boy snaps, he goes to swinging his fists like you're his damn punching bag? I won't do that again. I won't. I'll go to jail for shooting his ass before I let him back into your life."

She never did understand Hank. No one did. Not even the woman he shared a kid with. "I'm done saving him. He can't be saved. I know that."

Momma crushed her cigarette into the small dish sitting on the table and stalked over to the coffeepot. "I've told you since y'all were kids that he would end up in jail one day or he'd end up dead. You never listened to me, and he hurt you over and over again."

Hank had been a point of contention with me and Momma most of my life. Momma wanted me as far away from him as possible. I, however, couldn't seem to turn my back on him. "I know."

We sat there in silence as she sank down into the chair across from me. "You're beautiful. You've always been a looker. Use those looks, baby. Use them to get the hell out of this life. Don't waste them on the likes of Hank. This ain't a life I want for you."

"I went out with Jax Stone's brother last night," I blurted out. I hadn't been going to tell her that. I doubted I would ever hear from Jason again. I had tried hard to get him to make a move on me and he'd turned me down over and over. He had been so polite about it too. Like he didn't want to hurt my feelings. Which had only made it that much worse.

"Jax Stone, the rock star? His brother?" Momma asked, to clarify.

I nodded.

"So that's who you were skinny-dipping with last night?"

Rolling my eyes, I took a drink of coffee. Figures Momma would have already heard about that. "Walt come to Jugs last night?" I asked.

She nodded. "Yeah. Told me he gave you another warning. I made it go away, though. He's forgiven you."

I didn't want to think about how Momma made it go away. I tried not to think about that part of her life.

"So he wasn't here when Hank's stupid ass showed up?" she asked.

"No, Jason wasn't here. He had dropped me off and run." I shook my head.

"You invite him in?"

I could hear the unasked questions in her voice. She was wondering if I had slept with him. I stood up and walked over to the sink, then rinsed my cup before setting it down.

"Did you?" she repeated.

"Outta my league," I replied, wishing I hadn't told her about him. She would expect him to call me. She would question how I had messed that up. Momma didn't understand that I couldn't just make all men fall at my feet. Jason wouldn't be my ticket out of this life. She didn't need to get her hopes up.

"No one is out of your league," she replied angrily.

I started to argue, when my phone rang. Holding my breath, I picked it up from the table and looked down at it. I had texted myself from Jason's phone last night so I would have his number too. Not that I ever intended to use it.

His name lit up my screen. He was calling me. He had said he would call, but I hadn't believed he ever would. Why was he calling?

"Is it him?" Momma's voice snapped me out of my thoughts, and I glanced up at her curious expression. I simply nodded.

"Well, you gonna answer it or stare at it?"

She was right. I needed to answer it. I wanted to answer it. Didn't I? Nervously, I slid my finger across the screen and lifted the phone to my ear. "Hello."

A pause. One just long enough to cause my stomach to drop. I had waited too long to answer.

"Jess?" Jason's voice replied on the other end. It was him.

"Yes."

"Hey, it's Jason. Seems you left your bat in my car again," he said in an amused tone.

My small amount of joy plummeted. Of course. He was calling about the bat. It was why he had come back yesterday. "Oh. I'm . . . Yeah. Sorry about that."

"What are you doing today?" he asked.

"I have a class. I'm taking some summer courses," I replied.

He didn't reply right away. It was almost as if he was surprised. "What about later? Tonight?"

I knew I should tell him he could drop the bat off and that my mom would be here. But I didn't want to. I wanted to see him again. "I have to go to my cousin's kid's football game. He's eleven and he asked me to come. Rock would also come get me and drag me there by my hair if he thought I was going to let his boy down. But . . ." I stopped myself. Should I invite him? Was that stupid? It was a youth football league game.

"I like football," Jason said.

"Oh, well, then would you like to come . . . with me?" I had never been this nervous with a guy in my life. But then, I had never asked a guy to something that didn't involve me ending up in the back of his truck later.

"Love to. What time should I pick you up?"

He wasn't going to meet me there. He was going to take me. I stared at my mom, who was watching me with a pleased grin on her face. I couldn't think like her. It would get me hurt.

I had to remember who this was I was talking to. He wasn't permanent.

"Six," I finally told him.

"I'll see you at six," he replied. "Have a good day, Jess."

"Uh, yeah, um, you too," I stammered, before hanging up the phone and letting it fall to the table.

"So, he invited himself to the game. Guess he ain't so outta your league after all. But he's just for fun. Enjoy him, baby girl, but remember he's just a man. He'll marry a girl with a trust fund. Watch your heart."

I looked up at her, suddenly confused. "I thought you were all for me landing a wealthy man."

She frowned. "There's wealthy and there's filthy rich. He's just your Logan. Don't forget that."

Who was Logan? I started to ask and changed my mind. Listening to my mother's logic could confuse anyone. Momma didn't trust men.

JASON

There were things you expected from a girl like Jess. Her waiting on me outside when I pulled in the driveway and not giving me a chance to get out and open her car door before she jerked it open was one of them. Her wearing a tight-ass pair of jeans hugging every curve she had was another. But I hadn't been expecting to see Jess bend down and open her arms for a little girl to run into.

It made her softer. The walls she had built up around her seemed to vanish the moment the girl called out her name and wrapped her small arms around Jess's neck.

"You came to see me!" the little girl exclaimed happily.

Jess laughed and pulled back so she could look into the little girl's eyes. "I just saw you a few days ago, Daisy May. You act like we haven't seen each other in a month," Jess teased her.

Daisy May was Preston's little sister—I knew that much from my time with Amanda. Daisy had been the flower girl in Marcus and Willow's wedding. Rock had adopted Daisy May and her brothers when Preston's mother passed away. Which meant that Amanda and Preston were going to be here. Shit. I hadn't thought about that when Jess had said "my cousin's kid."

"Manda and Preston are here. Come see," Daisy May said. Jess, apparently, was unaware of my past with Amanda. I was relieved by that. I didn't want it to be awkward. Seeing Amanda and Preston the other night at Sadie's dinner party had been our first real encounter in a long time. The dinner hadn't been hard. It wasn't like I was hung up on Amanda. I just didn't think Jess was the kind of girl who would get along well with girls like Amanda. Even if Amanda had been the one openly defending Jess the other night when everyone was discussing her antics.

That was just Amanda. She was sweet and accepting of everyone.

"Lead the way," Jess told her, and she glanced back at me. "Rock's little girl," Jess explained.

I started to tell her I knew who Daisy was because of the wedding and then again at Sadie's dinner party the other night, but I closed my mouth. Bad idea. I just nodded. "She's cute," I replied instead.

"Yeah, she looks like Preston. Rock and Trisha couldn't have kids, so they adopted Preston's younger siblings when their momma died."

I nodded again, feeling guilty for not admitting I already knew all this. It was strange that Jess hadn't been at the wedding. I would have remembered her. She was hard to miss.

"Have you met Amanda? Marcus's sister?" Jess asked as we reached the bleachers.

Here it was. My time to lie or tell the truth and explain.

"He was her friend at Marcus's weddin'," Daisy May informed her for me. I was surprised the kid remembered me.

Jess stopped walking and looked up at me. "You were at Marcus Hardy's wedding?"

This was not where I wanted to discuss this

"Yeah," I replied, not able to lie to her.

She frowned. "I wasn't even invited to their wedding. How did you get an invite?"

I glanced up at the people in the stands and saw Amanda watching us. Preston wasn't there, but I knew he was here at the game. "I, uh . . ." Glancing back down at Jess, I forced a smile. "I was Amanda's date."

Jess's eyes went wide. "What? And you walked away from that without Preston Drake beating the shit outta you?"

She didn't seem mad. Maybe she liked Amanda. They couldn't be friends . . . could they? The two of them couldn't be any more opposite.

"Yeah, he wasn't a fan, but it all ended well. For everyone," I replied.

"Come see Manda," Daisy May said, tugging on Jess's hand. Jess glanced down at the girl, then back at me.

"Sadie fixed y'all up, didn't she?"

I just nodded. No need to tell her I had been the one to pursue Amanda. I'd had Sadie help me, but it had been my idea.

Jess laughed and shook her head, then turned to walk up the steps.

What was so funny? I didn't get a chance to ask before Jess's ass in those jeans caught my attention and completely distracted me. I followed her up the stairs, and she led us straight to Amanda.

"Hey, I'm so glad you're here. I haven't seen you in weeks." Amanda's voice distracted me from being fascinated by Jess's body in those jeans, and I jerked my gaze up to see Amanda standing up, smiling at Jess. She was shorter than Jess and thinner. Jess had curves that went on for miles. Amanda had the girl-next-door look.

"Drake's got you all wrapped up. Wouldn't be surprised if his possessive crazy ass wasn't keeping you as far away from me as possible," Jess drawled.

"Got that damn right," Preston said as he stepped over the seat in front of us and went directly to Amanda's side as if she needed guarding from someone.

Amanda slapped his chest. "Stop it. Jess is my friend and you know that."

Really? Interesting.

Preston scowled and pulled Amanda closer to him before shifting his scowl to me. Then slowly, understanding lit his eyes as he glanced between the two of us. A smirk touched his lips. "So that shit was true? Dewayne said the two of you showed up together at Live Bay. I didn't believe him," Preston said, looking more than amused.

"Shut up, Drake," Jess snapped, sitting down beside Amanda and then glancing up at me. "I'd introduce you, but seeing as how you dated his woman, Jason, I assume y'all have met."

"They didn't fucking date," Preston growled.

Amanda turned to whisper something to him, and I looked away. Let her deal with his insane ass.

"Ignore him," Jess said. "He goes apeshit whenever he thinks someone unworthy gets near her. Irony in its best form."

I couldn't have agreed more. I leaned down to her ear and asked, "How is it that you two are friends?"

Jess leaned back and cocked an eyebrow at me like she was offended. A slow smile finally took its place. "Because Amanda Hardy is hard to resist, even for females. She's always been good to me, from the time we were kids. And then, of course, there was the time she wanted to get Preston's attention and decided getting trashed and dancing at bars was the way to do it. So she of course came to see me for guidance."

What? That didn't sound like the Amanda I knew. Jess threw her head back and laughed. "If you could see the disbelief on your face," she said, grinning.

"She really did that?"

Jess nodded. "Yep. But remember, I like Amanda. So I made sure her bad-girl performance was monitored and she was safe. Besides, it didn't take long for her to figure out that that wasn't the life she wanted to lead. After that, we really became friends."

I knew that Jess didn't tell me this to impress me. She shrugged and turned her attention back to the game. But I couldn't take my eyes off her. She really was special and she didn't have a clue.

Chapter Seven

JESS

Amanda was the type of girl I could see Jason with. She made more sense. She was the kind he would have made it work with. She would have brought him back to Sea Breeze over and over again.

I wasn't.

I was the fling. I spent most of the game cheering Rock's boy Brent on and pushing these thoughts to the back of my mind. Amanda was the only one of the elite Sea Breeze crowd who gave me a chance. The rest of them stuck their noses in the air and treated me like . . . a stripper's daughter.

Amanda was different. Just like her brother, Marcus. They accepted everyone. So I refused to get jealous over Jason having dated Amanda. We were just hanging out, anyway. He would be gone soon.

Brent caught a pass, and I forgot my problems and jumped up to cheer. Rock was standing down on the field beside the coach. When Brent came running to the sidelines, he ran straight for Rock and threw his arms around him. I felt a lump form in my throat, and my eyes watered. Preston's younger siblings had suffered a lot when their mother was alive. The only reason they had survived was because Preston made sure to take care of them. He did things he would probably never forgive himself for in order to supply them with what they needed.

Preston had taken off running down the stands toward the field as he hooted and yelled. Somehow they made this all work, and seeing the happy smiles on the kids' faces would make anyone tear up. Rock and Trisha made excellent parents.

I reached up and wiped away the one tear that got loose, before sitting back down beside Jason. I could feel his eyes on me, and I glanced over at him and smiled. The curious expression on his face confused me. I turned my attention back to the field.

"When this is over, you want to go get something to eat?" Jason asked.

Looking back at him, I decided there was nothing I would rather do. Getting too attached to this guy wasn't something I could do, but I liked spending time with him. He wasn't constantly trying to grope me, and he didn't talk to me like I was beneath him. He was just as sweet in public as he was in private.

And he seemed to like me. He actually laughed at my sarcasm and he got when I was kidding. He didn't roll his eyes at me or ignore me.

It was a unique experience.

"Yeah, sounds good," I replied.

He grinned and turned his attention back to the field.

"Uh-oh, Jess. You might want to go get Rock," Amanda said in a worried tone.

I glanced over at her. "What?" I asked. Her frown was focused on something or someone else. I followed her gaze to see Hank walking across the parking lot beside Carrie, who was holding the hand of their little boy. He was just barely walking now. Hank hardly ever went anywhere with Carrie and their kid. Normally, I just saw him with the little boy. Me being here with Jason and him being here with Carrie was drama I didn't want tonight.

"What is it?" Jason asked.

I tore my gaze off my ex and his little family. "You ready to go eat now?" I asked. It was the beginning of the third quarter, but staying was a bad idea. I didn't want to explain Hank to Jason.

"I'm just hungry," I replied, standing up and reaching for his arm to tug him up too. He stood up beside me willingly. I tried hard not to let my hand dwell on his arm too long. The hard, defined muscles under my palm were a little distracting, so I dropped my hand. "See you later, Amanda. Let Rock and Trisha know that I had to leave."

She nodded and gave me an understanding smile.

When we reached the bottom of the stands, I glanced over to see if Hank had noticed me. Or worse, if Carrie had. She hated me and was very verbal with her hate for me. I didn't want to go near that with Jason here to see and hear it.

"You gonna tell me what's going on, or do I get to guess?" Jason said close to my ear.

Hank's eyes found me at that moment. I stopped walking and reached for Jason's hand. Shit. The anger in Hank's eyes wasn't good. This was going to be one big mess. I turned to Jason. "The guy's truck I bashed. He's here," I explained.

Jason's eyes went wide, and then a grin tugged at his lips. "Good thing I didn't drive the Porsche."

This wasn't funny. Why did he have to look so dang sexy and amused?

"Yeah, well, he knows it was me. Let's go."

Jason's hand found mine, surprising me. I glanced down at our hands as his fingers threaded through mine. What was he doing?

"You'll be fine. I promise," he said in a firm, calm voice that soothed me. Even if he didn't know how insane Hank could be.

"Thanks," I whispered, straightening up as we walked toward the parking lot. Hank had stopped walking. I wasn't going to make eye contact with him. Maybe he'd just let us walk by without saying anything.

Jason didn't say anything as we got closer, but Hank's heated gaze felt like it was burning a hole in my head. He was pissed. I didn't even glance at Carrie. I knew she'd go to screaming if I gave her any reason to think I wanted Hank.

I heard Hank's angry snarl. "Shut up." Fantastic. Carrie was saying something about me being here. I picked up my pace, and Jason tightened his grip on my hand but refused to walk faster. He forced me to keep his steady pace.

"Take the baby, Hank. I mean it. If you talk to that skank, I'll walk away. I won't have it. I swear I won't." Carrie was talking loud enough for people around us to hear her. She loved making scenes.

"Shut up, bitch," he roared, and I winced. I knew what that felt like. Hank's angry words. I also knew what Hank's fist felt like. Surely she realized getting him worked up was not safe.

"Excuse us," Jason said smoothly as we walked past them. Jason moved me to his other side so that he stood between them and me. It wasn't even obvious, he did it with such a casual ease.

"Who the fuck are you?" Hank demanded, and I thought Jason was going to ignore him. But he didn't.

He stopped, and moved me to stand behind him before he turned back to look at Hank. "Excuse me?" he replied. The warning edge in his voice surprised me. Jason was always so nice and easygoing.

Hank took a step toward us, and I tried to move in front of Jason but his hand held on to me tightly as he pulled me back behind him. The only way I could get free was if I jerked and shoved him. I wasn't going to do that unless I needed to keep Hank from hitting him.

"I asked who the fuck you are," he snarled.

"I don't see how that's your business," Jason replied.

Hank's hands fisted beside him and his face turned red. "Jess is my business, and if you don't get your fucking hand off her now, I'm gonna remove it from your body."

Okay, I had to do something. Carrie was screaming at him, and he was either going to slap her or punch Jason.

"Last I checked, Jess wasn't yours," Dewayne's voice suddenly warned. "Ain't been yours for a long time now. Why don't you go take your baby and his momma and move on along before I remind you just who the fuck her friends are." I looked back to see his cold, scary-as-hell expression focused on Hank.

"Stay out of this, Dewayne. Ain't your shit," Hank growled.

"I've been looking for a reason to smash your face in for a year now. Go ahead and piss me off," Dewayne replied, walking past us and toward Hank.

"Please, piss him off. I'd love to see him beat your ass," Preston drawled as he walked up to us. Amanda must have gone and told him what was going on. The playboy smirk that he always wore was gone. His eyes were locked on Hank. "Your boy's cry-ing. Best take care of that."

"Hank, please, come on," Carrie begged, pulling on his arm. Her ugliness toward me was gone now that they were sand-wiched between two of my cousin's best friends.

"Ain't over, Jess. Won't ever be over, baby. You know that," Hank said, staring straight at me.

I straightened my shoulders and glared at Hank over Jason's shoulder since he wouldn't let me get around him. "It's been over, Hank."

He shook his head. "We're endgame, baby. Remember. We are fucking endgame. Always have been."

I had told him that once. Back when I was young and fool-ish. Back when I thought he really did hate it when he hurt me. Not anymore. I didn't want that life. And I didn't love him anymore.

"No. He's your endgame," I replied, pointing to the little boy now in Carrie's arms. "Let's go," I said, tugging on Jason's arm. I had no doubt he was going to want to take me home now and drop me off. This wacked-up mess with Hank would send any guy running from me. But I wanted to leave anyway. I couldn't stay here.

Jason nodded and turned around, still holding my hand tightly in his as we walked back to his Hummer without a word. I wanted to apologize, but how could I explain that? Admitting that I had once been in love with that insane man didn't say a lot about me.

He opened my door and helped me up before closing it and walking around to get in the driver's seat. When he got in and closed the door, he didn't reach for his seat belt. Instead he looked over at me. I braced myself for his brush-off. I could handle it. I was used to it.

"I wish I'd gotten a chance to see his truck after you beat the shit out of it," he said.

I sat there and stared at him. *What?* I was confused.

A small grin tugged at his lips. All the worry and stress that had me wound tight released. I let out the breath I had been holding.

His expression had softened. "I want a good burger. You good with that, or do you want something else?"

He wasn't taking me home. I leaned back and smiled at him. "Burgers are good with me."

"You're the local. Where do I get a good burger?" he said as he started the engine and shifted the gear into reverse.

"Pickle Shack," I replied.

"Put on your seat belt," he said with a wink, then pulled out onto the road.

My heart did a little fluttery thing. Startled by my reaction, I reached for the seat belt and put it on.

"You want to talk about that back there?" he asked.

He didn't sound angry, nor was he demanding it. I wasn't sure what to do with him. He was so different. I didn't want to explain Hank to him. I never wanted him to see Hank again. That part of my life was embarrassing. "Not really," I replied honestly.

Jason nodded. "Okay. How do you feel about night swimming legally?"

I studied his profile for a moment. Was he really just going to drop this and not ask questions? I had been prepared for him to try a little harder, but he was changing the subject completely.

"I'm good with staying on the right side of the law if possible," I replied, wondering where he was going with this. I didn't do night swimming in the gulf, though. But then again, he might possibly change my mind.

"So you would be up for coming back to my brother's place after we eat? He's got a heated pool."

His brother's place. As in Jax Stone's vacation home? I was nervous. Over a guy. For the first time in my life, a guy was making me nervous. He was asking me to come to his place. Not the back of his Hummer. "Yeah, I'd like that." I hoped he hadn't heard the small stammer. I wasn't used to this.

"I'd offer to take you back to your house so you could grab a swimsuit, but I like the other option better," he said, sending my heart pounding faster in my chest.

JASON

It had been that small shudder when I held her behind me and faced off with her insane ex that had done me in. She'd been scared. It was like someone had flipped a switch in me. I had decided that she came with too much baggage and drama when Hank had sent her bolting out of her seat, ready to leave. I didn't like drama, so I had been preparing myself for how I was going to back out of her life just as quickly as I had stepped into it. That had all changed, though, the moment the terrified tremble had gone through her. All I could think about was protecting her. I wasn't letting the asshole near her.

Why would someone who looked like her settle for that asshat? He'd obviously mistreated her. The way he was treating the mother of his child was proof enough he had no idea how to treat a woman. Thinking about him getting near Jess pissed me off.

Jess had finally started smiling easily again while we ate. I did everything I could to get her mind off what had happened. I didn't want her worrying about it. I liked hearing her laugh. When she was relaxed, she was herself. The confident, flirty female who knew exactly how sexy she was.

"I've never been on the island," Jess said as we drove past the main gates and over the bridge that connected the private island to the mainland.

"I'm your first, then?" I asked teasingly.

She laughed and unbuckled her seat belt. I glanced over at her scooting closer to me. The self-assured girl I'd first met was back. "Guess you are," she said as her hand slid up my arm until her fingers wrapped around my bicep. I was immediately thankful for my personal trainer.

"Thank you," she said in a breathy voice as she moved closer to my ear.

"For what?" I asked, enjoying her warm breath against my neck.

"Today. Protecting me. Not judging me," she said as her hand moved from my arm to my chest.

As incredibly good as her hand on my skin felt and the images running through my head of her naked and in my bed excited me, I wasn't going to let her do this. She was used to guys expecting it from her. Or, from what I saw tonight, Hank expecting it of her. He seemed like he was a bit possessive. I wasn't sure many guys had been able to get too close to her and live.

"Don't thank me for that. Besides, it was Preston and Dewayne who kept him from doing anything."

Jess turned and slid a leg up higher on her seat as she pressed her chest against my arm. Damn, she was making it hard to be noble. "You stood in front of me. No one's ever done that," she whispered before her lips touched my neck. I gripped the steering wheel tightly with one hand and tried hard to remember she was doing this because she thought she had to. Not because she wanted to.

"This isn't why I brought you here," I told her. Even though the bulge in my jeans said something entirely different.

She stopped kissing my neck and moved back. "I don't understand."

Of course she didn't. How did I explain that I didn't want to be one more guy who used her body, without it sounding like I was judging her?

"I thought . . . I mean, from what you said, I thought you were attracted to me," she said, sitting back and leaving me cold.

We pulled up to the gate outside the house, and it opened when security saw the Hummer. Jess turned her attention toward the house, and I took another deep, calming breath. "There isn't a heterosexual male alive who wouldn't be attracted to you. I just don't want you to think that's what this is about."

"Then what is it about?" Her voice was soft. Almost a whisper, as if she was afraid to ask.

The fact that this was all she expected from me made a wide range of mixed emotions hit me at once. It infuriated me, yet it made her seem fragile. She wasn't what anyone would consider fragile, but seeing this side of her brought a whole new light to things. "I like spending time with you," I told her honestly.

She didn't seem convinced. I parked the Hummer and then

reached over to touch her hands, which she had tightly clasped in her lap. "Look at me?" I asked.

She lifted her head, and the insecurity in her eyes surprised me. How did someone who looked like Jess have any ounce of insecurity in her bones?

"I liked having you touch me. Hell, I loved it. But you weren't doing it for the right reasons. You think you owe it to me. But you don't. I didn't bring you here with any intentions other than getting to spend more time with you."

She frowned and a small wrinkle appeared on her forehead. It was cute. "So, you don't want to have sex with me?" she asked seriously.

I couldn't keep from grinning. "Jess, I want you naked and straddling me. I've fantasized about it more than once from the moment you crawled your sexy ass into my car. But when that happens, I want it to be because you want me, not because you think it's what's expected."

"Oh" was her simple response.

Chapter Eight

JESS

I was out of my element. Sitting on a lounger, I watched as Jason fixed me a drink at the outdoor bar. He picked up a remote and winked at me right before music filled the night air. Surprisingly, it wasn't Jax Stone's voice playing over the speakers.

"I don't have the best bartending abilities, but what I can do should be tolerable," Jason said, picking up two tumblers I was willing to bet were actually crystal. I had only had alcohol from cheap glasses at Live Bay or from a Dixie cup.

"Maybe I should have made the drinks," I replied teasingly.

He handed mine to me and sat down across from me. Our knees were almost touching. "You've had some time behind the bar?" he asked.

I could lie about my life, but there was no point. It was more than obvious. Besides, just because his pretty-boy smile made my knees weak didn't mean I would let a guy change me. "I was raised behind the bar of a strip club until I was old enough to stay home by myself at nights. Big Moose used to keep an eye on me while Momma was working. So, yeah, I got bored a lot of the time. Picked up a few things."

Jason's glass had stopped halfway to his mouth while he stared at me. I had shocked him. "A strip club?" he asked, then swallowed some of the bourbon that I could smell from where I sat.

I nodded. "Yep."

Jason leaned forward and rested his elbows on his knees. "I guess I'll let you make your own drink next time. Or you can teach me."

That wasn't the response I had expected.

Jason chuckled and set his glass down on the table separating the two loungers we were sitting on. "Are you done trying to shock me for the evening, or should I assume you're going to share some more juicy information about Jess? I was looking forward to the swimming, but I don't want to interrupt this conversation if it's just going to get better."

From any other guy that would have sounded obnoxious. From Jason it wasn't. His grin made up for it. "Let's swim," I replied, standing up and handing him my glass. I knew he was trying hard to be a gentleman with me, but allowing him to would only ruin me. When he left, that would be what I wanted. What I expected. What I measured every guy against. It would make future relationships impossible. As tempting as it was to see exactly how that felt, I couldn't.

Reaching for the hem of my shirt, I pulled it over my head and began taking off my boots and jeans. I could feel Jason's gaze on me, and it only propelled me on. He was attracted to me. He'd admitted it and even shared exactly what he was fantasizing about. Every good intention of his was about to be shot to hell. Because I was going to send them there.

When I reached up to unhook my bra, I looked directly at Jason, who had discarded his shirt and was working on his jeans. His eyes dropped to my hands, then shot back up to my face. "What are . . . ," he started to say as I let the bra fall forward and slide down my arms until it hit the cool, smooth stone below.

"You wanted to skinny-dip," I told him as I slipped my fingers into the sides of my panties and shimmied them down. Jason stood immobile, watching me.

"I didn't mean naked," he said in a low whisper.

I smiled at him and stepped out of my panties. "Oops," I replied.

Jason swallowed hard as his hands began working again on unbuttoning his jeans.

"It's warm, right?" I asked him as I turned to walk over to the steps.

"Yeah."

"Good. I'm cold, and after that talk in the Hummer I'm not sure yet if you're going to warm me up or if I'm going to have to let the pool do all the work."

Jason muttered a curse, and I bit down on my bottom lip to keep from smiling as I lowered myself into the water. He was right. It was nice and warm.

I swam over to a seating ledge in the deeper end of the pool and sat down, before turning around to see Jason right behind me. I dropped my gaze to the water lit by the color-changing pool lights. He was naked.

I lifted my gaze to meet his just as he got to the ledge I was sitting on. As he stood in front of me the water ran down his well-defined body. "You got naked too," I said, relieved that I wasn't going to have to work as hard as I had feared.

"You started it," he said, taking one more step toward me.

"Yes, but in the Hummer you weren't as accommodating," I replied.

Jason didn't smile. His hand touched my right knee, causing a jolt of pleasure to run up my thigh. I held my breath, unsure what he was going to do next, and then his other hand covered my left knee. Without a pause, he pushed my legs open and stepped up between them.

"That was before you got naked," he said simply as his mouth lowered to cover mine. The soft pressure was intoxicating. I opened my mouth and inhaled his minty taste mixed with the bourbon he'd drunk. It was so different from the cigarettes and cheap beer that I always tasted when I kissed Hank. There was a safety in it.

Jason's hands cupped my face while he continued to nibble my bottom lip, and then he plunged his tongue into my mouth again and slid it seductively against mine. I had been kissed many times over the years, but not like this. There was a strength to Jason's gentle touch. It also had me panting for breath and needing to squeeze my legs together for some relief from the throbbing need he was causing.

When he pulled back, he closed his eyes and took a deep breath. "Damn," he said in a hoarse whisper. "That . . . that was . . . Damn." The excitement from seeing him so affected only made the ache worse. I reached up and ran my hands through his hair and pulled his face back down to mine. I wasn't ready to stop this.

A low groan broke free from Jason's chest as his hands grabbed my waist and pulled me up against him until my chest brushed against his, causing me to gasp from the intensity and Jason to break the kiss again.

"Jess," he said, in what sounded almost like a growl.

"Hmmm," I replied, lifting my knees to wrap my legs around his waist. The movement caused his erection to press against me, and we both froze.

"I can't . . . ," he said as if he were in pain. "I can't stop this. Is this what you want?"

The fact that he was still trying to be noble made me even more crazy. I had never wanted anyone as much as I wanted Jason Stone at this moment. "Yes," I replied, trying not to beg as I moved against him. The friction made us both snap. Our kisses went from sweet and sexy to hot and wild. Jason grabbed my face again, but this time he kissed me like I was his oxygen supply.

He rocked his hips against me, rubbing his hard length directly over my swollen clit, and I broke the kiss to cry out from the pleasure. Jason's hands tightened on my waist right before he picked me up and sat me down on the edge of the pool. The cool air against my wet skin was the only thing keeping me from voicing my disappointment. I didn't want to stop this. He felt so good.

"I don't have a condom in here," he said with a predatory gleam in his eyes as he pulled himself out of the water and reached down to grab my hands. I let him help me up, and then his arms were wrapped around me again as he began kissing my neck and across my jawline before claiming my mouth again. His kisses were addictive. I had never wanted to curl up and kiss a man for hours, but this man . . . I could do that. I wanted to do that.

"My wallet," he said against my mouth, and picked me up. I

wrapped my legs around his waist, and he made a pleased sound as he walked over to the loungers we had left earlier. He sat me down, then bent over me to kiss me again with a hard promise of what was to come and reached for his jeans.

My wet skin and the cool night air were forgotten while I watched him find a condom in his wallet and put it on. When he came back down to me, I opened my legs so he could lie down on top of me.

"You're so damn sexy," he whispered in my ear as he pulled my earlobe into his mouth and biting it just hard enough to make me whimper.

I had been told that before, but it was different coming from Jason. Whereas I had wanted to roll my eyes at it in the past, hearing Jason say it made me curl closer against him. I wanted him to think I was sexy.

The way he held me and touched me made me feel special. Like I was some treasure he was getting to unwrap. It was the best high I'd ever been on. Jason Stone was going to be addictive.

Oh God.

This wasn't doing what I had meant for it to do. I thought getting him to have sex with me would make him just like the others—easy to walk away from. But he was setting a bar no one would ever be able to reach. Why was he so damn perfect?

"Your skin smells like honeysuckle. It drives me crazy. So

soft." His words were even addictive. The deep, turned-on sound of his voice was too much. I wouldn't be able to stop this now. I needed it.

I lifted my hips, forcing his erection to slip between my legs. He inhaled a sharp breath and moved against me. "You're so wet," he murmured, and shifted his hips so that he was ready to slide inside me. It had been a while for me, but that wasn't the reason I was clinging to him, pulling him closer.

"Fuck," Jason groaned as he sank inside me slowly. He ran the tip of his nose up my neck and then pressed an open-mouthed kiss on the tender skin behind my ear. "This feels too good," he said, lifting himself up and pulling back out of me, then rocking back inside of me, harder this time. I watched in fascination as his eyes focused on my breasts. His mouth lowered until he could pull a nipple into it. The hard sucking coupled with him filling me inside had me panting, on the edge of an orgasm entirely too quickly.

"Go ahead and come for me. I'll make sure you do one more time before I'm done," he said, then gave my other breast the same attention.

I trusted him, or else just hearing him tell me to come was what did it, but I grabbed ahold of his arms and screamed his name as the waves of release washed over me. Jason lifted his head and began pumping his hips faster as his eyes held mine. "You're like a damn glove," he said through clenched teeth.

The second orgasm hit me out of nowhere, and the surprised cry of pleasure came pouring out of me before I could control it. Jason's hands grabbed my head. "Look at me," he demanded.

I opened my eyes to see his eyes locked on mine. The uncontrolled desire in his eyes only made my orgasm continue pumping through me. My body trembled violently just as Jason's mouth fell open and he jerked against me. The ecstasy on his face as we held each other's gaze owned me.

When his head dropped to my neck and his unsteady breathing warmed my skin, I shivered and clung to him tightly. Never had sex been like that. My body was still feeling aftershocks, and each shudder that went through me made Jason's arms tighten around my waist as he held me against him.

Neither of us said anything while we both struggled to breathe again.

Jason pulled me up against his chest before shifting and rolling over on his side, moving me on top of him as our legs tangled. He wasn't getting up, or even pulling out, and making an excuse to go clean up. He just held me. His hand began to play with my hair as I lay in the security of his arms.

As the music played over the speakers and the waterfall in the pool filled the silence around us, I knew that, without a doubt, I had just been ruined.

JASON

Tonight wasn't supposed to be about sex. My plan had been to spend time with Jess. Then she'd gone and stripped. My brain had stopped working at that moment. But damn, was I glad. Sex with girls who were just in it for the fun or to say they had fucked Jax Stone's brother was the norm for me. It was what I was used to. Amanda was the first girl I'd pursued who I had considered having an actual relationship with. I didn't do relationships.

Jess was supposed to be like the others. But this hadn't been the same. Something was different. The way she had clung to me and fallen apart in my arms wasn't what I was used to. At some point she'd become my sole reason for breathing. I ran my hands through her wet locks of hair and enjoyed the feel of her sated body curled up against me.

I was still buried inside her, and I knew if I didn't move soon I was going to be ready to go again. Now I knew it wasn't just Jess's smart mouth and killer body that were hard to turn down. The sex was phenomenal.

Jess shivered against me, reminding me that we were still naked and wet.

"Come on, let's go inside," I told her as I shifted her so that she could stand up.

Watching Jess's body in the moonlight ranked right up there with the Seven Wonders of the World. Hank had to be the stupidest man on the face of the earth. Jess stood up and wrapped her arms around her stomach and turned to look back at me.

The nervous smile on her lips reminded me that underneath all that bravado was an insecure girl. One who had allowed herself to be mistreated by guys. I stood up and reached for my shirt, which I'd thrown off earlier.

"Lift your arms," I said, stepping in front of her.

She did as I asked, and I slipped my shirt over her head.

"Thank you."

I grabbed a towel that had been left folded on the table beside us and wrapped it around my waist. "Time to go warm up," I replied, reaching for her hand and leading her inside the house.

I took Jess to the bathroom closest to the pool and left her to go back and get her clothing. When I came back the door was unlocked, so I knocked once before opening it.

Jess stood in front of the shower, looking at it. "This is the biggest shower I've ever seen," she said with a smile, glancing back at me.

It wasn't even the biggest one in the house, but I guess it was a nice size. I walked over and reached inside to turn on the hot water. "Take a shower and warm up," I told her.

"If you take one with me," she replied.

The image of Jess soaped up in a shower was exactly what I was imagining at the moment. Climbing in with her would lead to more tonight. Would it be the same the second time? Was that first time inside her because I'd wanted her so bad? Getting attached to Jess was out of the question. I would be leaving soon, and Jess wouldn't be a part of that life.

Jess pulled my shirt over her head and dropped it, then reached out for my towel. "Please," she said as she tugged, letting my towel fall.

Maybe a second time would be a good idea. Getting her out of my system was the only way to deal with this.

Reaching for her waist, I pulled her against me and enjoyed the sweet taste of her lips and the soft, plump feel of them against mine. Telling this woman no was fucking impossible.

Chapter Nine

JESS

I lay in Jason Stone's bed, watching him sleep. I should have gone home. But he'd asked me to stay and I'd said yes. A dark curl had fallen over his eyes, and I wanted to reach over and brush it away, but I was afraid to wake him.

Sleeping wasn't going to happen for me tonight. I had too many thoughts in my head. Then, of course, there was fear. This was too good to be true. Jason was sweet, kind, smart, wealthy, and beautiful. He had shown me that sex could be soul shattering. Nothing with him was cheap. Especially not that.

But I wasn't the kind of girl who caught and held someone like Jason's attention. I wasn't a Sadie White. She was pure and sweet. Everyone loved her—even Marcus Hardy had. It was no wonder Jax Stone fell madly in love with her when he'd come to Sea Breeze. I had never lived in a fairy tale, and there was no sense in starting to now.

I eased out of Jason's arms and slipped quietly from the bed. Finding the bathroom we had used to take our shower was a little more difficult, but I eventually found it. Once I located my clothes, I put them on and then headed for the front door.

"If you open it, the silent alarm will go off," Jason's sleepy voice said from the dark staircase behind me.

I turned around just as his foot hit the bottom step. He was wearing a pair of shorts that hung off his lean hips, making it hard to concentrate on why it was I needed to leave.

"You don't have a car here," he pointed out.

I nodded. He was right. I hadn't really thought that through yet.

"If you wanted to go, all you had to do was tell me," Jason said.

"I didn't want to wake you," I lied. That hadn't really been it at all.

Jason smirked as if he knew I was lying. "I've called my driver, or the driver I use while I'm in residence here when needed. He's bringing the car around now. He can take you home."

I didn't respond. Jason walked toward me and stopped just a foot away from me. "Can I call you?"

Could he call me? Telling him I needed to think or that I

needed time was probably best. Reminding myself just where I stood in this situation was important.

"Yes," I replied before I could stop myself. I wanted him to call me. This thing, whatever it was, would mark me for life. Yet I couldn't seem to let it go.

Jason cupped my face and pressed a simple kiss to my lips. "Later, then," he whispered against my lips before stepping around me and opening the front door.

I fought to control my breathing. Just feeling him touch me was now making my heart do crazy things. "Okay," I managed to reply.

He didn't say anything else as I walked outside and toward the waiting car. The driver stood beside the car door and opened it for me as I approached. One more thing to remind me just how out of my depth I was.

Once I was inside the car, I looked up at the door to the house, but it was closed and Jason was gone.

The porch light was off, which meant my mother wasn't home yet to notice I was missing. Every light in the house would be on if she had been here. The driver opened my door and I stepped out.

I thanked him for the ride, and he nodded but didn't speak. With a smile I walked toward the house. There was no telling what the guy was thinking, about where he had dropped me off. No doubt this would be the gossip of the Stone employees' mealtime. Jason Stone slumming it in Sea Breeze.

"Jess." A hoarse whisper startled me and I jumped, searching the dark porch for the voice. Movement caught my eye, and I found Hank sitting on the floor, leaning up against the side of the house.

"What're you doing here?" I snapped. I was so sick of this. Why couldn't he just go away?

He shuffled his feet but couldn't manage to get up, which meant he was trashed. Again. "I came to see you. You were with him, weren't you?" he slurred before slamming his hand down on the porch.

"Where I was isn't your business. I'm not your business anymore. Please stop coming here. Just leave." I reached for the hidden key over the door and unlocked the door before he could figure out how to stand up.

"What happened to us, Jess? Used to be me and you against the world. We had each other. Didn't need anyone else. You were my reason for laughing. For smiling. I can't smile without you, Jess."

I squeezed the door handle tightly and fought back the need to scream. Once this had worked with me. Once I had wanted nothing but Hank. Now his words were too late. Years too late. "You happened to us. You used me one too many times. I'm done with that. And I'm done with us. Go home," I said with no emotion. Not because I was dead inside, but because he no longer touched my heart. He'd cut himself out. Or maybe I had finally cut him out.

"I won't let you go. I'll fight for you. He can't have you. He doesn't understand you."

This was about Jason. He hadn't liked seeing me with someone else. That was always the way I had gotten Hank back in the past. I'd made sure he saw me with another guy, and he came running back to my door. I'd trained him well. Now I needed to break that habit.

"He isn't the reason this is over. I just don't love you anymore. You made sure of that."

"Fuck YOU, Jess! Fuck you!" he roared, pushing himself up but staggering forward until he caught the rail of the porch. At least he had drunk enough that he couldn't hurt me. I could shove him and he'd fall over.

"You already did that, Hank," I replied, and slammed the door in his face.

It was over an hour later when the banging finally stopped. He had either passed out or given up. I wasn't brave enough to open the door and check, so I got in bed and closed my eyes, knowing that Momma would be home soon and that if he was passed out on our porch he'd pay for it.

JASON

I gave it three days before I called her. When I had opened my eyes the next morning, a part of me had decided to let it go. Not to call her. She had left, and it was the best thing for me.

After three very long days of reading and spending my time in solitude, I hadn't come to grips with anything in my life. All I had done was think about Jess. The only thing to do now was get her out of my system.

Jess had picked up on the second ring. The fact that she hadn't even been annoyed about me not calling her for three damn days made me more pissed off. Not at her but at me. I had just treated her the way she expected. The surprise in her voice had made my chest tighten. Why the hell was I wanting to protect her now? It wasn't my job to change the way this girl thought about herself.

Maybe it was the way she'd said hello or the smile I could hear in her voice. I didn't know what possessed me, but before I could stop myself I was asking her if she wanted to go to a party in Manhattan with me tonight. One of my friends from Harvard was turning twenty-one, and his girlfriend was throwing a huge bash at her parents' place. I had been planning on going for over a week now, but the sudden urge to take Jess with me had hit. I wanted to see her in that part of my life.

After a few moments of silence, she said yes

And I wondered if I had just lost my mind.

Taking her into my world was a bad idea. But then, facing those people who all wanted something from me without one person there who accepted me for who I was sounded so damn unappealing. I needed Jess there. Even if it was a terrible idea.

Chapter Ten

JESS

I set my suitcase down beside the door and looked over at Momma. She was sitting on the sofa with her legs crossed, studying me with a frown. The cigarette in her hand was forgotten, as was the coffee in her other hand. She was not happy that I was about to leave with Jason Stone on a plane.

"What? Just say it and get it over with. You're going to anyway," I said, wishing she would be done with it already. I knew what she was going to say. I just wish she didn't feel like she had to say it.

Momma took a long pull from her cigarette and then put it out in the plate beside her. She was running out of time, because I wasn't about to let Jason come to the door. I didn't trust Momma. She would test him and I wasn't sure he could pass the test.

"He's your Logan. Girls don't marry their Logans."

She was back to talking about him being my Logan again. That made absolutely no sense. I didn't even know a Logan. I crossed my arms over my chest and glared at her. "What are you talking about?"

Momma cocked an eyebrow at me. "Jason Stone is your Logan. He's wealthy and impressive and handsome. He's a fairy tale. But don't get serious. Guard your heart."

I let out a frustrated sigh and dropped my arms. "Why are you calling him my Logan?" I asked.

"*Gilmore Girls*, sweetheart. *Gilmore Girls*. If you had bothered to watch it with me like I asked you several times, you would know what I mean. Hank is your Dean. He wasn't meant for you either. He was just the first heartbreak you keep going back to. Now you've met your Logan. It's a shame, though. I wish you'd met your Jess next."

My head was starting to hurt. My mother could be insane at times. This was one of those times. She was obsessed with several old television shows. *Gilmore Girls* was one of them. Apparently, she thought it had all the answers to my love life.

"I am Jess, Momma. Why do I need to meet myself?" I asked, rolling my eyes.

She waved her hand at me like I was being ridiculous. "Not you. Rory's Jess. You haven't met your Jess yet."

I was done with this conversation. I didn't even know who

the heck Rory was, and who names their kid Rory? How was that show even popular? I turned to open the door.

"Logan isn't Rory's soul mate. He's the wealthy rich boy who she does love, but when it comes down to it he isn't the one. The show ended, but we all knew it was Jess she would go back to. He was her soul mate. He broke her heart once, but he had to grow up too, and he changed. I just don't want you to get wrapped up in this boy. I want you to reach higher and get out of this life, but a rock star's brother isn't the way to do it. Enjoy it and have fun, but remember he's just your Logan."

He's just my Logan. Words of wisdom from my momma. Shaking my head, I opened the door and picked up my suitcase just as the limo pulled into the driveway. I glanced back at her sitting there with her cup of coffee, staring out the window at my ride. She was right. Maybe not about the *Gilmore Girls* philosophy, but about enjoying myself and guarding my heart. I had been hurt when Jason hadn't called the next day, but I had chalked it up to the inevitable. He was a fairy tale. And I didn't live in a storybook.

The truck that pulled in right after the limo caused me to halt in my steps. This was not happening to me. Not right now. I didn't want to deal with crazy. I just wanted to leave and get on a private jet and have a once-in-a-lifetime experience.

"Shit," I muttered as I dropped my suitcase on the porch.

"What is it?" Momma asked, standing up and walking to

the door. "Well, hell. I just ran his ass off the other night. He was passed out on the porch. Told him not to come back here."

"Got any *Gilmore Girls* wisdom for this dilemma?" I asked.

Mom just snorted.

Jason stepped out of the limo just as Hank jerked open his truck door. Jason glanced over at Hank, then back at me. I had to step in and fix this before Hank scared Jason off.

I picked my suitcase back up and started down the steps.

"Rory would send Dean home," Momma called out behind me.

I just rolled my eyes and kept walking. I wasn't an idiot.

"She's taking him from me," Hank said in a panicked tone as he stalked toward me, completely ignoring Jason's presence. "She can't take my boy from me, Jess. She can't. He's mine, too. I need you to talk to her. Tell her she can't do this."

I stopped walking and looked at Hank. His face looked stricken. The drunken asshole wasn't present right now. He was the boy who needed me. I couldn't just ignore him. This wasn't the first time Carrie had threatened to take their son from him. She did it for leverage.

"What did you do this time?" I asked him, knowing that was what it all boiled down to. I turned to Jason and frowned. "I'm sorry. I'll make this fast."

He nodded and stood where he was, watching us with a bored expression. I wanted to hurl my suitcase across the yard at the unfairness of this.

"She knows I come over here when I've had too much to drink. She knows I love you, that I'll always just love you. I can't love her, Jess. She's not you. But he's my boy. She can't do that, can she? Go tell her not to. She won't listen to me." He was begging me. I wanted to ignore all this.

"I'm leaving. I'll be back tomorrow late, and I'll talk to her then," I told him.

"Don't leave me," Hank said, walking over to me and grabbing the suitcase I was holding. I saw Jason take a step forward and stop. He was waiting on me to decide what to do. I was thankful that he wasn't getting involved in this just yet.

"Marry me, Jess. I love you and I just want you. I'll stop fucking around. I swear it."

I shook my head. We had been here before. Same argument. "No. I'm not marrying you. Now go home, and I'll go see Carrie when I get back."

"Please, baby?"

"She said she'd help when she got back." Jason walked forward and took my suitcase from my hand, then handed it to the driver, who was behind him.

Hank shot an angry glare at Jason, and I watched as his hand curled into a fist. I took a step toward Hank and grabbed his arm. "Don't do this. You've got to let me go," I told him.

"He's using you. When he's done with you, I'll still be here. He won't be," Hank snarled, still looking at Jason.

"Go, Hank," I said, letting go of his arm and moving toward Jason.

It happened fast. Hank reached out to grab Jason, but the large driver was there instantly. The man had grabbed Hank's arm, towering over him.

"What the hell!" Hank roared, trying to get free of the driver, who held Hank still with what looked like little effort. The driver glanced to Jason for instruction.

"Let him go once I get her safely in the limo," Jason said in a matter-of-fact tone. His body was strung tight. I could feel the tension rolling off him, but he didn't act like he was tense.

Jason placed a hand on my lower back and led me over to the limo. I fought the urge to look back at the driver and Hank before climbing inside. Jason turned back to look at them.

"Make sure he moves his truck," Jason said before following me inside the limo and closing the door.

I just stared at him. I should have said something to Hank to make him leave before I'd gotten in the limo. I'd just left Jason's driver to deal with it like this was something he was used to.

"You did still want to go, didn't you?" Jason asked

"Yeah, of course, but I didn't . . . I mean, your driver shouldn't have to deal with my crazy ex. I could've made him leave."

Jason leaned back and stretched his legs out in front of him. "Your crazy ex is nothing compared to the insane fans that Kane is used to fending off for my brother. That's his job."

Frowning, I turned to look outside, as Hank's truck was actually moving and Kane was walking back to the limo. "I thought his job was to drive."

Jason chuckled. "He is also a bodyguard. He's the one Jax uses when he's here or traveling south. You thirsty?"

Was I thirsty? I stared at him as he lounged there comfortably like he didn't have a care in the world. Had Hank really not bothered him?

"What's causing the frown?" Jason asked with a grin on his lips.

"Did that not even bother you? I mean, you still want to take me with you after seeing that part of my life?"

Jason reached over to pick up one of my hands and threaded his fingers through mine. "I've helped you escape after you bashed your ex's truck with a bat, I've broken into a pool and watched you flirt your way out of trouble with the police, and I've seen your ex lose his shit right in front of his kid because you were with another guy. Do you really think at this point something like that is going to surprise me?"

I didn't reply. He was right.

"You're a nice change. You make life interesting. I came here to take a break from things, and you're helping me. When it's time for me to return to the pressures of reality, I'll have these moments with you to think of and smile." He said this with a grin before reaching over to an ice-filled silver bucket inside a glass bar. "Water?" he asked.

I nodded and accepted the bottle of water while his words sank in. I was his distraction for right now. He didn't see a future with me. I knew that already, but hearing him say it stung. The fact that it hurt reminded me that I was caring about him more than I should. This was supposed to be fun for me, too. I had to remember that. If I wasn't careful, he would break my heart.

JASON

I had almost left her. I wasn't going to let her know that, but she was right. Her life was a little more than I'd bargained for. The idea of going to that party without her hadn't seemed appealing, though. I also couldn't stand the idea of leaving her here with that idiot. I didn't trust the guy, and the way he played on Jess's emotions pissed me off.

"I'm a little worried about flying. I've never been on a plane before. Not sure if I will panic or not, but I thought I should warn you," she said, and twisted the bottle of water around in her hands nervously.

I couldn't help but stare at her. She had seriously never flown before? Wow. Had I ever met anyone who had never flown before? "Does that mean this is your first time to New York too?" I asked, assuming she wouldn't drive that far.

She smirked, and one corner of her ridiculously plump lips lifted. "Florida, Mississippi, and Louisiana are the extent of my travels. If I can't get there by car in about three hours, then I've never been."

Why did I like it so much that I was taking her somewhere she'd never been? Her tempting mouth had broken into a full smile now, and I couldn't seem to ignore it anymore. Reaching over, I cupped her face and reminded myself just how good Jess's lips felt pressed against mine.

Her hands went instantly to my hair, and she opened her mouth under mine, allowing me a taste without my even asking. The minty taste of her toothpaste met my tongue, and she pressed her chest against mine. We had a twenty-minute ride to the private airstrip, and I suddenly knew exactly how I wanted to spend it.

"Straddle me," I told her as I broke the kiss and reached for her waist to move her hot little body over mine.

She threw a leg over mine and made the transition so smoothly and with such ease, I pushed all thoughts about why she was so good at that away. I didn't like thinking about her with other guys, although I knew there had to have been many. Jess was a flirt, and I didn't know a guy who would turn her down. I stopped kissing her neck and took a deep breath. Shit.

The guys at this party were going to be all over her. I hadn't thought of that. She was different from the same group we always ran in. She would make all the other girls seem less interesting. I wasn't sharing her. I had just wanted her with me.

Jess pulled back and started to move off my lap. I held her there and she stilled.

"At the party, you're with me," I told her as I lifted my head to look at her.

She frowned, then nodded. "Okay," she replied. I could see the uncertainty in her face. She didn't understand what I was saying.

"It's different from your world. The partying may be in nicer places, but the crowd isn't more refined. They don't do well with boundaries. Guys are going to hit on you. A lot. A whole helluva lot."

Jess's eyes widened, and she sat back on my lap as her gaze hardened. "And what? I won't be able to resist throwing myself into the arms of any guy who hits on me? Really? That's what you think?" She started to move again, and I held her waist, making it impossible for her to move away.

"No. That's not what I think. I wanted you to be aware that they're going to be intrigued by you. You're not like the girls in our circle. I just . . . I'm not going to handle it well if you give anyone else too much attention."

Jess's body eased some as she studied me. I held her gaze and the anger seemed to be melting. Finally she placed a hand on my chest. "Why would I want to give anyone else attention when I'm with you?"

I liked that answer, but she still didn't understand the world she was about to enter. "You'll recognize some faces. Not everyone is famous, but they're all part of a world where they are connected to celebrities."

She leaned forward and pressed a kiss beside my ear. "I'm not saying I won't be silently blown away to be meeting famous people or those connected to famous people. But I'm with you because I like you," she whispered in my ear, then wrapped her arms around my neck. "Now kiss me again, please."

I glanced down, unable to ignore the low-cut shirt she was wearing, and I was pretty damn sure she was braless. Groaning as she rocked her hips and sank down in my lap, I leaned forward and pulled her bottom lip into my mouth and bit down before sucking on it. Damn lips of hers were driving me crazy.

Chapter Eleven

JESS

When the limo stopped, I was topless. Jason lifted his head from the attention he was giving my breasts and pressed a button. "Give us about five minutes," he said.

"Yes sir," Kane replied.

I had to bite my lip to keep from asking him if we could spend four of those minutes with his mouth back on me. His hands came up and cupped both of my swollen breasts. "Really don't want you to put your shirt back on," he said with a wicked grin on his face.

I didn't want him to either. "I'm thinking Kane would appreciate it," I replied.

Jason reached for the shirt he had taken off of me. "You're wrong there. Kane would appreciate this view. It would make his day." The teasing grin on his face made me laugh.

I let him dress me since he seemed to be intent on doing it. Once he had my shirt back on, he brushed my nipples through the fabric. "Damn, these are nice."

I had always liked my body. My momma had given me the body and looks that I used to my advantage. But right now I was thankful for them for a completely different reason. Jason was attracted to me. He wanted me.

"You ready to fly?" he asked, moving his hands down to my waist again.

I wanted to say yes, but I wasn't sure. So I shrugged.

Jason leaned forward and pressed a kiss to my mouth. "I'll distract you if you get nervous."

The idea of him distracting me made the thought of getting on the plane much more appealing. "Promise?" I asked, looking up at him through my lashes.

Jason chuckled and shook his head. "Don't flirt with me, Jess. I already want you. Flirting just makes it worse."

There was a knock on the door, and Jason moved me off his lap before knocking back. He reached for my hand as the door opened. We climbed out, and Jason nodded to Kane before we headed to the jet.

There was a lady standing at the bottom of the steps with her arms behind her back, standing straight. Jason stopped and looked at her. "We won't be needing you during the flight. I'd like privacy," he said as he moved me in front of him and I headed up the stairs.

I stopped just inside, and Jason came up behind me and slid his hands around my waist. "Go on in," he said close to my ear.

I walked inside and took in the place. Black leather sofas lined the inside, and a bar sat at the back. From here I could see it was completely stocked. A massive flat screen covered the wall on the other end. "Have a seat. Get comfortable," Jason said, taking my hand and pulling me over to sink onto the leather.

"Wow" was all I could think of to say. I knew I needed to say something, but this was beyond what I had expected.

Jason glanced over at the bar and back at me. "You want a drink? One that will calm your nerves?"

That would have been nice, but I also didn't want to get sick. What if I had motion sickness and didn't know it? I shook my head and looked outside the tinted windows.

Jason came over and sat down beside me. "Nervous?"

I nodded. "And excited."

"Good combination," he replied.

Yes, it was. The door we had entered through closed, and the lady he had spoken to locked it, then looked over at Jason. "The bar is stocked, sir. I'll be in the cockpit. If you need me, just ring."

"Thanks," Jason told her, then leaned back against the seat and stretched his arms across the back.

The lady left the room, closing another door behind her.

"I'm going to be good since this is your first flight. I want you to enjoy it. But the moment you need a distraction, just let me know and we'll take up where we left off in the limo."

My stomach fluttered. I loved the way Jason's hands and mouth felt on me. I tried not to look too anxious and kept my eyes focused on the window. But my body flushed. I didn't want him to get tired of me too soon. I knew that day was coming, and I wanted to postpone it. Being with Jason made me happy. He didn't judge me and he made me smile. When he touched me, it was different from how I had been touched before. He wasn't in a hurry or focused on getting himself off. He took his time as if he enjoyed touching me. Like he wanted to enjoy every second.

The jet began to move and all other thoughts fled. I reached for Jason and grabbed the first thing I could find, which was his leg. I held it tightly. Jason immediately moved closer, and his arm curled around me, but he didn't do anything more. His closeness helped but my heart was still pounding.

Soon we were speeding down the runway and Jason was holding me close enough that his warm breath tickled my neck. I sank back into him and closed my eyes as we left the ground.

"Breathe," Jason whispered in my ear, and I realized I was holding my breath.

I sucked in some air and he laughed softly.

"You sure you don't want that drink?" he asked.

I shook my head and opened my eyes to stare down at the ground, which was getting farther and farther away. When we broke through the clouds, I gasped and squeezed Jason's arm, which was now wrapped around me.

He nuzzled my neck. "God, you're too damn sexy to be this cute. It's supposed to be one or the other, not both."

Smiling, I leaned back into him and relaxed. No one had ever called me cute before. Why did I like it so much? His hands moved back up and over my breasts. "I want your shirt off again. It's all I can think about. Knowing you're not wearing a bra is messing with my head," he said as he kissed my neck and the curve of my shoulder.

"Take it off," I said, sitting up and lifting my arms.

Jason let out a groan and pulled the shirt up, then reached around the front of me and pulled me back against his chest again and continued taking small bites of my neck, then soothing it with a kiss. His large, warm hands held my breasts, and they felt heavy and needy. I was more than a handful even for his big hands, and I liked it.

"You smell incredible," he murmured as he kissed my shoulder and ran the tip of his nose against my skin.

I couldn't keep from trembling

"Stand up," he said, leaning back and helping me up on my weak legs. He stood me in front of him and began pulling the zipper on my blue jean skirt down, then tugged at it until it fell to the ground. I stepped out of it and waited on him.

He reached out and ran a finger over the wet spot on my

white satin panties. I had made sure to bring my sexiest underwear. These had very little fabric, and I loved the way they felt. Seeing his finger slide over the crotch, which was obviously soaked, made it harder to stand. Especially in the heels I was wearing.

As if he could read my thoughts, he slipped his hands into the sides of the panties and pulled them down slowly. I lifted each foot and he pulled the panties off completely. He stared down at the red heels I was wearing, then lifted his eyes to me. We stood there staring at each other for a long moment before he stood up in front of me and touched my body, gently running his hands down my sides, being sure not to touch me where I wanted him to the most.

When he stopped, I started to protest until I saw him pull his shirt off. Instead I stood there, transfixed by seeing his body in daylight. I was starting to touch the ripples on his hard stomach when his hands fell to his jeans and started unbuttoning them.

He had his jeans undone and hanging on his hips. I realized I was panting with anticipation. Then he stopped and let his gaze slowly caress me from my red heels all the way up until his eyes locked with mine.

"I want to take my time and enjoy every last inch of you, but right now all I can think about is putting you up on that bar over there with your legs thrown over my arms and these red heels still on your pretty feet. Next time I'll go slower, but I need to fuck you now."

My knees buckled and I reached out to grab his arms to steady myself. Jason muttered a curse, and in seconds his jeans were off. He picked me up and carried me to the bar, which put me at eye level with him, and sat me down on it. His eyes were smoldering with need, and it only made me more frantic. He lifted one of my legs and ran his hands down it before placing my foot on the edge of the counter, causing me to lean back. He did the same with my other leg, and when he had me laid out and spread open for him, he stood back.

"That's an image I'll never forget," he said as he tore open a condom wrapper and slid it on. "Fuck, Jess. That's a fantasy I've had for a long time," he said, taking a step toward me as his eyes roamed over my very exposed body. "But no one was ever right. I never wanted them like this." He sucked in a breath and let it out slowly. "You're fucking perfect."

My body heated under his praise, and I wanted to be perfect. For him. That scared me, but I wouldn't think about it right now. I knew this was temporary, and I wanted to enjoy it while I had it.

JASON

I had never wanted to worship anyone's body. I appreciated them and I enjoyed them, but they were always the same. Jess . . . wasn't.

She was different from every other girl I had been with. I had tried the sweet and innocent type, the wild groupies, and then the girls who were in my circle of friends. They were privileged and spoiled, but I understood them. I knew them. Each kind had been nice. The wild groupies didn't want anything but sex and attention. The good girls like Amanda were the kind you built a relationship with. Then the others understood my life.

Never had I been with someone as complex as Jess. She was wild and fun. But then there was this insecurity and innocence in her that, mixed with that body every man dreamed of, made her irresistible. I couldn't seem to calm down enough to take my time with her. I kept wanting inside her again, and fuck me if she wasn't willing. Her legs propped up on the bar without hesitation was the hottest thing I'd ever seen. And I'd seen a lot.

I wanted to slow this down. I wanted to make her feel special, because I was pretty damn sure after meeting her ex she hadn't been treated like she deserved. But my need for her was taking over.

Her legs trembled as her tongue came out and swiped her bottom lip. I wasn't going to be able to stop myself. I slid my arms under her knees and pulled her hips to the edge of the bar. Cupping her ass, I rested my head on her chest and inhaled the sweet smell of her skin. Her breasts rose and fell quickly with her breathing.

Lifting my head, I looked directly into her eyes as I sank

into her. It was so wet and tight my eyes wanted to roll back in my head, but I kept them locked on her. Her lashes fluttered and her head fell back as a moan escaped her. I couldn't think of anything other than how good this felt.

Then she did something that made her already tight hole even tighter as it clenched around me. I stilled and a wicked smile touched her lips. Then the extra tightness eased up, and I started to move when she pulled it tighter again.

"Jess," I said, trying to decide if she was doing this on purpose or not. I was going to come way too fast if she kept it up.

"Yes," she said sweetly, then pumped my dick again. She was doing it on purpose.

"You keep that up and this will be over before you want it to be," I told her in a strangled whisper.

She lifted her hips and did it again, causing me to tighten every damn muscle in my body to control my need to release. "I wanna make you come this way," she said, then pulled her plump bottom lip between her teeth.

"I'm real damn close," I warned her.

She squeezed me again and again quickly. "Then come," she whispered, her encouragement before starting a relentless pull with her body.

I was past the point of words.

Chapter Twelve

JESS

I felt like I was in a movie. Seriously. Just being in New York City after seeing it in movies for so long—it was as if I had stepped into one of those movies. I didn't want to look like a redneck bumpkin come to the big city, but I couldn't stop looking at everything through the window of the limo. The buildings were huge and people rushed down the streets just like in *Gossip Girl*. It was exactly what I'd expected.

"Welcome, Mr. Stone. I'll have your bags taken to your room," a man said, greeting us as we stepped out of the limo. Jason nodded and took my hand.

I was too busy watching the people on the street and soaking everything up to pay attention to anything else. I doubted I would ever make it back to New York, and I didn't want to miss anything. I needed to memorize it all.

"You want to go inside, or would you rather go explore?" Jason's amused tone made me blush. I was probably embarrassing him, but I decided I wasn't going to worry about it.

"Can we explore?" I asked, not wanting to look away from everything.

He chuckled. "Of course. Kane will get us checked in. What do you want to see?"

What did I want to see? Everything. Was that possible in one day? I stopped and looked up and down the street as horns blared and a cab driver shouted at another car stopped in front of him. I laughed. It was perfect. "I just want to see everything," I said honestly.

"That would be impossible, but we'll do our best to get in as much as we can. I'm getting hungry. What about a busy café crammed full of people?"

I nodded and grinned up at him. "That's perfect," I replied.

Jason just smiled and shook his head. Then he reached for my hand. "Come on. I know the perfect place."

I kept my hand firmly tucked in his as we walked past the people talking on phones or rushing from one place to another. Some had shopping bags and others were hailing cabs. How could I even begin to explain to my momma when I got home how unreal all this was?

"You like pickles?" Jason asked randomly.

I turned to look at him. "Pickles?" I repeated, confused.

"Yeah, pickles. This place has some of the best ones I've eaten."

Oh. I liked pickles. Even if I didn't, I would try them. I wanted to try it all. "I love pickles."

Jason opened the door to a small café that was, in fact, packed with people. He pushed through the crowd. "Most of them are waiting for to-go orders," he explained.

We walked toward a long table, where it looked like other people were sitting. The last two seats beside the wall were open. "Go on inside," he said.

I frowned and looked at the other people at the table. They weren't paying us any attention. "What about them?" I asked, confused.

Jason grinned. "They aren't using those seats."

"You share tables here?"

Jason moved closer to me. "Place isn't big enough not to use every available seat. It's the way it works. Promise. Sit down."

I did, and he pulled out the seat beside me and sat down. A waitress was there immediately, handing us two menus and asking what we wanted to drink.

I was too busy listening to the many conversations going on at our table to think about the menu. This was wild.

"I always get the Reuben. It's my favorite. But all their sandwiches are good. Just huge."

I watched as the waitress set an opened-faced sandwich down in front of the guy beside us. There was more meat piled up on the sandwich than I ate in a month. Holy crap.

"Want to share?" Jason asked with an amused smirk on his face as he watched me.

"Yeah, I like Reubens. That sounds good. I couldn't eat a fourth of that thing," I said, glancing from the sandwich up to Jason's pretty blue eyes.

Our drinks and a bowl of pickles were placed in front of us. The pickles all looked different, and Jason explained their differences. I didn't want to eat a whole one and started to cut off a slice when Jason picked up the pickle and held it to my mouth. "Take a bite, Jess."

I did as he instructed. Jason watched me as I chewed it up, and then he took a bite before winking at me and reaching for another pickle. He held each one and had me taste them. Once I had found my favorite, he handed it to me and told me it was mine. "Eat it."

The sandwich was the biggest thing I had ever seen, but I ate as much as I could. Jason finished off the rest, calling me a wimp.

After we left, he took me to Central Park and we took a carriage ride as he told me about different parts of the park. I felt like I had my own personal tour guide. He kept me tucked against him and played with my hair while he talked. Liking this too much wasn't smart, but I couldn't help it. I liked it a lot. I loved the way Jason made me feel.

Shopping on Fifth Avenue was another experience. The first thing I admired, Jason snatched up and bought me. I didn't want him doing that. So I was careful not to touch or look at anything longingly again. He still managed to watch me closely enough to see my interest in a pair of gray leather stiletto boots. Even with me insisting I didn't want to try them on, Jason somehow managed to get the lady to bring out my exact size. Giving in so I didn't make a scene, I tried them on, and Jason's eyes did that smoldering thing that made it hard for me to breathe.

"We want them," he told the lady without looking away from me.

When she took them and walked to the register, I grabbed his arm. "You don't have to buy those," I whispered. I had seen the eight-hundred-dollar price tag.

"Yeah, I do," he replied. "Trust me, that was a selfish purchase." He turned to hand the lady his card.

"They cost too much," I said through my teeth, not wanting people to hear me.

"Can't put a price on the way your legs look in those boots," he replied.

My face felt hot and my heart was doing funny things. When he said stuff like that to me, it was hard to remain calm. It also tore down more of my protective walls. The lady thanked him and handed him the bag and his card. Jason took the bag in one hand and then reached for my hand with his other one.

"What do you want to see now?"

"I don't know. I never imagined I would come here, so I don't know what to do."

Jason pulled me close to his side as a crowd of people rushed by. "We have about two hours before we need to head to the party. How long will it take you to get ready?"

"An hour," I replied.

"Then it's time you saw Times Square," he said.

We walked down the street, and I was careful not to look at items in the windows for fear he'd go in and buy them for me. I didn't know if all rich boys did that or if it was just a Jason thing, but I didn't want him to do it. He had already brought me here. That was enough.

JASON

I had been visiting New York City since I was a kid. Never once had I enjoyed it the way I had today. Jess had been so excited, and just watching her take everything in had been more fun than any other time I had been here. She was innocently amazed at things like the Gray Line bus and the Naked Cowboy—all things I took for granted. Whenever Jess saw something she wanted, I had needed to buy it. It was like some compulsion. I didn't buy girls stuff. It wasn't my thing.

Again, Jess was making me act out of character. She was all in my head, and I wasn't sure how safe this was. I couldn't forget that I wasn't planning a relationship with her.

The bathroom door opened and Jess stepped out of it, draining all other thoughts from my head. She was wearing a short red clingy dress that was strapless and looked like it was made of silk. The gray leather stiletto boots I had bought her hugged her legs perfectly.

She did a twirl and smiled shyly at me. "Will this do?" she asked. I could see the worry in her eyes. I hadn't considered the fact that she might not have something to wear, but she did. The dress she was wearing looked like icing.

"You're gorgeous," I replied honestly.

She beamed at me and reached back to twist her long blond hair up. "Should I wear it up or is it okay down?" she asked.

"Down," I replied, walking over to her so I could touch her. She stepped into my arms easily. "I like it down," I repeated.

She slipped her hands up my chest and behind my neck. "You look really hot all dressed up," she said, staring up at me through her lashes.

"Mmmm," I replied, tugging her closer to me. "We need to leave now or we won't be going," I said, letting her go and putting some distance between us. If I didn't show up for this party, Finn would be hurt. But with Jess looking like the fantasy in every wet dream I'd ever had, it was hard to give a shit about Finn.

Jess took a deep breath, and I suddenly wondered just how secure that dress was. Her chest rose and fell, teasing me with the idea that her tits might break free. "Jess?" I asked, unable to take my eyes off her generous cleavage.

"Yes?"

"How sure are you that your tits are safe from being freed?"

Jess let out a small laugh and walked over to me. She slipped her hand under my chin and made me look at her face instead of her soft, firm, tempting-as-hell breasts.

"Do you plan on tugging it down?" she asked.

I was real close to doing it now. I swallowed hard. "Not at the party," I replied. But as far as the limo ride back, I wasn't promising anything.

"Then I'm positive they're safely tucked away."

I hoped she was right. I didn't want to have to kill anyone for seeing what was mine.

A bucket of ice cold water couldn't compete with the icy chill that went through me. What did I mean by "what was mine"? Jess wasn't mine. I couldn't begin to think of her as mine. I would be going back to Harvard in the fall. I had a life that Jess didn't fit into. One I was currently trying to figure out. I didn't need more complications.

I turned and headed for the door, needing to get away from her. I couldn't talk right now, or think. I had to clear my head. This was a bad idea. I shouldn't have brought her. She was getting under my skin in a way I wasn't familiar with, and I didn't feel safe. It was also unfair to her.

"Jason?" she asked. Her voice wavered nervously.

I closed my eyes and mentally cursed myself. I had to distance myself from her, but I couldn't hurt her in the process. She was my date. She was in a strange city. Ignoring her completely was not an option, but I needed to remind her of exactly what we were. A fling. Just a summer fling.

I masked the panic on my face before turning to see her standing where I had left her. She was clutching her hands nervously in front of her. Damn. I couldn't be an ass. I held out my hand. "Come on. Time to go party," I said with a smile. She didn't seem sure, but she placed her hand in mine and I focused on getting us the hell out of that hotel.

The limo was waiting for us, and Kane stood at the door.

I didn't slide in close to Jess this time. Smelling her and feeling the warmth from her body was too hard to resist. I reached for a crystal tumbler and poured myself some bourbon before sitting back. Taking a long drink, letting it burn my throat and take the edge off, I remained quiet.

Jess didn't say anything, and looking at her was out of the question. I needed more to drink first. The ride to the party wasn't long, thankfully. When Kane parked in front of the building, I set my glass down and prepared myself for a very long night.

"Did I do something wrong?" Jess asked quietly.

I wanted to tell her that no, she had done nothing wrong. I had let this go too far. I hadn't been careful. But instead I smiled and shook my head. "Of course not. We're here," I replied as Kane saved me by opening the door.

Chapter Thirteen

JESS

I had done something. I just couldn't figure out what. Was he embarrassed by my dress? That was all I could think of. We had been talking about it when he had gone cold. I didn't have designer clothing. However, this dress was one of my best pieces. I wasn't talented at many things, but I was good with a sewing machine. When I had cried because I didn't have a nice dress to wear to the homecoming dance my freshman year, my momma had gotten out the old sewing machine that her mother had left her. She had brought me several dresses of hers that she no longer wore and told me to stop feeling sorry for myself and figure it out.

It had taken me a week of staying up most of the night to figure out how to work the machine. The designing had come easy. I was good at it. Making it work was more difficult, but I had worn an original dress to that dance. Making my own dresses had become a hobby. I enjoyed it. Momma brought me costumes from the club that needed mending, and they paid me for it. I even started making new stuff for them too.

This dress was my favorite creation. If he was embarrassed by it, then he shouldn't have invited me. I wasn't one of these people, but I refused to feel like less than a person because my label wasn't a designer one.

He was intent on not speaking to me, so I remained quiet. I'd asked him twice now if I had done something. He'd said no. I wasn't asking again.

When we arrived at the double doors of what I assumed was a penthouse because it wasn't a normal-size apartment, he rang the bell and the doors swung open almost immediately. The music was loud and the girl at the door looked like something out of a magazine.

"Jason!" she squealed, throwing her arms around him. "You're here! We've missed you."

I watched as he wrapped his arms around her and hugged her back. I would not care. Besides, she was probably the girl-friend of his friend who was throwing the party.

"Told you I'd be here," he replied, stepping back and scanning the room. I was almost prepared for him not to introduce us. I wasn't sure how I would respond if he didn't. It wasn't like I could leave. I had no money. I hadn't brought my purse because it didn't match this dress and wasn't nice enough.

"Vanessa, this is Jess. Jess, this is Vanessa, a friend of mine from school," he said, surprising me.

Vanessa's appraising gaze made me nervous and angry at the same time.

"Guess it's a good thing Jo isn't here," she replied, shooting Jason a look that made me cringe. "It's nice to meet you, Jess."

"You too," I managed to choke out.

Jason placed his hand on my back and led me inside. That small touch helped ease my fear a little, but the moment we were inside he dropped his hand.

"Jason, you've been hiding," a guy said. "Talked to Jax last night, and he said you were vacationing." The guy shifted his gaze to me, and a slow grin touched his face. "And who is this?"

"Cameron, this is Jess. Jess, this is Cameron," Jason said in a bored tone.

"Jess, huh? Well, Jess, how have we not met before?"

I wasn't sure how to answer that.

"Because you don't visit south Alabama," Jason replied, taking a shot glass from a tray as a waitress walked by.

Cameron raised his eyebrows. "You've been hiding out at Jax's summer place? Why no invite?"

"Been busy," Jason replied.

Cameron's eyes shifted back to me. "Yeah, I can see that."

Jason glanced at me. "I need something more than this to drink. You thirsty? I'm going to the bar."

Those were the first words he had spoken directly to me since we were in the limo. Startled, I just shook my head. Jason didn't ask if I was sure or take my hand. He just walked off and left me there.

Cameron, on the other hand, didn't go anywhere. "So, you and Jason been seeing each other long?"

I wasn't sure if we were seeing each other now. "Not really," I replied.

Cameron's grin changed, and I knew that grin. The guys here might be wealthy, but they were still males. I knew how to handle men. I also knew that just because Jason was bored with me, standing back and playing the victim wasn't my style.

"Since he seems to have left you," Cameron said, glancing over at the bar, "and is now preoccupied, why don't you dance with me?"

I looked over at the bar and saw a girl with dark brown hair pulled up in a classy bun, dressed like the elitist she no doubt was, curled up against his side. He wasn't moving away from her and he seemed to be deep in conversation with her. Had I been the means to make someone jealous? A rebound?

My stomach felt sick. How could I have been so stupid? Guys like Jason didn't take girls like me seriously. Momma had been trying to warn me with her screwed-up *Gilmore Girls* analogies.

"Sure, I'd love to," I replied, slipping my hand into Cameron's. Cameron pulled me out onto the dance floor as the live band played. Luckily, it wasn't a slow song. I wasn't in the mood to get close to anyone at the moment. I felt as cheap as my dress. Thinking about it would make me cry. I wasn't going to cry. Not here. I blocked it out, all of it, and danced. Forgetting myself, I enjoyed the sound of the music and moved my body to the beat. When Cameron's hand touched my hip, I didn't move away. I let him get closer. I might as well. If I was going to get through this night without being destroyed, I would have to deal somehow.

"I'm trying to decide if this is worth getting my ass beat over. I'm thinking it is," Cameron said, and I opened my eyes to look at him. He was dancing close to me, but his eyes were on my body. I could see the gleam in his eyes, and I knew he was turned on. He lifted his eyes to meet mine, and the lust was there.

"No one will beat your ass for dancing with me," I replied, hating the bitterness in my voice. A few times spent with Jason and I start expecting more from guys.

Cameron's other hand rested on my waist. "Yeah, he's watching us. He's considering it. I can feel his extremely jealous glare from here," he said as he pulled me closer.

"You're imagining it," I told him. I was pretty sure Jason would be glad to get rid of me for the night. The thought hurt, and I pushed it back. I wasn't going to think about it.

"If that were true, I'd call him a fool. But I've known him since we were thirteen. He's ready to rip my arms off," Cameron said close to my ear.

I wouldn't look for him. He wanted to ignore me? Then I could ignore him, too. I closed my eyes again and started to move to the next song that started up.

"Damn," Cameron whispered as his hand flexed on my hip.

Normally, knowing I was getting to a guy made me smile. I felt powerful. But not now. I was empty.

"Move." Jason's hard tone startled me, and I opened my eyes to see Cameron's amused grin as he winked at me and held up his hands and backed away.

"Sorry, dude. You looked otherwise occupied, and I figured if I didn't grab her up, someone else would."

Jason's angry snarl as he shot a warning glare at Cameron wasn't hard to miss. By anyone in the room.

Jason's hands were on my hips as he pulled me against him hard.

"Oh," I said, grabbing his arms to steady myself.

"You aren't wearing fucking panties," he growled in my ear.

No, I wasn't, because I couldn't with this dress. But what did that have to do with anything? "Uh, yeah, so?" I replied, wanting to be mad at him.

"His hands were on your hips. He could tell. He's fucking

you in his head right now, dammit," he said, tightening his hold on me like someone was trying to pull me away.

"We didn't talk about my panties," I told him.

"Every damn guy in this room is watching you. Is that what you wanted? To come out here and make sure they all wanted you? Because moving your body like that—it sure seems like you wanted attention."

The anger set in, and I stopped moving and shoved away from him. He may have brought me here and he may have been nice and kind before. But I wasn't going to be talked to that way. I would walk back to the damn hotel and get my purse. I had enough money for a bus ticket. I wasn't doing this. Turning, I walked away. I knew people were watching.

"If you're done with Stone, baby, I'm very available as of right now," a guy said as I walked by.

"Back the fuck off, Myles," Jason yelled, and I realized he was right behind me.

I was just going to ignore him. Once I was outside, he would come back in here. He just didn't want me in his world anymore. Asshole.

Jason's hand wrapped around my arm just before I reached the door, and he pulled me in the other direction. I considered making a scene and screaming, but I bit my tongue and followed him. We walked upstairs and then into a bedroom, and he closed the door.

He was breathing hard when he turned around to look at me. I couldn't read him. He had me so confused right now. Why hadn't he just let me leave?

I started to say something, and then I realized Jason was shaking. Oh shit. He was going to hit me. I had seen Hank shake from being so angry before. He always ended up slapping me or throwing me down.

Backing away, I wondered if I could possibly outrun him in these heels.

"They're looking at you. Cameron was touching you. He was too close to you," Jason said in a low, scary voice. I gripped the edge of a chair and decided I would use it for protection. I could hide behind it and maybe shove it at him before I ran. It would slow him down.

"Then Hensley points out that you aren't wearing panties. There's no line, and the way the dress is hugging your ass, there is no way you could be wearing panties. They were all looking then. And Cameron's hand was on your hip. His fingertips were brushing your ass. He shouldn't have touched your ass."

Okay, so he was upset over the fact that I was commando. I would leave if he would just let me. "I'm sorry. I don't wear panties with this dress. Didn't realize it was a big deal. Just let me leave. I'll get home. If you'll just let me out of here."

Jason frowned and stared at me. Why was this a confusing

145

concept to him? He didn't want me here, and I was going to leave. Very easy.

"What are you talking about?" he asked.

I took that moment to move behind the chair. His gaze flicked to the chair, then back at me. His frown turned to confusion. Good thing was, he wasn't shaking anymore. That was always a good sign.

"You regretted bringing me, and I should have left. But then Cameron asked me to dance and you were busy with that girl, so I said okay. I didn't mean to make you mad. I thought you'd be glad to get me out of your hair. I wasn't aware the panty thing was a big deal. Sorry. Just let me out of here and I'll go and we'll be good."

I had talked down an angry Hank enough to know the tone of voice to use. Jason didn't have the crazed look in his eyes that Hank got. That was a relief.

Jason's eyes went wide and he took a step toward me, then stopped. He ran his hand through his hair and cursed while looking at me in horror.

"Did you . . . ? Are you . . . ?" He looked down at the chair again, and then at me. "Why are you behind that chair?" he asked with disbelief in his eyes.

Did the guy have multiple personalities? He had gone from angry to horrified in a split second. "In my experience, getting behind something you can use as protection is the best course of action," I replied carefully.

Jason put both hands in his hair, and he froze as he stared at me. We just stood there like that. I wasn't sure what the shocked look was for.

"Motherfucker," he finally said, dropping his hands and hanging his head. "You thought I was going to hurt you?" he asked incredulously.

Of course I did. "You were shaking. Guys shake from anger before they strike," I pointed out.

"Strike?" he repeated, still staring at me. "God, Jess." He sank down on the bed and dropped his head into his hands. What was wrong with him? He looked upset. Like I had hurt him, not the other way around.

I didn't move, but waited on him to say something. Finally he lifted his head and looked at me. "I would never hurt you. I don't hit women. I've never . . ." He closed his eyes. "I'm sorry. I'm having a hard time dealing with the fact that you've obviously been hit by guys enough to assume I would do it. I can't comprehend the fact that someone would hit you."

Oh. Yeah, well, that made sense. He'd never seemed like the kind of guy who hit, but then, I tended to make guys so mad they snapped and lost it, so I wasn't sure if I had done the same to him.

"You were angry," I explained.

He nodded. "Yeah, I was angry. Cameron was touching you. Guys were watching you like you were their last meal, and I didn't like it, and I didn't fucking like the fact that I didn't like it. This . . . I can't . . . We can't have anything more than this. I don't want to care if other guys look at you." He stopped and fisted his hands in his lap.

"I know this is just a little fling. I'm not expecting more," I said, suddenly wanting to reassure him.

He just sat there staring at me. I moved over to sit beside him now that I knew he wasn't about to take a swing at me. "I wasn't dancing with Cameron to make you mad. I was trying to get out of your way. You seemed like you regretted bringing me, and I was trying to salvage your night for you by not being a burden."

Jason closed his eyes and let out a deep sigh. When he opened them, he looked at me. "I'm sorry," he said. "You felt that way because I made you feel that way. This is my fault."

I didn't argue with him. He was right. He had made me feel that way.

"I don't get possessive. I can't get possessive. I don't have time for that. You are making me feel that way, and it doesn't fit into my world. I was trying to distance myself."

He didn't want to share my body. So that was his problem. Well, I didn't want to share my body either. And I wouldn't be sharing it with him anymore. He needed to distance himself? Then fine. I needed that too.

"Okay. Then we get through the night. Take me home, and

that's it. You can even send me home tonight if you like. I don't mind the bus."

Jason groaned and turned away from me. "I'm not putting you on a bus" was all he said.

"Fine. Then you get me home however you want to."

Jason reached over and took my hand in his. "I don't like this," he said.

And he thought I did? I wasn't going to admit it, though. I shrugged. "It is what it is. And I've had fun."

Jason wouldn't look at me. "How do we distance ourselves?"

"We start with very little touching and of course nothing sexual. I won't dance with anyone else if that bothers you, but you can't dance with anyone else either. To keep it fair."

Jason turned his head to finally meet my gaze. "Nothing sexual?"

"Can't have distance if we're naked and wrapped around each other," I replied.

Heat flashed in Jason's eyes, and I stood up before he could act on that. As much as I loved to be in his arms, I also knew that no matter how many times I offered myself to him, he would be leaving me. I was not someone he would ever have a relationship with, and it was time I protected myself.

"That's gonna be fucking impossible," he said.

No, it wasn't. He wanted distance. He was going to get it. "It's the only way," I replied.

JASON

I placed my hand on Jess's lower back as we walked back into the party. I could feel the eyes on us—or more like, on her. Every damn guy here was looking at her, and I had no right to care. Which sucked. I wasn't going to think about it.

"You thirsty yet?" I asked her.

"If you go to the bar and get sidetracked, someone may approach me, and I don't want to be rude to your friends," she said.

I reached for her hand. "I'm not leaving you alone. They're all fucking vultures," I replied, taking her with me.

She went with me willingly. "What do you want to drink?" I asked her.

She glanced at the bartender. "Do you have whiskey?" she asked hopefully.

"Straight?" the guy asked, smiling at her like an idiot.

"Please, I need it," she replied.

He poured her more than the normal and slid it to her. Even the damn hired help was ogling her. "I can't believe you're drinking whiskey," I said.

She stopped with the rim almost to her mouth and gave me an amused grin. "Yeah, well, I don't know what else you expect from me. I'm not one of them," she said, waving her glass out at the crowd. "My momma ain't a trust-fund baby. She's a stripper."

I heard someone choke beside me, no doubt from her statement. She took a much longer drink of whiskey than I'd ever seen anyone take.

"Her momma is a stripper?" Hensley asked as he stared at her in openmouthed amazement. As if Jess hadn't already drawn attention, this piece of information was going to go through the room like wildfire.

"Shut up," I replied, and picked up my drink, needing to hover over her and protect her from the horny males who were just going to get worse when they found out her momma's profession.

"I can't believe you announced that," I said to her quietly as I led her away from the bar.

"Why? They're never going to see me again, and they'll all talk about you like you're a badass for bringing a stripper's daughter commando to one of their uppity parties. And whoever I'm supposed to be making jealous, I assure you, she is fuming. You'll have her back in your arms in no time. Just get rid of me first."

What the hell was she talking about? Make who jealous? Had someone told her about me and Johanna? That relationship had only been in Jo's head. All I had done was have sex with her once, months ago. "What are you talking about?" I asked her.

She took another long drink. "I'm talking about the reason you brought me to this thing. I couldn't figure out why you'd want me to come as your date when you could do so much better.

I get it now. I'm the bad girl from the wrong side of the tracks meant to drive the ex-girlfriend mad with jealousy."

That was what she thought? Shit. Of course it was. The insecurity that she was so damn good at hiding was still there. She had been used so many times in her life that she expected it. I had only wanted to spend some time with her and treat her differently. But in the end I had treated her the way she expected.

I grabbed her drink and set it on a tray as it went by, then led her to the door. I'd call later and apologize for leaving. Right now I was getting Jess out of here so we could talk.

"Where are we going?" she asked as I pulled her out the door and toward the elevator.

"We're leaving," I replied.

"Why?"

"Because I need to get you alone so I can explain to you how very wrong you are."

She stiffened beside me. "If that means sex, we aren't doing that anymore."

I started to say something, when the elevator opened and I watched her ass as she walked inside. Just imagining it bare under that silky material was driving me fucking crazy.

When the elevator doors closed, I backed her up against the wall and pressed against her so she could feel just how turned on she made me. "No panties, Jess. No fucking panties. Don't tell me we aren't having sex anymore."

She opened her mouth, but the elevator door opened and I reached for her hand and pulled her outside. I had forgotten to buzz the driver. I texted him and then pulled Jess over to a dark corner of the lobby.

"I didn't bring you here to make anyone jealous. I brought you here because I like spending time with you," I told her.

She bit her bottom lip and I watched, transfixed, as she let it free. "But you want distance now," she said, breathing hard.

"This can't happen. Us. It won't work. I don't have time. But that doesn't mean I don't want you," I told her, sliding my hand down her hip until I finally touched the silk-covered bare ass of hers. "Fuck," I whispered.

"Don't. Please. If we can't . . . If this is over when we get home, then don't." Her chest was rising and falling so rapidly I was positive she was about to pop free of that dress. If she could just wait until we were in the limo, I would make sure to give those sweet nipples all the attention they needed.

"But I want you. So damn bad," I whispered before lowering my head and pulling her lip into my mouth and sucking on it. Women paid thousands to have lips this full and plump. I couldn't get enough of them.

She kissed me back, pressing closer, and I felt my chest ease up. She was giving in.

"Your car is here, Mr. Stone," a voice said behind me. Jess backed away immediately. I tucked her hand in the crook of my arm and led her out to the waiting limo. After the door closed, I reached for her again and she moved away, shaking her head.

"No. Don't. I can't do this," she said. "It's just sex for you, but I'm afraid it became more for me. I didn't want to admit it, but after tonight I have to face it. I . . . This is going to hurt. You're leaving. It's going to hurt. I can't make it worse. So don't. Just, please, I need to go home."

Chapter Fourteen

JESS

The flight home had been lonely. I had tried to close my eyes and sleep, but my heart hurt too much. I hadn't even told Momma I was on my way home early. But by the time Kane had retrieved my bag from the limo and handed it to me, the front porch light had come on and the door opened.

I thanked Kane and walked away without looking back. I didn't want to watch the car pull out of my driveway. Even though Jason wasn't in it, I still felt like it was him leaving.

Momma stood at the door with her arms crossed over her chest, watching me. She was trying to figure it out. When my feet touched the bottom step, the first tear fell.

"Oh, baby," she said, rushing to meet me and pull me into her arms. "I was afraid of this." I let her lead me inside and to the sofa, where she held me close, patting my head like a child.

I needed the comfort. I had walked right into this, and I didn't regret the memories, but I knew I wasn't ever going to be the same.

"I know this hurts. But remember, he will never forget letting you go. It will be one of his biggest regrets," she said against my head.

I wanted to smile, because leave it to my momma to believe a rock star's privileged brother would regret letting me, of all people, go. A mother's love really was unconditional. "He was kind," I told her. I didn't want her to think I was crying because he had been cruel.

"I know. I saw it in his eyes when he came to get you. That's how I know he'll regret this."

I held on to her arms and let all the pain go. She let me cry and didn't say anything else. My chest felt like it had exploded, but the smell of her soap and perfume was comforting. Finally I closed my eyes and drifted to sleep.

I didn't leave my house for over a week. I worked on costumes for the club and sat in my room for hours, staring at the walls and remembering. It was ten days after I said good-bye to Jason that my bedroom door swung open and in sauntered Krit. He was the lead singer of the local band, Jackdown. He was also

Trish's little brother. We had grown up together. Trish and my cousin Rock had dated for most of our lives. Then they'd gotten married. Krit was the epitome of a man whore, but he was hard not to love.

"I fucking refuse to sing tonight if you're not there. Won't do it. Those motherfuckers can get their rocks off somewhere else. I'm sick of looking for your angel face and not seeing it," he said as he plopped down on my bed and stretched his legs out in front of him, then put his hands behind his head. "Place is pointless without your sexy ass out there dancing. I don't have you to make the girls jealous. Who the hell am I supposed to kiss like I'm fucking to drive the women mad if you aren't there to grab? You're screwing up my game, love."

I couldn't help but smile. I turned my head to look at Krit, who was now lying down beside me. "Did Rock send you?" I asked.

Krit made a mock face of horror. "Rock? Hell no, Rock didn't send me. When the fucking hell do I do anything Rock tells me to? Never. That's when. I came because I missed you. I need my tongue-fuck buddy. Come dance and give Green a hard-on. He misses getting one while we're onstage. You always did it for him. Although, that tongue of yours must remain mine. Besides, Green would come in his damn jeans like a schoolboy if you planted one on him."

Green was the bass player in Jackdown. Krit loved to harass

Green about the one time he and I had gone out in high school when I had broken up with Hank. Green had told me he loved me after one date, and once Krit found out about it, Green never heard the end of it.

"You don't need me to get women. They throw themselves, their panties, their bras, and anything else they can take off their body legally at you every night," I reminded him, as if he needed reminding.

"I miss you, though."

"How much are you getting paid to do this?" I asked teasingly.

"I was hoping to settle up payment with you. A hot fuck in the back room while I'm on break tonight. That always makes me sing better before the next set. Or hell, baby, we can do it here. I'm game," he replied.

I laughed this time. I knew Rock was behind Krit's showing up. There was no way Krit had noticed I was missing. He was just trying to make me laugh, and it was working.

"If I stripped naked and crawled on top of you right now, you wouldn't fuck me, and we both know it. It never ends well for us. We've been there, done that," I told him. We had tried that out when we were younger. It wasn't that it was bad, because it was actually really good. We were just both so unstable that we couldn't deal with a relationship. We were just good at the sex part. Then there was my inability back then to get over Hank.

Krit let out a hard laugh. "You wanna bet? Try me."

Well, maybe he would. The guy was a sex fanatic.

"Come on, don't tease me. Get naked and crawl on top, love."

I punched his arm and he groaned, then gave me an evil laugh. "If you're not gonna fuck me, at least come tonight."

Going to Live Bay with everyone there watching me and wondering about what had happened didn't sound appealing. I wasn't in the mood for guys, either. I didn't want to dance with any or have any of them grope me.

"I'm not in the mood for guys," I told him.

Krit shot up in bed and looked down at me. "Holy hell, love. Are you saying you want a woman? 'Cause I'll pay shitloads of money to see you with another woman. Fucking cut off my left nut to watch that."

I shoved him and grimaced, causing him to laugh. "You're so ridiculous. Of course not. That isn't what I mean. I just don't want the flirting and touching and all that."

Krit lay back down beside me. "I'll stake a claim to you tonight, and you'll be safe. Just let me do my thing and everyone will know you're taken. That way you can relax and enjoy the night."

I glanced over at him. "What about *your* hookup for the night? Acting like you're with me will screw that up for you," I reminded him.

He reached over and tickled my stomach. "Let me at this body and you can make it all up to me."

"Krit," I said, throwing his hand off me. "Stop it."

Krit tucked his hand back behind his head. "Fine. I get it. No touching. But tonight I'll lay one on you and probably grab your ass at least twice so people can see. It's the only way to show everyone you're taken."

He had used me more than once to get the attention of other girls before. I had used him to piss off Hank. It was a mutual-benefits thing. "If I do this, will you leave?" I asked.

He laid his hand over his heart. "I'm hurt. You want to get rid of me?"

"I don't know how long you can lie in bed with a female before making a move. Don't want to push my luck," I told him.

He turned his head and winked at me. "Love, if I thought there was any way I could convince you to let me in those shorts of yours, I would already have my head between your legs."

He had no filter on his mouth. I shook my head and shoved him off my bed. "Go on. I'll see you tonight."

Krit stood up. His shirt had ridden up, and the tattoos that covered his chest peeked at me. His arms were also covered, and so was his back. He pulled his shirt up and stuck his pierced tongue out at me and wiggled it suggestively. "You want some, love, you don't have to stare. Just ask."

I rolled my eyes and he grinned. He had the same startling blue eyes as Trisha, and his hair was just as white-blond, but he wore it short and sticking straight up all over most of the time.

Both his ears were covered in piercings, and his eyebrow was pierced too—and, according to talk from the females, his penis. But that was new. Back when I had been with him, his penis was metal free.

"Bye, Krit," I said.

He puckered up and blew me a kiss. "Tonight."

When he was walking out the door, I realized that he was the first person to actually try to help get me out of this funk.

"Krit," I called out, and he stopped and turned around.

"Yeah, love?"

"Thanks," I said.

His expression became serious, and that was a rare thing. He usually either had a naughty gleam in his eyes or a wicked smile. "That dickhead is a fool," he said, then turned and walked out of the room.

I fought back the urge to defend Jason. He wasn't the bad guy. He had been honest the whole time. I had known it was a short fling. My being a girl and caring too much was what had screwed things up.

Chapter Fifteen

Three months later . . .

JESS

It was finally Friday night. I needed a break. Between my classes and working every day, I liked to remember I was young and could have a good time. I loved my new job and my classes weren't bad, but they took up my entire day Monday through Friday. If the shop was busy, I had to bring things home to work on them in the evenings.

I still couldn't get over the fact that Mrs. Dillard had hired me to work as a seamstress in her store. Not that I wasn't good enough, because I was, but because Mrs. Dillard's husband was a Baptist minister and I was a stripper's daughter. She didn't seem to care, though.

I was making more money working for her than I would waiting tables or at a bar. She had sent the dance studio to me when they needed help with costumes, and I had been hired to design them after they saw some of my ideas. After they hired me, I got a call from the dance studio in the next town over, asking me to design for them, too. I kept pinching myself to make sure I wasn't dreaming. I knew that after this year at school it was very unlikely I could go to a four-year college. Junior college was all I could afford. All my momma could afford. But I was beginning to wonder if I could make a career out of this.

I parked my truck outside the back entrance to Live Bay. Jackdown was playing tonight, and it would be crawling with the college crowd soon. I stepped out of the truck just as the back door swung open and Krit came out, headed straight for me. I hadn't seen him in two days. Not from his lack of trying, though.

"About fucking time," he said before he grabbed me and pulled me into his arms. I laughed against his mouth and felt him smile in return. The cool metal from his tongue ring slid past my lips and entered my mouth. The mix of cigarettes and tequila hit my tongue. It was Krit's signature taste on nights he played.

Before he could get too carried away, I pulled away and pressed one more kiss to his lips so he wouldn't pout. "I had a test," I reminded him. He hadn't been very patient with my studies so far this semester.

"And all I could think about was your pussy," he said, slipping his hand into the front of my jeans. I reached for it and pulled it out before he got too far and I let him. Krit had many talents, and knowing how to make a woman come fast was one of them.

"Let me play," he begged, backing me against the side of the truck.

He wasn't normally this frantic with me. Maybe the monogamous thing was getting to him. It had been a month since I'd agreed to have sex with him only if it was just me and only me.

When he had promised me it was just me he wanted, I thought he was high. I also thought it would be short-lived. I needed someone to make me forget Jason. It had been two months then, and he had stayed in all my dreams and fantasies. So I had agreed to a friends-with-benefits thing with Krit if it was just me he was sleeping with.

For the most part it had helped. There were times I was guilty of closing my eyes and pretending he was Jason. Those were weak moments. Most of the time I was completely with Krit.

"You have to do sound check, don't you?" I asked as he slid his hands under my shirt and squeezed my boobs.

"Love, all I can think about is how fucking hot you are," he said as he started kissing my neck. He was horny. And it was because he was used to having sex a lot more often than I was giving it to him.

"Krit, stop," I said, putting my hands on his chest and moving him back.

He frowned. "What's wrong?"

"This. You. I'm busy with school and work, and you're used to more action. You've been good for a month, and I'll admit I'm impressed, but you're off the hook. Go sleep with the masses throwing themselves at you. It's what you need. I'm not enough for you. We both knew this was a short-term thing."

Krit started shaking his head. "Hell no. You're not doing this to me, love." He started pacing in front of me. "I waited fucking years to get you under me. Years. I panted after you. Beat off thinking about you, and then I get you and this? Fuck no." He got in my face and his eyes dropped to my lips, then back up to my eyes. "Just you, Jess. Just want you. Wanted you since we were kids. But you were fucking Hank's. Now he's gone and married Carrie and is playing house. He's out of your life. I got you. Don't you throw me out, because I want you so damn bad. Don't mistake that for something else."

I didn't have any words. I was speechless. This was not something I had ever expected to come out of Krit's mouth. Ever. About anyone.

"You've always teased me," I said, shaking my head, trying to understand this.

Krit ran a finger down the side of my face. His fingernails were painted black tonight. It always made me smile when he did that. "I had to do something. I couldn't have you. But not telling you how much I wanted you was impossible. So I let you think I was kidding."

How did I handle this? I liked Krit. He made me laugh. He was my friend, but I didn't think I was capable of more. I had given in and admitted to myself even before I'd started sleeping with Krit that I was in love with Jason. I didn't like thinking I could fall in love with someone so fast, so I wanted to pretend it wasn't true, but it was.

I couldn't think about Jason. He was off-limits in my head. "So you're satisfied with me?" I asked him.

Krit closed his eyes, and that wicked smile touched his lips. "Yes," he replied, opening his eyes. The dark eyeliner he was wearing tonight made him seem dangerous. The idea made me smile. Krit was so far from dangerous. "Now that's cleared up, can I play with my girl's pussy?" he asked, unsnapping my jeans and slipping his hand inside the front of my panties.

I was going to let him. I knew what he wanted, and with thoughts of Jason in my head, I knew I needed it too. He would drive them away.

The back door swung open and light surrounded us. "Put your damn dick away. Everyone's waiting on you for sound check. Then we need to warm up. Hey, Jess," Green said.

"Fuck," Krit groaned, looking up at me. "Did I get you wet? Are you gonna be left achy?"

"Damn, dude, whisper that shit," Green said from the door.

Krit glared over at him. "Then shut the damn door," he called back.

"If I shut the door, you'll finish what you started," Green argued.

"If she fucking needs me to, I'll finish it right now with the damn door open," Krit replied.

I moved his hand and started buttoning my jeans back up before they got any louder talking about my needs. "I'm good. I promise. Later," I told him, and kissed him.

"Break? Come back to the storage room," he said.

I nodded.

"I fucking hate you," Green swore as he held open the door.

"Hey, Green," I finally said.

Krit kept me close to his side as we walked into the bar. "Rock's already out there. I saw him earlier," he told me. I nodded and headed to find my cousin.

JASON

This was a bad idea. It had been three months. I had thought I was over it. Over her. When the guys wanted to come stay at Jax's beach house, I'd said sure. Why not? It was just a weekend. Then they'd all insisted we go to the local bar to hear the band. Someone had told them how good the band was, and they wanted to check it out. There was a good chance she wouldn't even be here.

I was overreacting. It wasn't like she had come to the bar all the time when I'd spent time with her. Hensley opened the door and Finn walked on in. Hensley followed him, and I stood there wondering if I went back to the limo if anyone would notice. Finn was already tipsy, and Hensley wasn't far behind him.

I stood there as the door closed and tried to convince myself to walk inside. The door opened again and Hensley looked at me. "Come on," he ordered.

Telling him it was about Jess wouldn't be good. They thought that was over and done. If they knew I couldn't get her out of my head, they would never let me live it down. I would have to hear them say her name all the time and talk about her body, and I couldn't deal with that shit. I had enough going on internally.

I followed them to the bar, which was the last place Finn needed to be. I wanted to scan the place for her, but then what if I found her? What did I do? Did I speak to her, or would she want to ignore me?

"Heard this band is fantastic. They played at a bar in New Orleans when Cash was there last spring. He got their CD and shit," Finn said as the bartender handed him a shot of tequila. It was too early for him to be doing shots.

"Hey, the hottie you brought to New York, she's fair game now, right? I mean, since you're dating Star?"

I tensed up. Had he seen her, or was he just looking for her? I turned to look at Hensley. "She's off-limits," I said. "Why?"

Hensley frowned. "You're dating a fucking celebrity. Why the hell is she off-limits?"

"I'm not dating Star. She's a friend. She's Jax's friend. Do you see Jess?" I turned, giving in and looking out into the crowd.

"Who?" Hensley asked.

I clenched my teeth. "The girl I brought to New York. Her name is Jess."

"Oh yeah, she's right . . ." He pointed, then stopped. "Whoa."

I followed his gaze past the area where her cousin and friends were last time, to the wall over by the stage. A guy with white-blond hair sticking straight up and covered in tattoos had her head in his hand and his mouth locked on hers.

"Fuck, is that guy with the band?" Finn asked. "Oh wait, he's fucking that chick from New York's face. Wait, I'm confused," Finn slurred as he set the empty shot glass down.

"Guess she's taken," Hensley said. "I'm not about to mess with that. The dude looks rough." He turned back to the bartender and picked up his beer.

"You guys know Jess?" the bartender asked, and I turned to look at him. My throat was so damn tight all I could do was nod. I wasn't sure I could speak just yet. I hadn't seen her since she got on the jet in New York. I'd let her go. It had been for the best. I just hadn't expected to see her like this.

"She's Krit's girl," the bartender said, as if that answered all the questions in the universe.

"Who?" Finn asked, still looking confused.

"The lead singer of Jackdown, Krit. Jess is his."

I turned back around to see Krit take the stage. He was shirtless, and his body was covered in tattoos. His jeans hung on his hips, and he was wearing eyeliner ... and nail polish. Really? She was dating that?

"Jess doesn't have a type, does she?" Hensley said from beside me.

I searched for her and found her just as she reached a table where Rock, Dewayne, Preston, and Amanda sat. I could ignore them, but one of them was bound to see me. Did that matter? Would Jess even want me to come over there? Maybe she would want me to ignore her.

As if she could sense my stare, she lifted her eyes and her gaze locked with mine. Her body went completely still. She didn't smile like everything was forgotten. She didn't move like it was no big deal. Instead she stayed completely frozen as she stared at me. She even blinked rapidly, as if she was in some sort of daze she was trying to snap out of.

Fuck. I was screwed.

"She sees you, dude. Might as well go say hello," Hensley said, stating the obvious.

I forced my legs to move and started making my way over to

her. She seemed to snap out of her trance, and she looked away from me. I could see her mouth move even though she wasn't looking at anyone exclusively. Apparently, it had been the entire table, because all their gazes turned to zero in on me.

Rock started to stand up and Jess grabbed his arm and said something to him. Then she moved around the table and made her way toward me. She didn't want me near her friends, so I stopped.

"She's coming to us," Finn said, leaning against the bar.

"Me, she's coming to me," I corrected him. "Stay here," I said before walking toward her. I didn't want those two listening to us.

She stopped a few feet away from me. I didn't want her that far away. All those emotions she had evoked in me and scared me with roared to life. I had missed her. I knew I had missed her, but seeing her made it all the more real. "Hey," I said.

She gave me a small smile. "Hey." Then she glanced up at the stage. The band had started playing, but I wasn't paying attention to them. She'd been all I could focus on.

"How are you?" I asked, wanting to hear her voice.

"Good, and you?"

I could lie and say good. It would be easier if I did lie. For both of us. "Miss you," I said instead.

She tensed and her gaze shifted to the stage again. Did she love him? Fuck, just thinking that hurt like hell.

"I saw you with him," I told her.

She moved her gaze back to mine. "Oh" was all she said.

"You look happy." I was reaching. It was wrong and I should let this go, but I couldn't.

She started to say something, then closed her mouth and shook her head. "No. I'm not going to do this with you. I'm not ready yet. I thought maybe I was, but I'm not," she said, then turned to walk away. That was the reaction I wanted. Something to tell me she still gave a shit.

"Wait," I said, reaching for her arm.

She stopped and looked down at my hand wrapped around her arm, then back at me. "What do you want from me?" she asked, looking defeated. I hated that. I didn't want to hurt her. I didn't want to make her sad. I just wanted her.

"Can we go outside and talk?" I asked.

She looked back at the stage and I followed her gaze. The guy was singing, but his entire focus was on Jess. "I think he loves me. He hasn't said it, but he treats me like no one ever has. He acts like he can't live without me, and he never makes me feel unworthy or not good enough." She looked back at me. "I'm enough for him. Don't mess it up for me. Because I'd hurt him for you. And in the end you'd hurt me."

She pulled her arm free and walked away. I let her go this time. I stood there as she walked past her friends at the table and to the stage. Then she opened the back door and disappeared. Krit left the band to finish without him as he hurried off the stage.

He was willing to put her first. I never had been. He made her feel special, and I hadn't. He wore eyeliner and had more piercings than one human should, but he knew what he had and he wasn't willing to lose her.

Problem was, she had said she would hurt him for me. It was me she wanted.

How the hell was I supposed to walk away from that?

Chapter Sixteen

JESS

The stage door had barely closed behind me when Krit came stalking backstage. His eyes searched my face, and I felt like crumpling to the floor. He was worried about me. Jason was out there and I had all but told him I still wanted him, and Krit was worried about me.

"What the hell did he want?" Krit asked, looking ready to strike.

"He's here with friends. He just wanted to say hello. I don't think he expected to see me," I told him.

"Does he know you're with me?" Krit asked, taking another step toward me like he was scared I would burn him if he got too close.

"Yes, I told him. But he saw us earlier too."

Krit studied me. "Now you've seen him, are you over it? Is this your closure?"

My closure? Could you get closure for something like this? Loving a man who didn't love you back? "I don't think there is anything to close. We were a mini fling."

"Bullshit! He screwed with your head. Then that motherfucker has the nerve to walk into this bar." He started pacing again.

"Krit, get out here," Green said in an aggravated tone as he stepped backstage.

"Leave me the fuck alone," Krit snapped at him. Then he looked back at me and cupped my face. "You okay?"

"They want you, Krit," Green yelled over the crowd.

"I said to back the fuck off," Krit yelled back at him.

I put my hand on Krit's chest. "Go. I'm fine. I just want to stay back here and watch until your break," I told him.

Krit nodded, then pressed a kiss to my lips before walking back onto the stage.

The door behind me closed, and I turned to see Trisha standing there. "Did he go back on?" she asked me, and I nodded.

Trisha walked over to stand beside me, and we watched him as he entertained the crowd. "He loves you," Trisha said.

He hadn't told me he loved me, but after the way he had acted outside earlier, I was beginning to wonder. "Why?" I asked. I hadn't done anything to deserve it.

Trisha grinned. "Because you're you. He knows the real you. Not the wild party girl you show the world. But then, you've not been that girl since the beginning of the summer."

I hadn't been that girl since I met Jason. We were both thinking it, but neither of us said it out loud.

"He's not ready for what he feels. He wants to be, but he's not. He'll let you down. He'll mess up." I looked at Trisha, surprised by her words. She adored Krit. "I love him. But I know him. He's a free spirit, and for the first time in his life he's got someone he wants to hold on to. He's never had that before. But he isn't ready for it. It will ruin you both eventually."

"I can't hurt him," I told her just as Krit turned to look back at me. He winked and licked his lips, causing the crowd of females to squeal.

"He'll hurt you if you don't. He'll hate himself for it, and I'll end up having to protect him from Rock. I don't want to say all this, because for the first time in a very long time I can see he is really happy. You make him happy. But it's not going to last. He can't keep this up. He'll crack. The right girl will throw herself at him and not take no for an answer and he'll have had too much to drink. Then he'll hate himself." Trisha stopped talking and sighed. "I hate doing this. But if there is anything to that guy out there and you, he's your ticket out, Jess. He's the one who will pull you out of the life you were born into. Don't let that go."

What was out there would hurt me more than Krit could ever

hurt me. I looked at Trisha. "Jason has the power to destroy me completely. I can't let him. He broke me once. I can't chance that."

"You love him?" she asked.

I wanted to say no and for it to be true. I couldn't. "Yes."

"Krit has a club full of females willing to soothe his broken heart. He loves women, Jess. You know that. He'll be hurt, but he will get over it. The females who adore him will help him."

"When he's ready, I'll let him go. I can't love him. My heart's already taken."

Trisha reached over and squeezed my arm. "And you're sure you don't want to see if this thing with Jason deserves a chance?"

Jason wasn't here to give anything another chance. He just happened to be in town with friends and saw me. He hadn't come looking for me. "I'm sure," I replied.

Trisha nodded. "Okay."

She turned and walked back out the door. I thought about sneaking outside to be alone, but if Krit looked back and didn't see me, he would leave the stage again. So I leaned up against the wall and waited.

Fifteen minutes later Krit announced a break and left the stage without talking to the girls hanging around for his attention. He came directly to me and grabbed my hand. "To the back. Now."

I knew what this meant, but could I do it after seeing Jason again made me so raw? I started to follow him and stopped. "Wait," I said.

Krit stopped and looked back at me. I could see the fear flash in his eyes, and I hated it. I couldn't let him think this was because of Jason.

"I'm . . . vulnerable right now. My emotions are all over the place. I'm not in the right mind-set to go have a quickie."

Krit let out a defeated sigh. "I can make you forget him. Just give me five seconds, love."

"That's not the problem. I just need more than a quickie."

Krit walked back over to me and pulled me into his arms. His chest was damp from sweat. "Fuck, yeah. Okay. I get that."

He didn't get it, but he thought he did. I was just glad to get a reprieve.

"I'm gonna need a drink, then," he said. "You good to go out there with me?"

I nodded. If I had him beside me, I could deal with it. Jason was probably gone by now anyway.

"The douche is still out there," Krit said, opening the door and putting his arm around my shoulders as we walked into the crowd. I knew it was his form of showing ownership, and any other night I would have shoved it off. Tonight I needed the protection. My heart needed protection. Krit was supplying that.

We walked over to Rock's table, and Dewayne was grinning

at me as I approached. "If it ain't the heartbreaker. Got all them boys lining up tonight, don't you, Mess?"

Dewayne had been calling me Mess instead of Jess for as long as I could remember. He and Rock had been friends since elementary school, so there wasn't a time in my life Dewayne wasn't in it. That went for Marcus Hardy and Preston Drake, as well.

"Shut it," I snapped at him, shooting him the bird as Krit pulled out a stool for me.

"Sit, love. I'll go get you a whiskey," Krit said before laying one of his claiming kisses on me. They weren't meant for me. They were meant for everyone else in the club. When I had first agreed to him kissing me to keep other guys away while I nursed a broken heart, I hadn't expected things between Krit and me to progress the way they had.

"Thanks," I said when he pulled back, and he sauntered over to the bar. Krit had cornered the market on walking to draw attention. Girls stopped in midsentence to watch him. Something about his bad-boy charm and ego did it for the females. Then there was the fact that he could sing.

"We were wondering if Krit had chained you up backstage when he did that disappearing act in the middle of the song," Dewayne said, leaning back with a taunting grin on his face.

"Leave it," Rock warned him, but Dewayne just laughed.

"Amanda wanted to stay and check on you," Trisha said, "but

Preston was having a hard time keeping his hands off her. Their classes are keeping them apart this year, more so than before, and he's not dealing with it well."

"Dumbass needs to go ahead and marry her. They can move in together, and that will fix that shit," Dewayne drawled.

"Oh, hell, Jess. Stone's coming this way," Rock muttered.

I knew looking was a bad idea, but I couldn't help it. Surely he wasn't stupid enough to walk over here. But then, he had no idea how badly I had been hurt. It had been a fling to him.

"It's fine. He's probably coming to say hello to everyone," I said under my breath.

"Would have been smarter had he done that when you weren't here," Rock replied, shooting an annoyed glare Jason's way.

"But it wouldn't have been nearly as much fun," Dewayne added.

Trisha slapped his arm and scolded him.

"Krit's gonna go apeshit," Dewayne said in a singsong voice.

"Shut him up," I whispered to Rock.

Jason approached the table, and I did my best not to stare at him. I smiled. "Hey again."

He didn't look as easygoing as before. "Hey." He turned his attention to the others at the table. "Rock, Trisha, Dewayne, good to see you," he said, then looked back at me. "I was hoping we could talk."

"Bad idea. Her man won't deal well with it. Just let it go and save me the hassle," Rock answered for me.

Krit's arm settled around my shoulders again, and he set my drink down in front of me. His gaze was locked on Jason, but he lowered his head to kiss the side of my face. "Company?" he asked in a bored drawl, even though he knew exactly who Jason was.

"Krit, Jason Stone. Jason, Krit," I said, unable to look at either of them. I glanced to Rock for rescuing.

"Jason, it's good to see you again and all," Rock said. "Hope life's treating you well, but due to your past with Jess, this isn't the best time."

"When is a good time?" Jason asked, looking at me and ignoring the glare I knew Krit was directing his way.

"Never," Krit replied.

This was not me. I didn't hide behind men to protect me. How had I let this one guy completely change me? I was stronger than this. I grabbed Krit's hand and made him look at me. I had been going to tell him to let me talk to Jason, but the look in Krit's eyes stopped me. He didn't deserve that.

"It's okay," I told him softly, then pressed a kiss to his lips to try to ease some tension from his body. Then I turned my attention to Jason. "We talked, Jason. You've said all you wanted to say to me before. Let's just be friends and leave it at that," I told him.

Jason started to say something else, but I shook my head and then stood up. I wasn't arguing with him in front of everyone. I didn't want him to say anything around them that would prove what an idiot I was. How I had taken something so small and made it much bigger. It was my humiliation. I wanted to keep it that way.

"Dance with me," I told Krit.

"Gladly, love," he replied, and I watched him cockily salute Jason as I pulled him toward the dance floor.

JASON

"She's a hot little number. Completely blew you off, though, for the singer dude with the eyeliner," Finn said as he leaned over in the limo, unable to sit up straight.

I wasn't in the mood to discuss Jess with either of them. They didn't know what had happened with us, nor would they understand.

"Don't know why you didn't dance with one of the many other babes who asked you," Hensley said. "Hell, that redhead was hitting on you so hard she was about ready to crawl into your lap. Sucks that I can't have a rock-star brother. That one group of girls knew you right away. They were squealing and shit, like you were the fucking rock god, not Jax. 'Course, I got to fill that girl up. When you weren't showing interest, she moved on over and climbed into my lap. Sweet tits. Really sweet tits."

I closed my eyes and tried to block the guys out. But then again, if I thought too hard, all I'd be able to see was that fucker's hands all over Jess like she was his. But then, she was his. I didn't have any claim to her.

"I don't know why we can't take home those slutty ones. I woulda been getting lucky right now," Finn grumbled.

"Oh, I don't know, Finn, maybe because we're staying at Jax's summer place, and he doesn't want rabid fans to know where it is," Hensley replied.

"We coulda drove around and fucked in the limo," he complained.

"You need to sleep this off. No orgies in the limo. We aren't that drunk," Hensley said.

She had said that she'd hurt him for me. I had thought that meant she wanted me more than him. That she didn't love him. But then she'd chosen him over me at the table. I couldn't figure her out. Had she gone to the back and changed her mind? Was my fuckup in New York it for her? I had sent her home like she asked and not contacted her once. I had stared at her number enough times, thinking about it. But I'd never actually gone through with it.

"She was watching you when she thought you weren't looking. When she was dancing with him, the rocker dude," Hensley said.

I opened my eyes and lifted my head to look at him. "Jess

was looking at me?" I asked, needing to make sure I hadn't just imagined that.

"Yep. She looked at you a lot. But then the rocker dude caught her one time and she stopped. Then we left."

Shit. This was all kinds of fucked up. I needed to let this go. She had obviously moved on. I had to get back to school Monday, and staying in Sea Breeze to make something happen with Jess was impossible.

"Doesn't matter. She doesn't fit into my life," I said, more to myself than anyone else.

"Yeah, you're right," Hensley agreed.

"Dude could sing, though," Finn said with his eyes almost closed and his body leaned over so far his head was touching the seat.

Maybe I needed to get that drunk. Then I wouldn't care.

Chapter Seventeen

JESS

Throwing myself back into school and work was the only thing that got me through the next week. Krit realized I was pulling away, and he was letting me. I wasn't sure why, but he wasn't holding on so tight after Jason's showing up at Live Bay. Part of me felt like I should go apologize to him, tell him I was sorry about how I was acting, but I couldn't. I needed time to deal.

When Friday night came back around, Krit called three times. I didn't answer. I wasn't in the mood to face Live Bay tonight. I had brought home some things to alter from the shop. Focused on that, I almost ignored my phone the fourth time it rang. But it could have been Momma. Glancing over at it, I saw Jason's name flash on my screen, and I dropped the pants I was holding and grabbed my phone.

Standing in my room, I stared at it. Why was he calling? I didn't think about it too hard. I just answered.

"Hello," I said, wondering if he had accidentally called me. Maybe he had meant to call a Jessica or a Joclyn.

"Hey, can you talk?" His deep voice came over the line and my insides went all warm, despite my better judgment.

"Uh, I . . ." Could I talk? Could my heart handle it? "Yeah, sure."

He let out a relieved-sounding sigh. "Good." There was a smile in his voice. I could visualize the way his lips curled up in amusement. "I'm sorry about last weekend. I shouldn't have put you on the spot like that. I just . . . I hadn't been prepared to see you again."

I wanted to laugh at that. He hadn't been prepared to see me? *Ha.* Did he have any idea how he had affected me? "You surprised me," I replied.

"You surprised me, too."

"How did I surprise you? Surely you knew I would more than likely be there."

I sat down on the edge of the bed, trying to calm my shaking hands. Talking to him like this was making me nervous. It was silly and ridiculous and I should have ended this call, but I didn't.

"I wasn't expecting . . . him."

Oh. So he'd thought I was sitting here pining for him. Even

if it was for selfish reasons and it made me a terrible person, I was thankful for Krit at the moment. If Jason had expected me to still be alone, I was glad he saw I was desirable to some people. "Why?" I asked, needing to hear him explain it.

"I don't know." He let out a hard laugh. "I'm a dick."

That still didn't answer my question. "Krit is different. I never imagined anything serious with him when it started, but his feelings ran deeper than I thought possible. So, yeah, he surprised me."

Jason didn't respond right away. I wanted to ask him what he was thinking. I wanted to see his face and smell his clean scent, so different from Krit's.

"How's school?" he asked finally.

"Uh, good. I guess," I replied, confused by his change of topic.

"You guess? Sure it doesn't suck? Mine sucks."

No, mine didn't suck. It was the last semester I could go to junior college. Which meant it was the last of my college education. I would be getting my associate's degree in December.

"Why does yours suck?" I asked, my nerves finally easing as I lay back on my bed and relaxed.

"I'm doing what my parents want me to do. Not what I want to do."

"What do you want to do?"

"I want to have time to decide. I'm . . . I'm thinking of taking next semester off. They don't know it yet, but I want to be free to travel. Find myself. Figure it all out. I tried that this summer . . ." He stopped.

"But I messed that up," I finished for him. He hadn't come back to Sea Breeze after our trip to New York.

"No. I messed that up. None of that was you, Jess." His voice had gone gentle, as if he wanted to reassure me. The smile on my face was ridiculous, but it was there.

"I didn't expect you to answer," he said.

"Why?"

"It's a Friday night. I figured you'd be out."

"No. I'm staying in tonight. I have work to do," I told him. I didn't want to tell him I had been hiding out since I had seen him last Friday. That wasn't something he needed to know.

"Work as in school?" he asked.

"No, I'm working for a seamstress in town now. I have some work I brought home."

"You sew?" he asked. I had surprised him. It was in his voice.

"Yes. I also design clothes. I'm working on Christmas recital costumes now for the local dance studio."

He made a choking sound, like he had been drinking something. "You design stuff?" he asked after he'd caught his breath.

"Yep. The red dress I wore in New York—that was one I designed and made."

"Holy shit, really? That's amazing. That dress was . . ." He trailed off.

"It wasn't a designer label and I know I didn't fit in, but it's my favorite piece," I told him. He didn't have to feel awkward.

"No, you looked beautiful in it. There wasn't another girl there who even compared."

I didn't know how to respond to that. He had also sent me home without an argument that night.

"I need to go," he said. "Jax is sending a car to get me. I'm eating with him and Sadie tonight while they're in town. But can I call you again?"

Could he call me again? No. "Yes," I replied.

"Have a good night, Jess," he said, the smile back in his voice.

"Yeah, you too," I replied.

After we hung up, I stared at the phone for a long time. I shouldn't have told him he could call again. Would that mess with my head completely? Could I move on if he was calling me and reminding me how I felt? No. That would be impossible. The wound would never heal. I had to tell him the next time he called. This wasn't going to work.

JASON

Jax was sitting in the limo with a bottle of water, watching a football game when I climbed inside.

"Where's Sadie?" I asked when I realized we were alone.

"Meeting us there. She's picking up Star at the airport. I would have sent you to pick her up, but Star said you're acting weird lately when she calls. So I figured it might be best if we talked before this thing tonight."

Jax had agreed to do an event at Harvard tonight. It was for charity, and because I attended here he had agreed to it. He just had to sing a few songs and then sign some things for them to auction off. Star was also performing with him. After their appearance, we were going to head out to dinner.

Star was the female counterpart to Jax in the music industry. She was also a longtime friend of Jax's, since they both started young and had been thrown together so much. Once Jax and Sadie went public, they stopped getting thrown together. Star and Sadie had had a rocky beginning, but they were friends now. And when Star needed a last-minute date and didn't want anything that would cause problems for her, she called me.

"Bad week," I replied, reaching for a water.

"Why?" he asked, studying me.

"Went to Sea Breeze last weekend," I told him.

"Yeah, I know."

Of course he knew. I had stayed at his place. He was still watching me.

"I saw her," I said through clenched teeth as the image of what she had been doing flashed in my head.

"Ah, so the town's bad girl still gets to you," Jax said, grinning.

I hated it when he referred to her as a bad girl. He didn't know her. He had never met her. He only knew the stories. She was so much more than that. "Don't," I warned him, and he stopped grinning.

"Wait . . . are you really hung up on her?"

I opened the water and took a drink. I wasn't talking to him about this. He wasn't any help. He had made it work with Sadie, so none of my excuses would stand with him. His life was different. Our parents weren't trying to control him since he held their purse strings.

"You like her . . . a whole damn lot, from the looks of it."

I glared at him. "Yes. I like her. But I fucked it up. She's with some alternative-looking dude in a local band. He had his hands all over her." Just remembering the way Krit had kept his arm around her shoulders like she was a possession pissed me off.

"Is this a mutual thing, or did you get in too deep with a girl who likes to play the field? From what I've heard, she's a flirt."

I slammed my water down. "What you've heard? You've only heard shit about her. You've never met her. You don't know that she's fun and when she gets embarrassed she blushes. You don't know that she can design and make her own fucking clothes. That she pays her tuition at a local junior college and won't get a chance to go any further because she can't afford it. Her momma is a stripper, and the boy she grew up loving hit her and broke her heart and knocked up another woman. Yet when his drunk ass needs something, he comes to her and she sets him straight. You don't know shit. So don't act like you do."

I was breathing hard when I finished, and I jerked my head around and stared out the window. I had said too much.

"Holy shit," Jax finally said under his breath.

"What?" I snapped, still angry.

Jax shook his head. "Nothing," he said.

I wanted to demand he explain himself, but I was afraid he'd piss me off and I'd hit him. Not a good idea since he was about to go onstage.

"I called her tonight," I told him. I needed to say it. I needed to admit it.

"Did she answer?"

"Yeah, she did. We talked. She said I could call again."

"Which member of Jackdown is she dating?" he asked.

I looked at him, confused. "How did you know it was Jackdown?"

Jax smirked. "I found Sea Breeze first."

Oh. Yeah. And Sadie would know about Jackdown.

"Lead singer," I replied, trying to block out the guy's face.

"Krit? Really? That's Trisha's brother. Huh . . . ," he said, surprised.

"What do you mean, 'huh'?"

He shrugged. "Krit is Trisha's brother. Trisha is married to Rock. Jess is Rock's cousin. I would think those two grew up together. Known each other for years. Surprising they're just now dating. Weird, almost."

I hadn't known that. Could he have been there just to make me jealous?

"You don't think . . . ," I said, but stopped myself.

Jax didn't need me to finish. "Might be," he replied.

I had to get back to Sea Breeze.

Chapter Eighteen

JESS

On Tuesday I finished my last class at two and headed home to change and get the clothing I had taken home to work on. I was supposed to work from three to seven tonight. Krit had called twice today, and I hadn't been able to answer it. He knew I had classes today.

We had talked Sunday night, and I had explained to him I needed to cool off. What we were doing was going too fast, and he was free to sleep around. He hadn't handled it well, but according to talk, Krit had taken not one but two girls backstage Monday night, where he had performed in Destin, Florida. Several of Jackdown's groupies followed them around. They also made sure I heard about it.

I would call him on my way to work. Pulling up to the house,

I realized I wouldn't need to. Krit was sitting on my front porch. I wasn't in the mood for him to apologize, if that was what this was. I had told him he could sleep around, and he hadn't wasted any time. Proved to me he wasn't as into me as he thought he was. Which eased my conscience. At least he didn't love me.

I stepped out of my truck and headed toward him. He sat there and watched me approach, but he didn't look apologetic. He looked pissed. But I hadn't done anything.

"Hey," I said, studying him.

"You didn't answer my calls," he replied.

"I was in class. I was going to give you a call on my way to work. What's up?" I tried to make it sound casual.

He shook his head as if he couldn't believe me. "Really? That's it? We're back to being fucking friendly?"

He was going to make me late for work. "We talked about this. You were okay with it," I told him.

"Okay with it? Who the fuck told you I was okay with it?"

I leaned on the railing and sighed. "I know about the girls Monday night. Word travels fast. I would say that makes you okay with it," I told him.

Krit threw down some paper he was holding and stood up. "Fuck that! You said I could sleep around. You needed fucking space. You can't get mad because I did what you told me to."

I reached out and grabbed his hand, hoping to calm him down. "I'm not mad. I didn't say I was mad. I was pointing out that you taking girls backstage means you're okay with this. With us."

Krit crowded me and reached up to cup my face. "They weren't you. So no, I'm not fucking okay with this. It sucks. It hurts like hell and they can't make it go away."

I reached up and pulled his hand from my face. "You did it, though. You wanted them enough to fuck them. That means you were attracted to them. If you had been heartbroken over this, you wouldn't have been able to sleep with other girls. That's all I'm saying."

Krit closed his eyes and swore. "Don't you fucking say that. Don't you turn that shit on me when you said it was okay. All you had to say was you didn't want me with anyone else, and I wouldn't have."

If I didn't think it would make him angry, I would have smiled. He was so confused. He did have feelings for me. I knew that. But he wasn't in love. He hadn't experienced that yet, so of course he thought this was as bad as it got.

"If you just wanted me, then you wouldn't have been able to sleep with anyone else. With or without my consent. That's all I'm saying."

Krit shoved away from me and started pacing. "Fuck that. It's not fair, Jess. I was drinking. I get horny as hell when I'm onstage. It gets my blood pumping. You know that."

I grinned this time. I couldn't help it. "I know. And I'm telling you it's okay. I just have other things going on right now I have to deal with."

Krit stopped pacing and bent down and picked up the papers he had thrown down: several articles from an event this weekend, where Jax Stone and Star had performed for charity. But the photos weren't of Jax. They were of Star, and on her arm was Jason.

"This is what you're dealing with. This little shit. He used you. He's fucking with your head. I saw you looking at him last weekend. You wanted him. I could taste it on you. Don't let him fuck you up. He can't be what you want, love. Hell, I have a hard time being what you want. You want a fucking lot. You deserve it, but he won't be the one to do it."

Krit started to say more and stopped. Instead he turned around and walked to his car. I didn't watch him go. I was too busy staring at the photo of Jason and Star taken on Friday night. The same night he had called me. He had said he was going out with Sadie and Jax. He hadn't been lying. He'd just left out the small piece of information that he was dating Star.

Krit was right. I was wanting a fairy tale. I wasn't getting a fairy tale. I was a stripper's daughter. Nothing more. I was trying to be someone I wasn't. Someone I would never be. I started to wad the paper up and stopped myself. Instead I smoothed it out. I would put it away, and when I needed reminding of just how stupid I was when it came to Jason, I would pull it out again. Remind myself.

Friday night I spent extra time getting ready. I wore my shortest skirt and my tightest top. I even finished it off with the expensive boots Jason had bought me. I hadn't been able to wear them again. But I was tired of acting like they were some shrine to him. I should be enjoying something from our time together.

My hair looked good down tonight, and I put extra eye makeup on to give me a sultry look. By now everyone would know Krit and I were over and I was free to flirt and be flirted with. It was rebound night for me, and I planned on drinking too much and dancing all night.

When I walked into Live Bay, the night was already in full swing. I stopped by the bar and grabbed a whiskey before heading over to the table where Rock was watching me with a concerned, fatherly frown. I just winked at him, which made his frown deepen. I shifted my gaze to Dewayne, who was the only other person at the table right now. Licking my bottom lip suggestively, I set my glass down and leaned forward, knowing that even though he viewed me as Rock's little cousin, he was going to look at my tits.

"Wanna dance?" I asked.

"No," Rock answered for him.

"Hell yes," Dewayne replied.

"Stand up and I'll make you sit down," Rock warned him.

Dewayne just laughed and took a drink.

"What are you doing, Jess?" Rock asked.

"Drinking, then dancing," I replied with a smile I didn't feel.

"It's not like you," he replied.

"No. It's exactly like me. This is me, Rock. I'm done pretending to be someone else. Now, why can't Dewayne dance with me?" I asked, turning to pout at Dewayne, who looked very amused.

"Stop flirting with Dewayne," Rock said, annoyed.

"I'm enjoying it. Please, let her continue," Dewayne said, leaning back to look at me through half-hooded eyes as he smoked a cigarette.

Maybe I should be careful with him. He seemed like he might just be more than I could handle. "Fine. I'll go dance by myself," I told them, taking a long swig of my drink before turning and walking out to the dance floor.

I made sure to swing my hips just enough to draw attention. I wouldn't dance alone for long. This was what I was good at. I had watched my momma control men my entire life. It came easy to me.

"Heard you and Krit are over," a deep voice said as warm fingers circled my arm. I turned to see Justin Monroe. He had been the senior quarterback in high school my freshman year.

"Yeah, we are," I replied with a flutter of my eyelashes and a slow smile. "But I just want to dance."

Justin grinned. "Lead the way," he said.

I walked us into the center of the crowd. Luckily, this was Green's song. He sang the solo on it, so I didn't have to hear Krit singing while I adjusted to my life after Jason Stone.

Justin rested his hands on my hips, and I moved to the music while smiling up at him. He was a safe distraction. Nothing dangerous. He'd been engaged to the preacher's daughter in town once, but that had fallen through. Not sure why. I didn't hang out in their circle, and they were older than me.

Green announced a break, and I stopped dancing when the radio took over playing music.

"Need a drink," I told him, and then I left him there while I went back to the table. I didn't ask him to come with me. It had just been a dance, and he'd be one of many.

Rock was shaking his head at me when he saw me coming.

I picked up my drink. "What?" I snapped.

"You're stirring up trouble," Rock said.

I rolled my eyes and took a drink. "I'm dancing," I replied.

"And here he comes," Dewayne drawled.

I glanced back, expecting to see Justin, but Krit was headed our way instead. Hadn't expected him. He normally had quickies backstage first.

Krit's hand wrapped around my arm and he pulled me to him. "We need to talk. Now."

I shook my head.

"I'll cause a fucking scene," Krit warned.

"We discussed this. What's wrong with you?"

Two girls came up to Krit and grabbed on to both his arms and started telling him how good he sounded. He shrugged them loose. "Thanks. Now go," he said, pulling me again. "I need to talk to you, love. Don't make me do it here."

The girls walked away, scowling at me. I pointed my glass at their retreating backs. "You should go get them. I bet they'll do a threesome," I said.

"Fuck, Jess," Rock groaned.

Krit got in my face, and I felt Rock move behind me. "Back up," Rock warned him.

"Is that what you want, love? You want me to leave and go fuck someone else backstage?" He wanted me to say no. I could hear it in his voice. But he needed me to say yes.

"Yes, that's what I want," I replied, and he stepped back like I had slapped him.

He wiped his thumb over his bottom lip and shook his head in disbelief. "That's it, love. That's it. I'm done." He threw his hands up and stalked off. I didn't watch him go. I turned back to the table and met Dewayne's eyes.

"He'll get over it. You did the right thing. He ain't for you," Dewayne said.

"I just hope we can be friends again one day." I did. I shouldn't have let things get out of hand with him. I also shouldn't have come here. I didn't belong here. I didn't want this anymore. I set my glass down. "I'm gone," I said.

"You okay?" Rock asked.

I looked up at him. "Yeah. No. I don't know. I just . . ." I looked around at the place. "I don't want to do this anymore," I told him. "I want more now."

Rock pulled me into a hug. "You'll get more," he whispered into my hair.

I pulled back and forced a smile. "I hope so."

Turning to leave, I walked to the door and ignored people who called out my name. I just needed fresh air and time alone. Right before I reached the door, it opened and Jason Stone walked in. His eyes locked on me, and we stood there staring at each other. I hadn't spoken to him all week. Not since his call.

He stepped back and opened the door for me. I walked through, keeping my head down. Should I say something? Or was he going to stay inside without a word?

The door closed behind me. I spun around to see Jason outside. He nodded toward the parking lot. "Can we talk?"

All I could do was nod. Even if I should be leaving here and protecting myself.

We walked over to his Hummer. This time there was no limo, no driver. Just him. He opened the door for me, and I climbed in, realizing that this was something Krit had never done. Opened my car door. I had missed it.

I thanked him, and he just smiled before closing the door and walking over to the driver's side. The Hummer smelled like him. I breathed in deeply and enjoyed it before he opened the door and climbed in.

"Were you leaving?" he asked.

I turned to look at him, and seeing his face only made my heart speed up. His gaze was focused on me, and just being this close to him made everything seem better.

"Yeah," I replied, not sure how much I should tell him.

He glanced out the window, then back at me. "Is he going to come looking for you?"

I shook my head. "No. We ended that . . . whatever it was."

His eyes widened and his shoulders visibly relaxed. "Why?"

Did he want me to tell him it was because of him? Not that I would. I shrugged. "We don't fit, I guess," I replied.

Jason nodded like he agreed. I bit back a smile.

"Where were you headed?"

"Home," I replied honestly, even if it made me sound pathetic.

"Could I convince you to come back to my place?"

God, how I wanted to say yes. He could convince me of anything if he tried hard enough. But the regret that would come when he left and didn't call . . . The pain was something too fresh. I wasn't ready for that again. "I don't know if that's a good idea."

Jason leaned toward me and kept his intense gaze focused on me. "Why?"

"Because you'll make me miss you." I said it before I could stop myself.

He reached over and touched my hand. "That's why I want to talk. The way we left things . . . I don't like it."

I didn't respond. I didn't want to misunderstand him.

"I miss you, Jess," he said in a husky whisper. That was my undoing.

"Okay."

He raised his eyebrows. "Okay . . . you'll go back to my place?"

I nodded and he let out a sigh. "Good. I was trying to weigh my options and abduction seemed risky." The grin on his face brought the first real smile to mine in a week.

JASON

I had never been more relieved to get out of a car in my life. If Jess crossed her legs one more time in that ridiculous excuse for a skirt, I was going to lose my mind. Damn, why did she have to be so fucking sexy?

I tried not to look at her as we climbed the steps to the house. The outfit she was wearing was more adventurous than anything I'd ever seen her wear. How the hell she'd walked out of the club alone was beyond me.

I opened the door and she walked inside. The staff was gone for the night since Jax wasn't in residence. I liked it better alone. Especially now that I had Jess here.

"You wanted to talk," Jess said, not walking any farther into the house. She seemed nervous now. I wasn't sure what had changed from the car to here. She had been fine in the Hummer.

"Yeah, uh, not here. We could go outside." I stopped when she started shaking her head.

"No, let's not," she said softly.

The last time we'd been outside was memorable for both of us. She was right. That was a bad idea. I needed to focus. "Uh, yeah. Let's go . . ." Where the hell to take her? "Downstairs. It's more comfortable down there. Less formal," I finally said.

Jess nodded, and I started toward the stairs. Hearing the click of her heels on the marble floor made it difficult not to turn around and look at her legs. Not that I didn't have a very clear mental image of them.

I started down the stairs and Jess stopped. Glancing back at her, I noticed she was gripping the railing tightly and having some internal battle with herself.

"Jess?"

She looked at me and shook her head. "I can't. I shouldn't have come here."

What the hell? I walked back up to the step underneath her. "Why?"

She took a deep breath. "Because—we will—we will—do stuff, and you'll leave for Boston and I'll be here and I'll be sad and I'll be alone and I can't do that again," she said in one long, rushed sentence, then turned to leave. I reached out and grabbed her before she could get away.

"Don't leave. That's why I want to talk. Yeah, I'm gonna have to leave, but I want to come back. Like I'm doing now. Like I did two weeks ago. I want to come see you. And I sure as hell don't want you to be sad."

She got very still and stopped trying to move away from me. "What do you mean, you want to come back?"

"Exactly what I said. I want to see you. I miss you."

She didn't look at me. "But why? You're dating Star. Why do you want to come here?"

Those stupid fucking pictures. I shouldn't have let them take those. I had witnessed firsthand how pictures like those had almost ended Jax and Sadie's relationship. "She's a friend."

"Oh" was all she said.

"Please come downstairs and talk to me," I pleaded, sliding a hand around her waist.

She tensed at first, then seemed to melt back into me.

"Okay," she finally said after a moment.

I didn't take my hand off her this time for fear she'd decide to run again. We made it downstairs and I directed her to the closest sofa to get her comfortable.

She looked around the place. "It's nice down here," she said.

It was where Jax and I had hung out when we were younger. He had been limited to our small portion of the beach when we visited, so we had spent a lot of time down here playing video games and pool.

"I haven't been down here in a while," I admitted.

She glanced down at her hands, then finally up at me. "So, you want to visit me," she said slowly, as if trying to understand what I had been saying.

"Yeah, I do. A relationship would be impossible, but that doesn't mean we can't still date. I can come visit. I can bring you to visit me if you want to. I just . . . This thing with us not talking sucks. I miss you."

Chapter Nineteen

JESS

A relationship would be impossible. That's all I heard. Everything else he said didn't make sense. What was it he wanted? A booty call?

"So you just want to hook up when you're available and do what? Have sex?" I asked bitterly.

His eyes went wide and he shook his head. "No! God, no. That's not what I mean. I meant just . . . date. The sex, well, yeah, it's amazing, but that isn't what I came here for. I wanted to see you."

Just not in a relationship. He wanted to be free to go on dates with Star and whatever A-lister came his way and also come see me. Yes, this pissed me off, but it shouldn't have. He never promised me anything. Just because I wanted more didn't mean he had to. He liked me. He wanted to date me. I was used to the possessive-type guys who wouldn't share, so casually dating wasn't something I had done much of.

Seeing him with other women would hurt. But was it worth it to have him, even if only for a little while? Could I do that? Maybe I needed to. Maybe it was time I learned how to date different people, to leave my options open. It wasn't like I was looking for marriage and babies.

"Okay," I finally said. This would probably come back to haunt me, but I wasn't willing to let him go.

A slow smile spread across his entirely too handsome face. He'd gotten what he wanted: me and whoever else. I guess he had something to smile about.

"Okay. You're open to seeing me when we can? And we can talk on the phone," he added.

I was going to the long-distance-nonrelationship-while-in-college place. That made me sound weak. For giving in to something like this. It was as if I had settled for less. But I wasn't ready to let him go. Not yet. Maybe soon I would be, but I wanted Jason Stone. Damn him.

His gaze dropped to my feet. "You're wearing the boots I bought you," he said with a pleased grin.

I nodded and swung the leg out that I had crossed. "Yep."

His eyes trailed up my legs and stopped to spend extra time on the tops of my thighs. I was dressed like a hooker. I knew it. I had done it out of stupidity. Of course he was looking.

"I'll wear more clothes the next time," I told him, trying to make a joke out of it.

His gaze jerked back to meet mine. "Sorry. I was, uh . . ."

"You were checking out my short skirt. I know. I was in a mood tonight."

He cocked an eyebrow. "And that mood would be to see how insane you can drive every male you come in contact with?"

I shrugged and leaned back on the sofa. "Pretty much," I replied honestly.

Jason laughed. "You succeeded."

"Thanks. I think," I replied.

He leaned closer to me and picked up a strand of hair from my shoulder, then began playing with it. "I love your hair," he said as he let it fall through his fingers.

I tried to say thanks, but I couldn't manage to form the words.

"I want to kiss you. But I don't want you to think that's why you're here," Jason said.

My heart was speeding up, and I wanted to sigh from the way it felt to have him run his fingers through my hair. "I wouldn't think you brought me here just for a kiss," I assured him.

He leaned forward and nuzzled my neck, inhaling me. "If I kiss you, I'm gonna want more. We'll do a lot more than just kissing," he whispered.

I shivered from his warmth. I wanted that too. Maybe that was why I had come. It would be a lie to say I hadn't thought about it. I turned my head and caught his lips in a kiss. His breathing stopped for a moment and his hand stilled in my hair. He was thinking. Trying to decide. I was going to have to push this.

I turned my body and slipped my leg over his before wrapping my hands around his neck. That was all it took. His hand was on my thigh, pulling me closer, before he took control of the kiss.

After months of thinking this was over and I'd never feel this way again, I couldn't get close enough to him. All I could think was that if this was limited, then I wanted more. If it was possible to get my fill of this man, then I wanted to. Maybe next time it wouldn't hurt as much.

Jason pushed me back on the sofa and covered me with his body. His mouth kissed my collarbone and the tops of my breasts, which were now pushing up from the top I was wearing. I closed my eyes so I could breathe. It was hard to take deep breaths when I could see his tongue dart out and lick my skin.

I reached for my shirt to pull it off, but his hands grabbed mine and stopped me. "Don't," he said as he rested his head against my chest, breathing hard. I didn't move, waiting on him to do something or say something more. His hand trailed down my side and cupped my hip, but he didn't do anything else.

"Jason?"

"Yeah," he replied in a hoarse whisper.

"Are you okay?"

"Give me a minute."

"Okay . . . but why?"

He pressed a kiss to my chest, then lifted himself off me. "Because this isn't why you're here. And as much as I want to take whatever you're willing to give, I can't do that."

I sat up beside him. "But it is why I'm here. We decided to date."

Jason grinned and rubbed his jaw. "Still need a minute, Jess."

I reached up and grabbed his arm. "Explain to me what you mean."

He turned and looked at me. He reached out and moved the strap of my top back up to my shoulder, where it had slipped from, then ran his finger down my arm. "When I go back to school Sunday and you're left here all week to think about this, I don't want you convincing yourself that all this was a ploy for me to get in your pants."

Damn, he was sweet. I leaned toward him, wanting him to touch me some more. "I won't think that. Besides, I'm not wearing pants," I reminded him teasingly.

He let out a short laugh. "How could I forget?" he replied.

I leaned over and kissed his neck, and he groaned. "I want this," I said.

"I want it more. Trust me. But I want you to know that's not all I want."

This whole not touching me to prove he cared thing was doing it for me. He could teach a Seduction 101 class. Or one on the fastest way to get a woman naked. "I'm not ready to go home yet."

Jason put his arm around me and pulled me against his side. "Me neither. Tell me what I've missed the past three months, but leave out the details with the singer."

He wanted to talk. But he was still going to hold me. I moved closer to him, and he reached for my legs and threw them over his lap. This was by far more dangerous to my heart than if he had screwed me tonight.

"Not a lot," I replied.

"That's not true. You said you got a job sewing. Tell me about it."

I laid my head back on his arm and smiled. I liked talking about my job, but no one ever asked me.

JASON

It was soft and warm and smelled fucking amazing. I pulled it closer and buried my head against it. A soft moan and a shift in just the right area woke me from the dream to reality. Opening my eyes, I realized Jess was the soft, delicious body I was trying to climb inside of. She was tucked against my chest. At some point we had fallen asleep on the sofa and had managed to spoon. I moved my hand, to find it full of bare, soft flesh. Shit, I was feeling her up in my sleep.

She pressed the boob I was holding into my hand and let out a soft moan. The semi hard-on I had went to full blown in seconds. I knew I should move my hand. She was sleeping and vulnerable. I knew I shouldn't be touching her tits. Although they felt like heaven.

Her legs were tucked in between mine, and her perfect, round ass was pressing against my erection. How the hell was she sleeping through this? Slowly I moved my hand away from her, using all my willpower not to go back and play with the hard nipple that brushed my palm. Slipping my hand out of her shirt, I moved her top down as far as it would go, which wasn't very far. It left a small portion of her stomach bare. I rested my hand over her shirt and as far away from her extremely tempting chest as possible.

We had talked for hours. Then she had started yawning and I had started playing with her hair. The idea of taking her home wasn't appealing. Not when I had to leave on Sunday. I wasn't willing to give her up just yet. So we went to sleep on the couch. We were still in our clothes.

The only things she had told me that made me remotely happy were that she had a job she loved and that the ex boy-friend who had been harassing her was now married. He had been forced to marry the girl he'd gotten pregnant to prevent her from moving off to Arkansas with his kid. She hadn't talked about the other guy, though. Not once. But then, I'd asked her not to.

Jess cuddled closer to me and shivered. I reached behind me and grabbed a white blanket to pull over her. I wasn't moving, though. According to the clock it wasn't even six in the morning yet. I had hours left of this.

Jess pressed back against me. "'S cold," she mumbled.

I gave up trying not to touch her too much and used my body to warm her up by getting under the blanket with her. She made a pleased sound and began wiggling her ass again. I bit back a groan and tried to think about anything other than her body.

"You're warm," she said sleepily, and settled back down once she had burrowed against me so hard all I could feel was her body.

I pressed a kiss to her temple. As much as I wanted to promise her more, I knew I couldn't. It would be wrong to ask for a relationship when I never knew if I would have time away on the weekends. Then there were my parents, and I had to deal with them. My mother was going to go apeshit when she found out I was taking off next semester and traveling.

Jess needed her freedom, but I had to have some sort of connection to her. I missed her. I liked being near her. While she was willing to give me this much, I would take it.

She began moving her ass against me again. But this time there was a rocking movement to it. I grabbed her hip to still her.

"Don't. You like it, I feel it," she said. Her voice had the thick sound of sleep. She reached for my hand that was on her stomach and moved it up to cover one of her tits. I squeezed it gently, and she arched into it, then threw her hand up and slid it behind my head. I could see my hand on her as the creamy, smooth flesh rose up out of the top of her shirt.

"Are you awake?" I asked, wanting desperately to slip my hand back under her shirt.

"Yes," she breathed, and threw a leg over mine so that when she rocked back, my erection brushed closer to the heat between her legs.

I started to slip my hand under her shirt but grabbed the bottom of it instead and pulled it off. Her breasts bounced free from the tight halter top, and I filled my hands with them. I'd seen a lot of boobs, but never had I seen any this perfect. Jess arched her back, giving me an even better view of how good they looked in my hands.

She opened her legs wider, trying so hard to get the friction she needed for a release. Slipping my hand down her stomach, I pulled the short skirt up, and Jess cried out in anticipation. I played with the top of her panties, running my finger back and forth as she squirmed.

"Please," she begged.

"What is it you want?" I asked, pressing a kiss to her ear.

"Touch me, God, please, touch me," she panted. Her legs were wide open, and I could smell her arousal, which was about to push me over the edge. I slid a finger inside the lacy fabric, and Jess gasped and stilled. Her breasts rose and fell, causing them to bounce beautifully while she waited for me to move lower.

When my finger brushed her clit, she cried out my name and threw her head back. Fuck, that was hot. I ran one finger down the slick folds, and then I brought it up to my mouth to taste her as she watched me.

"So sweet," I whispered, then moved my hand back down to touch her through the soaking-wet cotton crotch of her panties. "We need to take these off," I told her, and she nodded frantically.

I reached up and unzipped the skirt because it was going too. Then I shoved them both down until she had to shimmy them the rest of the way and then kick them to the floor.

"Jason," she breathed, opening her legs to me again. The room smelled like sex with her open like that. I was beginning to think I didn't have to go back to school. I could just live down here with Jess naked on this couch with me.

"Yeah?" I asked, kissing her neck while I moved my hand back to cover her smooth, wet mound.

"Take off your pants," she said, moving her hips against my hand.

"Why? I'm taking care of you," I told her as I pressed my thumb over her clit.

"Not the same. I want you inside me," she said, grabbing my arm and holding on tight as she bucked against my hand. "Just like this. Slide into me from behind," she said.

The image in my head had me unbuttoning my jeans. I reached in my pocket and grabbed the condom I had stuck in there last night when we got back to the house. I hadn't planned on it then, but I also didn't want to be unprepared. If Jess put her mind to it, she could make me do anything.

I handed Jess the condom. "Open it," I told her, then pushed my jeans down until I could kick them off.

"Here," she said, handing it to me.

I grabbed it, then pressed a hard kiss to her lips before sliding it on. I was past the point of being hard. I was in pain. Reaching for her leg, I pulled it up high on my hip, then eased into her. She was more than ready as she pulled me inside, causing us both to cry out.

She moved her hand back behind my neck again and arched back into me. "You're so deep," she said on a moan.

"Forgot how fucking amazing you feel," I told her as I fought to keep from losing myself right then.

Jess's hand touched my cock as it slid in and out. I held my breath as she then ran her fingers over her clit before circling them around me again. Having her play with me while I fucked her was pushing my resistance.

"I'm about to come," she said, tensing up as I pumped into her hard. "Oh, God, Jason. I'm going to come. It's . . ." She stopped talking and her head pressed against my chest as she bucked wildly against me, screaming my name, until I followed right behind her.

Her body started to tremble, and I held on tight as I jerked while filling the condom with my release. I had almost convinced myself that sex with Jess hadn't been the most epic experience of my life. That because I had lost her, I had put sex with her on a pedestal. I realized now that it had been epic. It had never felt like this with anyone else. Ever. And I wasn't willing to lose this again.

Chapter Twenty

JESS

I didn't go home until Jason dropped me off on his way to the airport Sunday. Momma hadn't been thrilled with the idea of me spending time with Jason again, but she didn't argue with me about it over the phone.

However, I knew she would be waiting on me to get home so she could confront me about making stupid decisions. It was the reason I had told Jason not to walk me to the door even though he had tried really hard to. Eventually, telling him it would wake my momma and she needed rest before work had kept him standing at the limo instead. He had watched until I'd closed the door before he turned and got back inside to ride away.

He hadn't told me when he would be back. He'd made me

no promises. He had just said that he would call me. If this weekend had been even a tenth as special to him as it had been to me, then he would be back soon.

"Fire, baby girl. Playing with fire," Momma said as she walked into the living room in her blue silk wrap.

"Don't, Momma. Please. Let me enjoy this."

She walked over to the window and watched as his limo pulled away. "You gonna sulk in your room again when this goes south? I can promise you Krit won't come running back to save you." She paused. "Then again, maybe he will. Maybe Krit is your Jess. Come to think of it, that makes complete sense."

She was back to the *Gilmore Girls* thing again. I wasn't doing this with her. Not today. "I have some things to do for work," I told her before walking back to my bedroom.

"Did you love Krit?" Momma called after me.

"I wasn't in love with him, no."

She sighed loudly. "Well, I guess there's always time for that. You did do this backwards, after all."

I closed my bedroom door on my mother's crazy relationship advice, then turned to my bed and lay down. Staring at my ceiling, I let the silly smile free that I had been trying to hold in. Jason had been different this weekend. He hadn't been as standoffish. He had let me in. We had talked about his friends at school and his brother. I felt connected to him in a way I hadn't before.

My phone started ringing, and I reached in my pocket to get it. Jason's name was on the screen, and the happy giggle that erupted was one I hoped no one heard.

"Hello," I said, unable to mask my happiness that he was already calling me.

"I wanted to hear your voice one more time. Once I get back, I have to study."

"I need to do the same thing. I'm glad you called," I replied.

I heard a soft laugh. "Good. I was afraid it might be too soon."

"Hmm, maybe, but it's cute," I teased.

"Cute, huh? Do I need to remind you of my sexiness?"

This time I laughed. "Definitely not. I'm very aware."

"Thought so. I'm hard to forget," he replied.

"Agreed."

He sighed. "I have to go. I'll talk to you soon."

"Okay, be careful," I replied.

When he hung up, I dropped the phone to my stomach. It was hard not saying anything more than that. Remembering that this was a casual thing was hard. There were no strings. Not that I intended to date anyone else, but still. The fact remained he could. And I wondered how I was going to handle it when he did.

The first part of the week, I stayed clear of all entertainment news and tabloids for fear I would see something with Jason in it that I didn't want to see. When he hadn't called me by Thursday, I caved and googled him to see if there was any news on him. But only old stuff popped up. There was news about Jax Stone's new single and some photos of him and Sadie shopping on Rodeo Drive.

Friday I seriously considered going to Live Bay but changed my mind about five times during the day. By the time three o'clock rolled around, I had decided to stay home and work.

When my phone rang, it was almost four, and I ran for my phone. The sinking feeling hit when I saw Amanda's name instead of Jason's on the screen.

"Hey," I said, trying not to sound too disappointed. I didn't get calls from Amanda very often.

"Hey, Jess. It's Amanda," she said.

"I still have your number. Just because you hooked up with Preston and ruined all our partying fun doesn't mean I disowned you as a friend," I teased her. She was the kind of girl I would never be but often wished I could have been.

Amanda laughed. We had actually done very little partying. I hadn't let it get too far. Back when Amanda had a wild streak, she had come to me to help her learn to have some fun. One night when she had gotten drunk, she'd let it slip that she was trying to get Preston Drake's attention. He was the last guy she needed to be messing around with. Or at least, I had thought so. In the end she had wrapped Preston so tightly around her little finger that he'd cleaned up and stopped screwing his way through life.

"Yes, well, speaking of partying," she said, "I'm having a birthday party for Preston tonight at the house. I just found out that even the single guys coming are bringing dates. And Preston just ran into a former teammate of his in town for the weekend and invited him. He has no date, and I don't want him to feel like the odd one out. So I was hoping . . ." She trailed off.

"That I would come and make this an even number," I finished for her, thinking that I would rather poke needles in my eyeballs.

"Yes, please? Rock and Trisha will be here. I know you aren't a big fan of this whole crowd, so if you don't want to, I understand," she said.

That was typical Amanda. She was giving me an out in case I didn't want to do this. She hated making anyone uncomfortable. I knew Marcus Hardy's wife, Willow, didn't much care for me, and honestly I didn't blame her. I'd been an ass to her once. I had been so full of anger back then with my life in general, thanks to Hank. Probably time I apologized to the woman. Then there was Cage York's wife, Eva. We had only had one run-in, but I had been a bitch then, too. I'd never had my sights set on Cage. He'd been more screwed up than Krit, but then he'd met Eva. Cage was so completely different now.

"I'll come," I said. This had always been a crowd I didn't fit into but watched from the outside.

"You will? Thank you so much!" she replied happily. I listened to her tell me about the details and wondered if this was a major mistake. What if Jason had planned to call tonight and I was at this party and couldn't talk to him?

After I hung up the phone, I sat there staring at it, wishing Jason would just call.

JASON

I had a test to study for and a paper to write. All week I had focused on my classes and making sure I was caught up and ahead of the game. My goal was to be available to leave for Sea Breeze by next Friday to spend time with Jess. Tonight I intended to call her, but I was going to get done with my course work first. I knew once I heard her voice I would be too distracted to think about anything else.

Only an hour into my studying, my phone rang, interrupting me three times in thirty minutes. I reached over and picked it up to see that Jax was the determined caller.

"What?" I asked irritably. He was wasting my limited time.

"Glad you could answer. I called three times," he replied.

"I'm busy. What do you need?"

"Studying, I gather. You always act like an ass when I interrupt your study time."

"Yet you kept calling after I ignored you the first time."

"Did you get my text?" he asked.

"No. I was ignoring you."

"I was just passing along some information that I thought you might find interesting, but then again, maybe not. I just figured since you were using my beach house so much lately, there may be someone bringing you there."

Was he talking about Jess? "You have my attention. What is it you know or think you know?"

"You haven't talked about it since that night in the limo. You were pretty upset about the alternative-looking guy. But since you were back in Sea Breeze last weekend and I have it on good authority that you took Jess into the house and kept her overnight, that things between you two are back on again."

Since when did Jax have time to stalk my private life? "Get to the point."

"Touchy. So you two are back on again," he replied. I pulled my phone back and checked my text messages. I wasn't in the mood for this.

Jax had sent me a photo of Jess sitting beside a guy, smiling up at him while he was saying something to her. Jax had texted: *Look who's got a date to Preston Drake's birthday party.*

"What the hell is this?" I asked, standing up and taking several deep breaths while I tried to decide what to do.

"You saw the text? That's who sat across from Sadie and me during dinner tonight."

"Where are you?" I demanded, walking to grab my keys and wallet from the dresser beside my bed.

"Sea Breeze. Preston and Amanda's place. Everyone else is inside still eating, but I thought you should see that. Not sure what your relationship is with her, but you need to know she isn't sitting around Sea Breeze waiting for you. But then, you had heard the stories about her. Don't want you to get hurt."

I opened the door to my apartment and slammed it behind me.

"What are you doing?" Jax asked.

"Going to the airport," I snarled, unable to mask my anger.

"So you two are seeing each other. Is it exclusive?"

I stopped stalking toward the elevator. Was it exclusive? That one question had been like a slap to the face. What was wrong with me? I had been ready to go get on a plane and demand Jess explain herself. But I couldn't do that.

"No," I replied, and leaned up against the wall to let the heaviness settle on my chest. "We aren't. Exclusive, that is."

"Then I guess she isn't doing anything wrong. Didn't think she would right in front of me, but I still wanted to make sure you weren't being screwed over."

She was with a guy. Someone else. Was she going to kiss him? Had she already kissed him? Was she seeing him, too? Fuck.

"You still there?" Jax asked.

"Yeah. I'm here."

He sighed, and I felt the big-brother lecture coming on, from the sound of his sigh. "Guess it's time you deal with reality, then. I gotta go. Sadie will start wondering where I went."

"Yeah, okay. Wait, did she . . . did Jess say anything to you about me?" I asked, holding on to the hope that I was on her mind.

"No, she didn't," he replied.

I hung up, letting the phone fall to my side. She was on a date. This was my fault.

I turned and went back to my apartment. Studying was going to be impossible now. I grabbed my overnight bag and threw some things into it while calling to book a flight.

Chapter Twenty-One

JESS

Under any other circumstances, having a rock god like Jax Stone staring at me would be thrilling. However, this was entirely uncomfortable. Twice tonight I had come close to telling him that I wasn't doing anything wrong. That I wasn't sure what he knew or what he thought he knew, but Jason and I weren't exclusive. Not that I didn't want to be.

Sadie apparently noticed Jax's interest in me and Jeff, Preston's friend who I had been seated with during dinner, and she kept trying to break the tension by talking to me. To make things even more uncomfortable, Willow Hardy wasn't exactly happy with me being here. I felt like pointing out that Marcus was holding their kid in his lap while gazing at her like she fell from heaven just for him.

"Excuse me," I said to Jeff before standing up. He was talking baseball with Preston, and Amanda had slipped out a few minutes ago, followed by Sadie. I was going to find Amanda and make an excuse to leave.

"Sure," Jeff replied with a dimpled smile. He was cute and had those pitcher's arms going for him, but he wasn't Jason.

I walked in the direction that Amanda had gone in and overheard her and Sadie talking in the kitchen. Knocking on the door frame, I stepped into the kitchen. Both girls' heads snapped up, and Amanda put a much-too-bright smile on for me.

"Hey, Jess," she said.

I didn't wait for her to say any more. "I think I'm going to head out, if that's okay. Since dinner is over."

Amanda took a quick glance at Sadie, then back at me. "Oh, um, okay. You sure you don't want to stay for cake?"

"No. I think I'll forgo the cake, but thanks for the invitation. I . . . enjoyed the evening." Which wasn't exactly true, but I didn't want to be rude.

I could feel Sadie studying me, and I moved my gaze to hers. I wanted to say something to her about my relationship with Jason, but then if he hadn't told them, he may not want me to. Instead I forced a smile, then turned to leave.

"I didn't know about Jason," Amanda said before I could walk out of the room.

I stopped and turned back around. "What about him?" I asked, trying to sound as if it was no big deal.

Amanda shifted her gaze from Sadie to me. "That y'all were dating," she said, looking at me apologetically.

I shrugged. "Not many people do. It's a casual thing." I hoped my voice didn't give me away.

"Oh. So y'all aren't serious?" Amanda asked.

"Who's not serious?" Eva asked, walking into the kitchen with Willow. Both of them were carrying dirty plates. Willow was the first one to notice I was in the room. She tensed up and glanced at Eva. I had pissed them off, and although they were now married, they still hated me for flirting with their men back then.

I ignored Eva's question since she hadn't been speaking to me, and looked back at Amanda. "Nope. He's got his life at Harvard, and I'm here in Sea Breeze. Jason isn't interested in serious with me." I hadn't meant to say it like that, but trying to fix it would only make me look more pathetic. "Thanks again, Amanda. I'll see myself out," I told her so I could escape before they asked me anything else. Just before I walked out, I turned to Willow and Eva. "I'm sorry. I know y'all don't like me, and I deserve it. Just wanted you both to know that I'm sorry about how I acted back then."

Willow's eyes went wide in surprise. I decided to just leave it at that and walk away. I had said what needed to be said. They really didn't owe me a response.

"Okay. Thanks," Willow replied in a soft tone. Her expression was still one of amazement.

"Yes, thanks for . . . that," Eva said, her face almost friendly and slightly amused. I smiled and decided I liked having that weight off my shoulders.

"Bye," I said, then left the kitchen.

On my way out I called out a bye to everyone in the living room. I didn't make eye contact with Jeff. It hadn't been a real date, and I had no desire to get to know him more.

Driving home, I tried not to dwell on the fact that Jason still hadn't called me. He did say he would be busy this week. The fear that he'd gotten back to Harvard and forgotten about me was nagging at me. I hated feeling this way.

Tonight had been a mistake. That wasn't my crowd. I loved Rock and Trisha, but his friends weren't my friends. I didn't really have friends. Hank's friends had been mine for so long that when it was over I had pushed everyone else away.

Hank hadn't been back to my house since he'd had to get married to keep his kid. It was a relief not to have to worry about him beating on my door in the middle of the night. Talking him down from being an angry drunk was tiring. I knew this wouldn't last—he would get tired of doing what Carrie said, and he'd be back. I was enjoying the break while I could.

The knocking on the door started just after midnight, and I stared at the ceiling in my bedroom, thinking this couldn't be happening. I had just been thinking about how great it was not having to deal with Hank.

He wasn't banging on the door, so there was a good chance he wasn't drunk. That could be even worse. At least when he was drunk I could calm him. Sober, he was dangerous. When my phone started ringing, I reached over and picked it up. Jason's name was on the screen. Sitting up in bed, I cleared the sleep from my voice and took a deep breath before answering. I had been waiting on this call all week.

"Hello," I said, a little too anxiously, into the phone.

"Are you gonna make me stand out here all night?" he asked.

It took me a moment to understand what he was saying.

"Is that you knocking?" I asked.

"Yes."

I jumped up and ran to the door. When I jerked it open, Jason stood outside with his phone still at his ear, but he wasn't smiling. He stuck his phone in his pocket and stepped inside before putting his hand on my hip and backing me against the wall. My heart had just enough time to flutter before his lips touched mine.

This made up for no calls all week. It more than made up for it. I opened my mouth when his tongue slid across my bottom lip. The pleased growl that came from his chest made my entire body feel hot and flushed. I slipped my hands into his hair and leaned into him as his minty taste invaded me. He always tasted so clean. I loved that. It made me want to crawl into his arms and never leave. There was a security with it that didn't make sense. Just because he tasted good did not make him less dangerous to my heart than anyone else.

"You had a date tonight," he said against my lips as his hand tightened on my waist.

I started to shake my head and stopped. He meant Jeff. Jax had called him and told him. Was that why he was here? Could he get here that quickly? I grabbed his shoulders and broke the kiss enough to catch my breath.

"Did you come because I was at Amanda's with Jeff?" I asked. I was torn on how I wanted him to answer this. He had said he wanted to keep this casual. We were doing that. Me dating someone else was okay, but if he had come all this way because he was jealous, then I liked that. I liked it a lot. I just wasn't sure if I wanted him here because he missed me or if I wanted him jealous.

"Yes," he replied. I could hear the frustration in his voice. He didn't want to care. But he did. He cared enough to come all the way here unplanned.

"You said . . . ," I started to say, but he cut me off when his mouth covered mine again.

I had to hold tight to him because his hungry, aggressive kissing was making my knees weak. He took from me like he couldn't get enough. I tilted my head back and let him. I wanted this. I wanted him to desire me, but I also wanted him to claim me. We had been down this road before, and when he had gotten jealous it had ended. I didn't want to lose him again.

"I don't like it," he said as his mouth left mine and started moving down my neck, kissing and tasting my skin. "Did he kiss you?"

I shook my head, unable to speak from my need to breathe.

"I don't like it," he repeated as he stopped his delicious onslaught at the curve of my neck and shoulder. He kept his lips brushing against the sensitive skin there. "I can't share," he said.

"We just ate together. Everyone had a date. She needed someone for Jeff to make it an even number," I explained.

Jason moved closer to me and slowly lifted his head. Dark blue eyes stared down at me. "Don't do that again," he said, then brushed his thumb over my bottom lip. "They're always so damn plump. Like they're swollen from kisses," he murmured as he continued to touch my lip.

I had to concentrate to respond to his demand. Seeing him so fascinated with my lips wasn't helping me. "We aren't exclusive."

He stopped touching my lip, and his eyes lifted from my lips to meet my gaze. "No. We weren't. I'm changing that. Now," he replied. He moved his leg forward until it was firmly wedged between my legs. "Do you want to date other people?" he asked.

His muscular thigh was pressed against me just enough to

make me light-headed. I wanted to rock against him and reach that release I knew was there. His kissing had sent my body into an excited frenzy. It wouldn't take me long. Just a little more pressure.

Jason pressed a kiss to my ear. "Answer me. I'll give you fucking orgasms all damn night, but right now I need you to answer me."

I moved my hands down to grab ahold of his arms. "Just you," I told him.

Jason slipped his hand down the boxer shorts I was wearing, and his finger slipped easily inside me. Crying out, I rested my head on the wall and closed my eyes. I was already on the verge of an orgasm just from his caveman aggressiveness.

"I want this getting hot and wet just for me," he said with labored, heavy breathing that caused me to shiver.

I nodded, because he could rest assured he was the only one getting anywhere near it these days. He had ruined me for everyone else.

"Tell me," he urged, slipping his wet finger over my clit and causing my knees to give out. He held me up with his knees still between my legs and held on to my waist with his free hand.

"What?" I asked, unable to remember what we were talking about. My body was trembling, and all I could think about was the pleasure about to rip through me.

"That you're mine, Jess. That you're only mine," he said as his hand went still.

I whimpered, needing him to keep touching me. I was so close. "Please," I begged, desperate.

"I want to, baby. Nothing I want more than to feel you come on my hand," he said, making me cry out in frustration. "But I need you to tell me. This is just us now. No more dating. Just us," he said. His voice sounded far away, but I understood him.

This was what I wanted. Silly man thought he had to get me so worked up I couldn't think straight to get this answer. All he had to do was ask. I had been waiting on this. Too scared to hope for it.

"Yes. Just you. I've always"—I gasped as his finger slowly slid inside me—"just wanted you. I love you," I managed to say before the waves of release washed over me.

I heard his name rip from my lips as I lost conscious thought, no longer caring if I crumpled to the floor. It felt too good. I could feel the trembles still racking my body and moaned as the ecstasy held on tight, not letting me go just yet.

The ground beneath me moved, and I tried to open my eyes but I only managed to wrap my arms around Jason. I never felt the hard ground beneath my feet, but Jason's warmth grew stronger, and I curled against him. This was what safety felt like. I had never truly understood what it felt like to be safe.

Finally able to open my eyes, I looked up at Jason's face and realized we were outside and walking. Before I could manage to ask him what we were doing, he slid into the back of the limo with me still in his arms. The door closed behind us, and I sat up and looked around before I turned back to him.

"What are we doing?"

Jason grabbed my face and kissed me with an urgency I immediately reacted to even though he had just sucked most of my energy from me inside the house. He pulled away first and shook his head with a grin. "Damn, Jess."

"What?" I asked, still not sure what was going on.

He continued to cup my face in his hands like I was some precious object. "You're going to kill me or drive me insane. I can't seem to care. I'm looking forward to it," he said.

I returned his smile and covered his hands with mine. "I'm glad you're here."

He chuckled softly. "I might have gotten a little possessive when I heard you were having dinner with another guy."

I wasn't going to lie to him. I was glad he had cared. "It was really nothing," I assured him.

Jason leaned forward and pulled my bottom lip into his mouth and sucked on it. I loved that he was so enamored with my lips. No one had ever been so obsessed with them before.

"I have fantasies about these lips," he said when he leaned back.

I wanted to know all about his fantasies so I could make

them a reality. But first I wanted to know where we were going. "Where are we going? And I didn't lock the door to the house."

Jason gave me a crooked grin. "I locked it and put the key back in the very bad hiding place you keep it in. And we're going to my place. I want you in bed with me all night."

Oh. I liked that. A lot. "So you aren't going back yet?"

"You've got me the rest of the weekend," he replied.

I couldn't keep the silly grin off my face.

JASON

Watching Jess sleep was like crack. I couldn't get enough. She was so unbelievably beautiful, and once you got to know the real Jess, you realized she was fucking sweet. The badass smart mouth who thumbed her nose at rules and skirted the law whenever she could had a kind heart. She'd been hurt in the past, and her life had been hard. It gave her an edge. But there was still an innocence there I hadn't expected.

She loved me. She had said it several times last night, and I hadn't been able to say anything back. Each time I'd reacted by bringing her pleasure simply because I wanted to hear her say it again. I didn't deserve it, but I wanted it nonetheless.

I had also been dealing with the realization that she'd never felt safe. I wasn't even sure she realized that she had been mumbling about finally feeling safe when I'd held her against me. But it had struck me like a damn brick to my chest. No man had taken care of her and her mother. The guys in her life had only taken from her. No one had taken care of her.

It caused an ache in my chest so intense it had been hard to breathe. She was vulnerable, but no one realized it. She hid behind a strong, brave facade, and it pissed me the hell off that Rock let her. He was her cousin. From what I could tell, he was a good husband and he was great with those kids. Why didn't he protect Jess the same way? He let people talk about her and guys treat her like shit.

Jess's eyelashes fluttered, and I enjoyed that perfect moment when she opened her eyes and her gaze found mine. A small, sleepy smile touched her lips. In that moment I knew nothing was more important to me than keeping this woman safe and taken care of. I loved her. I hadn't expected that, but it had happened. She'd become my world, and I intended to give her the life she deserved. She wasn't going to be scared and alone again. I would make damn sure my girl always felt safe.

Before I could say any of this, there was a swift knock on my door before it swung open and my mother stepped into the room.

Well, fuck.

Mother's eyes went to Jess, then swung back to me. I could see her compose herself. She hadn't come in here expecting to find a girl in my bed. It was obvious by the shock on her face.

240

"Jason," she said in her businesslike tone, which meant she was angry and trying to keep it under control.

"Mother," I replied.

Jess had gone completely still beside me, and I was thankful I had the covers pulled up, covering her very naked body. I looked down at her. "Jess, meet my mother, who has forgotten her manners this morning about respecting others' privacy," I told her, then pressed a kiss to her nose to reassure her before looking back at my mother. "Mother, this is Jess, my girlfriend."

Chapter Twenty-Two

JESS

Meeting a guy's mother while naked in his bed was never good. Especially when the guy was someone like Jason. Hank's mother would have been shocked, then made a comment about not knocking me up. Maybe even called me a whore.

Jason's mother reeked of money. She hadn't expected to find a girl in bed with him. That much was obvious. And honestly, a relief, in a way. At least I knew he didn't do this often. I hoped that proved to her that I wasn't some slut after him because of his brother.

Jason's arm stayed firmly tucked around me like he was keeping me out of harm's way and protected. It was sweet and eased my mind some. But the disappointment in his mother's eyes was hard to ignore. She expected more from Jason than . . . me. I couldn't blame her, really. Jason was brilliant and had a future ahead of him so much bigger than me. I wanted to reassure her that I wasn't going to hold him back. I wanted all his dreams to come true too. I didn't say anything, though. She didn't look like she wanted to speak to me.

"Girlfriend?" she repeated, distaste in her voice as the word rolled off her tongue. "I was unaware you had a girlfriend. Johanna was under the impression you would be accompanying her to the cotillion next weekend. Her mother called to let me know the color of her dress so you could order her corsage."

Jason's body went rigid beside me, and his arm tightened as he pulled me even closer to him. "I told Johanna I would be her escort before things got serious between Jess and me. I'll still take her, but it will be a friends-only thing."

I was trying to figure out what a cotillion was and why it was okay for Jason to still buy a girl flowers and take her to this thing when he'd gotten upset over me just having dinner with Jeff.

"Yes, well, we will talk about this later. You need to get dressed." She paused and looked at me. "Both of you," she said, again with the disgusted tone in her voice. "We can continue this conversation over breakfast."

"We'll be down shortly," he replied.

His mother nodded and stepped out of the room, closing the door a little harder than necessary.

Jason let out a frustrated sigh and laid his head back down. "She lives to control me. I swear I can't get away from her. Not even here."

I turned to look at him. "Your mother?" I asked, wondering if we were talking about his mother or Johanna.

"Yeah, my mother," he said, then leaned over and kissed me. "I'm sorry about that. Not how I wanted you to wake up. I had some really good plans that she just shot to hell."

I wanted to know what those plans were, but I was afraid his mother would come back and demand we get dressed if we took too long. "We need to get dressed," I said.

He frowned, then nodded. "Yeah, she'll be back if we don't get down there soon."

I slipped out of his embrace and started to get out of bed when his arms slid back around my waist and he pulled me back against his chest. "You look gorgeous when you wake up. I've been watching you sleep for an hour, imagining how good your skin tastes in the morning."

I wanted to melt into him and let him keep telling me what he had been thinking, but his mother's presence in the house and the name Johanna were keeping me from doing that.

I reached for his hands and pulled them off of me, then stood up and reached for my clothes, realizing he had brought me over here last night in a pair of boxers and a tank top. I couldn't go downstairs dressed like that.

Turning around to look at Jason, I found him still sitting on the bed, staring at my naked body. That was hard to ignore. I wanted to forget Johanna and his mother and just crawl back into bed. But this was important. I wanted her to like me.

"I don't have anything to wear," I told him, feeling my skin heat up under his gaze.

He lifted his eyes to meet mine after they lingered on my breasts. "Have I mentioned that I hate my mother?" he asked. Then his lips curled into a sexy smile.

I put my hands on my hips, knowing it only made my breasts look better, and frowned at him. "I am pretty sure she hates me, too. So finding me something other than my tank top and boxer shorts would be wise."

Jason's eyes were back on my chest. "Jess," he said slowly.

"Hmm?"

"You need to cover yourself or I'm not going to be able to focus on anything other than bending you over my bed."

Oh. My nipples went taut and he muttered a curse. I wrapped my arms over my chest and Jason shook his head as if he were trying to clear it. "Okay, right, uh, clothes," he said, looking anywhere but at me. He opened a drawer and pulled out a T-shirt and a pair of sweatpants. "These are too small. I've had them here for a couple of years. They also have a drawstring," he said, handing them to me without looking at me. "Put them on fast, please," he said.

Smiling, I took the clothes and pulled on the tank top I had worn, since I didn't have a bra, then finished dressing myself. The clothes were baggy but not too bad. "I'm dressed," I told him as he pulled on a pair of jeans. He turned back around and his gaze traveled down my body. When his eyes met mine again, a pleased look was on his face. "I like you in my clothes."

I liked wearing his clothes. I was doubting his mother was going to like it, though. But there wasn't much I could do about that.

Jason pulled a shirt over his head, then held out his hand for me to take. I let him pull me against him before I put my hand up to stop him from kissing me. "Wait."

His frown was instant. I knew he didn't realize the thing with Johanna bothered me. He was acting like it wasn't a big deal. He hadn't even brought it up after his mother left the room. But it was a big deal. I wanted to know who she was. What a cotillion was and why he was still planning on taking her.

"Who's Johanna and what's a cotillion?" I asked.

Jason sighed and ran his hand through his hair like he was frustrated. If I wasn't so completely obsessed with him, that would piss me off. But where Jason was concerned, I was weak. I loved him too much.

"A girl from home. Our parents are friends. They have a place in the Hamptons next door to ours. We've grown up together. And a cotillion is a stupid thing they do at the country club my parents are members of, where girls enter society. They get all dressed up, and it's a dance thing. Like I said, it's stupid."

He was taking her to a dance. A girl who his mother approved of and he had known his whole life. My stomach felt sick. She would be all dressed up in a fabulous, expensive dress, and he would put his hands on her as they danced. I stepped back from him, needing some space.

I had asked for this when I had decided to enjoy Jason while I had him. I should have known there was a Johanna. There always was.

"Jess," he said, reaching for me, but I pulled my hand away and put it behind my back.

"I should go," I told him before walking to the door.

"Oh, no, you don't," he said, running in front of me and blocking the door. "You aren't walking out of here mad at me. You're the only girl I want. If I could get out of this thing with Jo, I would. But it would leave her in a bind for an escort, and she's a friend. That's it. A friend. She knows it, even if my mother would like to pretend otherwise."

I wanted to believe him, but it still stung. I felt like he was choosing "Jo" over me. Which didn't surprise me. No man had ever put me first. Why I should expect that from Jason just because I'd told him I loved him, I didn't know.

"Fine. I still want to go home. Can you have your driver take me, please?"

Jason grabbed my waist. "No. You aren't leaving like this. You're upset, and I can't fucking handle that. I don't want you upset. What do you want me to do? Tell me how I can fix this, and I'll do it, Jess. Just please don't be mad at me."

He looked determined. I wanted to believe him, but I had already voiced my concern. He had ignored that. I couldn't ask him not to take her, because I knew he would give me the same excuse again. "What night is it?" I asked him instead.

"Next Saturday," he said, almost wincing as he said it.

I wasn't a whimpering, pathetic female. Something about Jason was making me weak. The protective walls I had lived behind were crumbling, and I was letting myself be pushed around. I was tougher than this. I looked him directly in the eye.

"Fine. She's your friend. Take her to her cotillion," I said, and relief touched his face, but I wasn't done yet. "I'll have Dewayne take me to the music festival next Saturday night on the beach, since he's a friend I've had since I was a kid and I never miss a music festival. Especially since Blake Shelton will be there this year."

Jason's entire body went rigid, and I flashed him a smile. "We should probably go to breakfast now," I said sweetly.

"Why Dewayne?" he asked in a low, even voice. I could tell he was trying to control his reaction.

He had been dealing with the lovestruck Jess. He'd forgotten that I could play dirty. "Because I know if I ask him to, he'll not only get me a ticket, he'll take me." I added a shrug. "And, of course, he's an old friend."

Jason grabbed the door handle and took a deep breath. "Okay" was all he said before opening the door and standing back for me to exit first.

I walked into the hallway and had no idea where to go next. "You're gonna have to lead. I'm lost," I told him.

He was still standing at the door, staring at me, when I glanced back at him. There was a pained look on his face, and I silently cheered that my threat was getting to him. If he wanted me to live with his world, then he'd have to learn to live with mine.

"How's he gonna get tickets this late?" Jason asked.

"We're locals," I replied with a grin. "We know who to call."

Jason's frown was verging on angry, and I couldn't keep the grin off my face. Guess it didn't feel too good to him, either.

He didn't say anything else on our way down to the dining room, and I became more and more aware of the fact that I was way underdressed for breakfast with his mother the closer we got. I had been busy making sure Jason knew how it felt to be left on the sidelines that I hadn't thought about my clothing.

"She's not going to like what I'm wearing," I said, pausing outside the door.

Jason touched my arm and gave me a reassuring squeeze. "You're fine. I'll handle this."

The safe feeling was back, and I nodded and walked inside

when he opened the door for me. His mother's eyes were on me immediately, and the distaste on her face was obvious.

"I'm glad you could finally join me. I thought I was going to have to come back up there and remind you." Her haughty voice was like ice.

"No, Mother. We remembered. We just aren't working on your schedule. We have our own," Jason replied, and held out a chair for me to sit down.

I was seriously considering running out of the room. This woman was scary as hell.

"Don't talk to me with such little respect," she said in a warning tone.

"Don't provoke me," he replied, taking the seat to my left and placing himself between me and her.

She set her cup down and fixed her now angry glare on me. "Could she not dress more appropriately?"

Jason's hand was immediately on my leg, holding it firmly. "She wasn't aware that she needed to bring clothing for eating breakfast with my mother. I didn't know you were coming."

"Johanna called me when she went to your apartment and you told her you were headed to Sea Breeze for the weekend. She wondered if it was a family gathering."

We were back to Johanna again. I hadn't realized she also went to Harvard. The sick knot in my stomach was back. My victory was short-lived.

"Johanna needs to mind her own business," Jason replied.

"She was concerned because you were supposed to be at a special study group tomorrow that she said was mandatory."

Jason's grip on my thigh was the only thing giving away his mounting frustration. "It isn't mandatory. She knows that," he replied.

"Does she know that you have a . . . a thing with this girl?"

I winced at her tone and didn't even attempt to acknowledge the food in front of me.

"Does she know I have a girlfriend? No. But she will as soon as I see her again. I wasn't aware she and I were close enough to discuss my life outside of school."

His mother cocked one of her perfectly shaped eyebrows. "Please tell me that comment was for your girlfriend's benefit, because I'm the one who caught you and Johanna having sex last spring while we were vacationing in the Hamptons on your break."

He'd had sex with Johanna. I was done. I couldn't sit through any more of this. I was afraid of what else his mother would enlighten me about. I started to stand up, but Jason's hand held me down.

"That's enough, Mother. You managed to push me to my limit. You've not only made Jess feel unwelcome and uncomfortable, you've upset her. I don't like her upset. Thank you for changing my mind. I won't be attending the cotillion with

Johanna. I'll let her know today so she can find a replacement. Maybe you can help her with that." Jason stood up and held his hand out to me. "Let's go," he said, fixing his gaze on me.

"You aren't leaving. We aren't done here," his mother snapped, and I jumped up, grabbing his hand tightly.

"Yes, we are," he replied, then turned and walked us out of the dining room and directly toward the front door.

"Bring the car around. We're ready to leave," Jason spoke into his phone, then slid it back into his pocket. He opened the front door and stepped back, letting me walk outside.

The limo I was accustomed to seeing pulled in front of the house, and Jason's hand was on my back, leading me toward it. The driver had barely had time to park when Jason was opening the door himself and motioning for me to get inside.

After he crawled in, he looked toward the opening between the driver and us. "Just drive until I tell you otherwise," he said, then pressed a button that raised the divider.

I was afraid to let him talk first. I didn't know if the anger rolling off him was because of me or his mother or both. "You don't have to cancel with Johanna," I said, surprising myself. Especially after I now knew he had slept with her. That changed everything for me.

"No," he said, picking me up and putting me in his lap. I straddled him and placed my hands on his chest, unsure of what he had planned for this position. I wasn't feeling very affectionate at the moment. "Jo has turned into one of them. Just like my mother and hers. I have no desire to do anything for her."

"But you wanted to," I reminded him.

He put his hands on my thighs and stared up at me. "I promised her last spring I'd take her," he said, as if that explained it. Must have been during the sex they were having. "Canceling on her now was mean. I didn't want to leave her without an escort. But now I don't give a shit."

"Because she called your mom," I said, trying to figure out what exactly had made him mad.

Jason laid his head back on the seat and closed his eyes. "No. That just gave me an excuse. I'm glad she gave me a reason, because I was going to cancel on her before we walked into that dining room." He lifted his head back up and looked at me. "I wasn't letting you go anywhere with Dewayne or anyone else. The thought of you dressed sexy, drinking and dancing on the beach where anyone could see you and think you were available, was more than I could handle. I'm taking you to that damn festival. Me. They all need to know you're taken."

Oh. My heart did that flutter thing again, and my hands on his chest turned into fists to keep from pawing at him in appreciation. It had taken me fighting back, but he had put me first in the end. That was almost as good as being picked first. It would have been better if he'd chosen my wishes over hers without my having to threaten him with another guy.

The fluttering stopped. When I realized how I had won this battle, it took away all the joy. He had originally chosen her. He hadn't wanted to hurt her, but he'd been okay hurting me.

"I won't go with Dewayne. Take her to the cotillion. It's what you originally wanted to do. I played dirty, and I shouldn't have," I said, shifting to move off his lap. I needed some space.

Jason grabbed my waist and held me there. "It's not what I wanted to do," he said. "It's what was right. She didn't deserve to be ditched at the last minute."

He still didn't get it. I nodded. "Take her. You don't want to hurt her."

I could feel him studying me, but I wouldn't look at him. I just wanted to go home and lock myself in my room. I could cry then and no one would see me. "I don't like hurting people in general," he said slowly, as if he was trying to figure out the meaning behind my words.

"I know. You're a better person than I am. Actually, than most people I know. You're thoughtful and kind. It's one of the things that I find so insanely attractive about you."

Jason moved his thumbs so that they brushed my stomach in a gentle caress. "Then why won't you look at me?" he asked.

Because you didn't choose me first. Those words sounded shallow, yet they kept repeating in my head. I wish it wasn't important to me. I wish my self-esteem was better and that kind of thing wasn't a weakness of mine.

"This morning has been intense, and I just want to go back to sleep," I told him, forcing myself to look at him so he wouldn't push that issue.

Jason reached up and took my chin between his thumb and forefinger so I couldn't look away. "You aren't telling me something." He sounded frustrated.

"I don't want to talk about it. I'll be okay. Just give me some time to deal with my own insecurities. I'm working on them," I explained, trying to sound flippant.

"I never want to make you feel insecure. If I have to dedicate my life to making sure you know where you stand with me, I will. So don't give me that shit. If you have something to deal with, tell me. I'll fix it."

He couldn't fix this. He didn't realize that it had already been done. His immediate impulse was to protect Johanna. Not me.

I wondered if he had loved her. If he had ever told her he loved her. I loved him, but he hadn't told me he loved me. Maybe that was it. He didn't love me but he had loved her. She had that hold on him. I started to move again, wanting to get away from him, but he continued to hold me still.

"Talk to me, Jess. Please," he begged.

"You had to choose, and you chose her. When pressed for an answer, you chose her feelings over mine. Nothing that happened after that matters. Because it was after I manipulated you." I stopped and looked out the window because I couldn't stand looking at him while I admitted this. "I wanted to be your first choice, so I forced you to pick me. It was wrong. I don't want you to put me first because I use your jealousy against you. I want you to think of me first because it's the way you feel. I'm tired of trying to be someone's first choice. I've done that, and I'm exhausted. I won't do it anymore. I just won't." Jason's grip on me loosened, and I used that opportunity to get off his lap and put some space between us. I didn't look back at him, and I didn't say anything else.

He had wanted me to talk, and now that I had he had nothing to say. I wished I could reach the button so I could let the driver know to take me home. I wanted out of this car. I wanted to run until I couldn't run anymore.

"I didn't realize it hurt you. You acted like it wasn't a big deal," he said in a pained voice.

"Really? That's what you're going with?" I asked angrily. "If I were to go to a dance with a guy friend because I had promised him I would and you knew his hands would be touching me while we danced, just how would you feel? Would you be okay with that?"

He didn't reply. I knew he couldn't honestly tell me he would be fine with it. When I had thrown it back in his face, he had cracked. So how could he say that he didn't think it would bother me?

"You're right. I didn't think," he said. "My first thought should have been to protect you and your feelings. I'm so sorry,

Jess. I'm not good at this. I don't do relationships, and I obviously suck at it." He sounded so defeated.

I couldn't stay mad at him. It wasn't his fault that he didn't love me. He cared, and that was all I would ever get from him. I knew that already. I was expecting him to react the way a man in love would. He couldn't.

"It's okay," I said, turning to look at him. "I was expecting too much. I'm sorry."

Jason's frown only deepened. "Don't apologize. This is all me. You deserve better than the way I treated you this morning. But if there is any way you can forgive me, I swear I'll be better. I'll figure this relationship thing out and get it right."

He was willing to try, which counted for something. He still didn't get that his first instinct should have been to choose me. But then, he wasn't in love, so that wouldn't be what he first thought of. I wasn't looking for someone who would put me first, I was looking for someone to love me.

The realization was sad and pathetic. I had let this thing with Jason mean too much. I didn't want to lose what little time I had with him until a Johanna came into his life and he fell head over heels in love with her and I was forgotten.

"Okay," I said, fighting back the emotions that the thought of losing him stirred up.

"Okay?" he repeated. "I'm forgiven, okay? Or you'll think about it, okay?" he asked.

"You're forgiven," I replied.

He let out a sigh of relief and bent his head to capture my mouth with his. I closed off all other thoughts and enjoyed him. Enjoyed this thing we had that I had let myself believe could be more. I accepted what was real and kissed him back, knowing I was going to need every memory I could make with him to keep me warm one day.

JASON

When her body melted against mine, I felt like I could take a deep breath again. I had been so damn scared. The hurt look in her eyes was going to haunt me for fucking weeks. I had to come up with a way to prove to her how important she was to me. Until then, I needed to reassure myself that she wasn't about to walk out of my life in search of that guy who puts her first.

The unknown guy only made me more desperate. I lay her back on the seat, pushed my shirt that she was wearing up, and slid my hands under her tank top until her breast filled my hand. Her soft moan was so damn sweet. "I want you naked," I told her, and she leaned up so I could pull the shirt and tank off of her.

"I swear, Jess, your tits get more perfect every damn time I see them."

Her nipples hardened from my praise. "Those things you were thinking of to wake me this morning," she said, smiling up at me. "Why don't you show me?"

I pulled a nipple into my mouth and sucked hard until she grabbed my head and cried out. When I let it go, she was panting and her cheeks were flushed. "I'll have to take these sweats off in order to show you, because when I was talking about how you tasted I had a specific area in mind."

Her mouth formed a small O and she trembled underneath me. I was about to show her just how important her happiness was to me. Over and over again.

Chapter Twenty-Three

JESS

Mondays had never been my favorite day of the week, but now I hated them. After spending my weekends with Jason, facing Monday was hard. Especially knowing he had gone back to a world with Johanna in it. I didn't want to be jealous of her, but I couldn't help it. Jason Stone had me tied up in knots.

After my morning class, I had time to come home and eat lunch and then work on the things I didn't get a chance to finish this weekend for the shop. I needed that job, but I hadn't wanted to give up any of my time with Jason to work. Not when I had an entire week without him to work on it.

Sitting down at the sewing machine, I pushed all thoughts of Jason from my head and tried to concentrate on other things. It was short-lived, however, because the doorbell rang. Momma had gone to run some errands that she had been evasive about, which led me to believe she was messing around with a man and didn't want me to know about it.

I went to the door and opened it. The cold, hateful glare that I was sure Mrs. Stone only reserved for me met my gaze, and I wished I had looked out the window first. I really needed to start doing that before I opened the door.

"Can I come in?" she asked, raising that one eyebrow as if she was daring me.

I wanted to say no and slam the door in her face. But she was Jason's mom. I couldn't exactly do that. Besides, I needed to win this woman over. If that was even possible. "Um, okay, yes." I stumbled over my words and stepped back to let her inside.

You could see the living room, my bedroom, my momma's bedroom, and the bathroom from the entrance. The only room you couldn't see the door to was the kitchen, and that was because you had to walk through the living room to get to it. Thanks to my momma's smoking habit the place smelled like stale smoke, but it was clean. Momma wasn't one for filth.

Mrs. Stone's nose visibly scrunched, like she was smelling something bad. I didn't notice the smell much since I'd lived with it, but I knew that to those not around it, it smelled bad. I was suddenly wishing I had made her stay outside and just walked out there to talk to her.

"I'm not here to waste my time. I have the jet waiting at the airport, so let me get to the point," she said, turning to level her haughty glare at me. "You won't do for Jason. I realize Jax will end up marrying beneath him, but he is a celebrity and will be a legend. He can make as many mistakes as he wants, and his success is intact. However, Jason is different. He can't get involved with someone like you." She let her gaze flicker to the blue sofa that I knew was worn and old—but again, it was clean.

"Jason has a bright future. He's brilliant and he has connections. In the world of politics, Jason can't have skeletons like you in his closet. You won't help him reach his goal. You'll only bring him down. He's been in love with Johanna since he was a child. Johanna was groomed to be the wife of a senator. She has grown up in the home of one of the best. I know she will be willing to overlook Jason's baser urges that led him to you. But it has to stop before you affect his life any more. His grades can't suffer, and he will attend that cotillion this weekend as her escort. It's too important for him. If you hold him back, he will hate you for it later. I've dealt with your kind before, and I know you don't go away easily. I'll have one hundred thousand dollars wired to your account within the day. In return, you need to end it with him and disappear from his life. Do whatever you need to do to send him away if he comes back."

I had seen this in a movie once. But having it actually happen to you was different. The dirty way it made you feel was indescribable. To think someone expected you to take the money and agree to something like this was like a slap in the face. Several slaps in the face.

She had seen my home and assumed I was in this for the money, because someone like her couldn't fathom that I would have the ability to love someone more than money. Being poor didn't mean I was soulless. I managed to shake my head no. Words had left me as I stared in horror at this woman who had given birth to the most beautiful, kind, giving, selfless person I knew. How was that possible?

"You'll change your mind." She handed me a small card. "Call me when you realize the stupidity of your decision. Unless he's tired of you by then. I may not have to give you a dime. Now that Johanna knows she has competition, she'll be working extra hard to make him happy," Mrs. Stone said with an evil smirk.

She turned and walked out the door without another word. I stared at her back until she climbed into the limo and drove away. Reaching for the handle, I closed the door, then looked down at the card in my hand. She had left me her contact information. I wanted to burn it, but I didn't. As much as I didn't want to tell Jason about this, I feared that I needed to. I didn't trust her. I wanted him to know that I had never accepted this from her, if it got back to him.

Needing to hear his voice, I walked to my room and dropped the card to my desk before picking up my phone. I wasn't sure if he would be in class right now, but I could at least hear his voice mail.

It rang three times, and then a female answered. She was giggling and telling someone no. I just sat there and listened to her. She said hello again, but I was still too confused to speak.

"Jason is indisposed at the moment. You'll need to call back later," she said before hanging up.

I didn't need someone to tell me who that had been. I just needed Jason to explain it to me. Apparently, Johanna was more than he had admitted to. There had to be some truth to his mother's words. I knew that already. He had feelings for Johanna. I'd already come to terms with it.

Was he in love with her? Was that it? He couldn't love me, because he loved her, and he was sewing his wild oats first. The idea of being his wild oats made me want to curl up in a ball and die.

JASON

"Give me the damn phone, Jo," I demanded, snatching it out of her hands and shoving it in my pocket. I needed another study group. Seeing Jo pissed me off after her duplicity with my mother. She had known calling my mom would send my nosy mother to Alabama looking for me.

"Stop being so nasty to me." She pouted and batted her eyelashes. Jo and I had grown up together, and last spring after I'd had too much to drink she'd gotten naked and crawled on top of me and I'd made the mistake of screwing her. Ever since, she'd been acting different. I never liked the Hamptons. Like Jax, I had always preferred the Sea Breeze house. But the place in the Hamptons had been handed down to us from my grandfather. It would actually become mine in a couple of years. It was the vacation home Mother used when she wanted to be seen. Sea Breeze was where we always went when Jax needed to be hidden for a while.

Johanna was a part of the Hamptons life we had always known. The fact that she had ended up at the same university as me was my bad luck. She was hard to get rid of. At least nicely.

It was obvious Johanna had grown fond of this idea that we should get married and I should be a politician. It wasn't happening. For starters, she annoyed me. Her giggling got on my nerves. She kissed like a fish and she was spoiled rotten.

I grabbed my books and headed for the door.

"Wait, what about Saturday night? When are you picking me up?" she asked, slipping her arm in mine.

"I already told you I couldn't do it. Stop acting like you didn't hear me," I said.

She shrugged. "I know you'll come. You won't stand me up." The cheeriness in her voice made her sound as crazy as the giggling did.

When I stepped outside the library, a voice called out from across the lawn. "Jason."

I shook Johanna's hold on my arm loose and walked away toward Morris.

"Where did you find the girl with you in the picture that you tweeted this weekend, and where can I get one? Because, dude," Morris said, "she's smokin'." He gave me a nod, his eyes wide with appreciation. Jess did that to all men.

I couldn't keep from smiling. She was mine, and damned if that didn't feel good. No one knew the Jess I did, and that felt even better. "Yes, she is," I agreed. "She's fucking perfect."

Morris followed me to my next class, and I got to talk about Jess. It wasn't until later that evening when Jax called that I remembered the call that Jo had answered. Checking my recent calls, I saw Jess's name at the time Jo had answered my phone.

"FUCK!" I roared, ignoring the people around me, and dialed Jess's number. I needed to find some privacy. I had some explaining to do.

I called three times and it kept going to voice mail. I checked the time. She was still at work. There was a chance she didn't take her phone in with her. I left her a message telling her to call me, then sent a text message saying I was sorry about earlier. If she hadn't called in two hours, I was calling again.

Chapter Twenty-Four

JESS

He had called three times while I was at work. I had sent it to voice mail each time. His message said for me to call him. So did his text message. Why had it taken him so long to decide he needed to contact me and explain?

I pulled into the driveway and momma's car was still there. She should have been at work by now. She hardly ever missed work. I climbed out of the truck and headed for the house quickly. My thoughts focused on Momma.

Opening the door, I started to call out for her when I saw her sitting on the sofa. The look on her face told me something was, in fact, wrong. Had Jason's mother talked to her? Threatened her? No, Momma would be in jail, not sitting on the sofa missing work. She didn't take shit from anyone.

"What's wrong?" I asked, dropping my book bag to the painted cement floor and walking over to her. "Are you sick?" I asked, unable to sit down. I needed her to ease my mind. I had a million different scenarios going through my head.

Momma motioned to the chair behind me. "Sit," she said.

I shook my head. "No. Tell me what's wrong," I demanded. The worry and concern had exploded into full-blown fear. This wasn't right. The last time she had acted like this, my best friend in kindergarten had been hit by a car riding her bike and died. That alone told me something was terribly wrong.

"I got a lot to say, and you standing there ain't gonna make me talk faster. So sit your ass down," she said.

"Is someone dead?" I asked, needing to know that Rock, Trisha, and the kids were okay.

She shook her head. "No, ain't no one dead. Now sit down," she said, pointing to the chair again.

I noticed that the ever-present cigarette in her hand was missing. Had she lost her job? Surely not. They loved her there.

"I didn't have no errands to run today. I had a doctor's appointment," she said, then cleared her throat. "It was my fifth one this month. About six weeks ago I noticed a lump in my breast when taking a shower. It was hard to feel since I have the implants, so it was pretty big when I noticed it. I got me an appointment and went in, and they had to run some tests. Today they got back the final results, that it is breast cancer, and 'cause it's been there awhile it's spread some. They're gonna need to do a mastectomy, and I'll need chemo treatments."

I couldn't move. All I could do was sit there and stare at her. This felt like death. This was just as bad. "Can they get it all?" I asked, unable to ask her if this would kill her. I couldn't accept that.

She nodded. "Yeah. They can. They think I'll be fine once they do the mastectomy and I go through chemo. They're positive about my recovery. So don't go worrying about that. Problem here is, I ain't got insurance. I make too much to get government help and not enough to afford the monthly costs of it. The hospital is going to let me make monthly payments. They actually start this month because all that testing wasn't cheap. We're gonna have to move. We need cheaper rent. I'll also need to find a job that I can work and make enough money to support us. My old one isn't gonna be possible no more."

She was going to live. That was all that mattered. I didn't care about moving. We'd made it through hard times. Momma never let us go hungry. She'd done whatever she could to pay the bills.

Now it was my turn to take care of her. I loved my job, but it wasn't nearly enough money. I needed something that paid more. "I'll get a job. Something that pays well," I told her.

She grimaced and wrung her hands in front of her. "Ever since you was a little girl, I wanted big things for you. That beauty of yours was a gift. Then you ended up with a smart head, too. That brain and those looks were meant to give you the world. You shouldn't be here with this burden on you. I didn't get insurance. Now I'm paying for it, and so are you."

My momma had fought hard my entire life to be a single mom and not lean on a man for anything. She used to say you can only depend on yourself. I disagreed. She could depend on me. "I'll use this brain and these looks to take care of us," I assured her. "We'll be fine. I promise. It's time to learn to depend on someone else. I've got this."

I stood up and walked over to the sofa and sat down beside her. This time I pulled her into my arms, instead of the other way around, and held her. The only person in my life who I never doubted loved me was my momma. I would do whatever I had to in order to make sure she got better. "We can do this together," I said, more to myself than her.

My phone was ringing in the pocket of my book bag, but I ignored it. I knew it was Jason, and I would deal with him later. Right now the fact that Johanna was answering his phone was the least of my worries.

"Can't believe I'm about to say this," Momma said, "but you know they'll hire you at Jugs. You'll get top pay, and if you go that route, you'll be safe there."

I hadn't wanted to admit to myself that using my body was the only way I could make the most money. Waiting tables wouldn't be enough. The only way I could use my body to make the most money was to follow in my mother's footsteps. I would lose Jason, though. He would never allow it, and I couldn't let him stand in my way. My heart took another hit at the realization. Our time together would be shorter than I had imagined. But my momma's life came first.

The easy answer was lying in my room. I could have it all paid for with one phone call to Mrs. Stone, but I would never do that. I wasn't using Jason to fix my problem. I loved him. As much as I loved my mother, she wouldn't want that money either. I would get money the only way I knew how.

"What if we moved farther away from the beach? About an hour or so away, the rent will be cheaper for small apartments, and we'll be closer to the hospital. And because I'm young and I have the body, I can probably get a job at Delilah's. It has higher-paying clientele."

Momma looked defeated, and I hated seeing her like this. She was always so tough and ready to take on the world. "Delilah's is the big time in that world. Hard to get a job there because they only accept the best. You'll be hired. Probably make three to four times what I make now," she said.

It was hard for her to accept that I was about to do what she'd worked so hard to keep me from. I wished I had another answer but I didn't. I wouldn't be finishing my two-year degree after all. Might as well face the fact that my future was mapped out for me a long time ago. No use in fighting it.

"That boy ain't gonna be okay with you stripping," Momma said.

I nodded. "Yeah, I know. We were gonna be over soon anyway. He has a girl at college I think he's in love with. I was just the walk on the wild side before he graduates and becomes a politician."

"Well, he never did realize what he had. But then, most politicians are idiots, so that's not surprising."

I managed to laugh even though it was the last thing I felt like doing. I would much rather have cried at how unfair life was. Why some people were born with all the luck, and then others were given one punch after another. I wasn't going down just yet. I had more fight left in me.

Tonight, I wasn't calling Jason back. I couldn't do it without breaking down and crying. This wasn't his business. I wasn't his future and he wasn't in love with me. I had to deal with it on my own. The hardened wall I had let come down slowly began to erect itself as I sat down and made a list of things I needed to handle this week. By Saturday I would be ready to go get a job and an apartment.

JASON

I had been calling Jess for two days and left several dozen messages, but she hadn't responded once. If she was listening to my messages, she knew I had the tickets to the music festival thanks to my brother. She also knew exactly what had happened when Jo answered my phone and how it would never happen again.

Either she wasn't getting my messages or she didn't believe me. I made arrangements to leave Thursday night. My Friday class was just going to have to be missed. I had someone getting me notes. I couldn't wait until Friday night to see Jess. I had to fix this. Knowing she was upset made it impossible for me to concentrate on anything.

When my phone started ringing, I jumped out of the shower soaking wet and grabbed my phone. It was Jess.

"Finally," I said into the phone. "I've called a million times."

She didn't respond right away, and I felt a moment of panic. Was she still pissed?

"It's been a busy week. I'm sorry I haven't been able to call you back." Her voice sounded off. Almost like she was fighting back tears.

"Jess, what's wrong? Is this about that shit with Jo? Because I swear to you . . ."

"No, it's not about her. Don't apologize. It's okay, really. I'm not angry about that."

Then what the hell was wrong? "What's going on?"

She let out a sigh, and I walked over to my computer to see when the next flight headed south was. My classes could all go to hell. I wasn't losing her. If she needed me, then I was going to be there.

"I . . . Your, uh . . ." She stopped, and it sounded like she sniffed. Then she took a deep breath. "Your mom came by on Monday to see me. She made it very clear how you feel for Johanna."

"What the fuck? She came to your house?" I asked, standing up and staring straight ahead as fury rolled through me. How could she do this? What was wrong with my mother? It was my fucking life.

"She wanted me to understand how things were with the two of you and your hopes for your future. I don't fit in to that world. Your world. It is just too much. And I understand now why you picked Johanna's feelings over mine that morning. It makes sense. I was confusing sex with something more."

"Jess, stop talking now. Just stop fucking talking. None of this is true. I don't know what she said, but—"

"You chose her feelings when put on the spot. I knew that meant something. I get it, and I accept that I was never meant for more than a fling. I let the needy female in me want more, and that was my mistake. But it's all irrelevant now."

"I'm booking a flight now. I'm coming to see you. I thought we cleared that shit with Jo up. I never would choose her feelings over yours. Please, just—"

"I slept with Krit last night," she blurted out, and my world stopped turning. The fire inside of me was immediately doused as I stood there unable to speak.

"I've always wanted a man to love me for me. Because he's

wild I always ignored his declarations of love. But he loves me. He always chooses me first. He will turn down anyone and anything if I ask him to. That's the kind of devotion I deserve. It's what you have with Johanna. I was ruining that for you. Go change the world. I'll be fine here in this life I was born into."

I couldn't even tell her bye. When she hung up, I stood there holding the phone in my hand, completely cold inside. She hadn't called me all week because she was fucking that lowlife again, not because I had hurt her. My mother tells her one batch of lies and she believes her. No questions asked, she fucking believed her and then went running to a guy who wears motherfucking eyeliner.

The pain slowly turned to rage and hate. I would make sure I never saw her face again. If she wanted to be a whore, then so be it. I should have known better. Girls like her aren't the kind who change. They don't have good hearts and the ability to fall in love.

The sad fact was, now she had ruined me. I had tasted that kind of passion and nothing else would ever compare. Jess had made sure she broke me. I wouldn't be able to need like that again. I didn't fucking want to. A loveless marriage to a woman who was raised to know that you didn't control a man with your body was the safe route. No wonder so many men married boring women and only fucked the wild ones. You couldn't hold the wild ones. Guess I'd learned that the hard way.

Chapter Twenty-Five

JESS

I held on to the tree in front of me while I dry heaved over and over again after my stomach was completely empty. My face was wet with tears and my throat burned. None of it mattered. Every time I'd replayed the lie I had told Jason, I threw up again. My plan to end things with him had gone much differently in my head. I had worked on what I would say to him for two days while I ignored his calls.

When the time had come to actually tell him something I knew would drive him away, I hadn't realized how it would completely destroy me. It had been a last resort, but the determination in his voice had been more fierce than I'd expected. He hadn't been going to go away easily. It had only made me love him more.

Then I had told him a lie that ripped my heart out. He hadn't said another word. Not even good-bye. His silence had been enough. I knew then that he was done. I had guessed right. He wouldn't forgive me for something like that.

Krit didn't even know I had used him. I hadn't seen him in two weeks. And once I moved, I wouldn't be seeing him at all anymore.

When I went back inside, I didn't tell Momma about my phone call. I just got in the shower and let the tears fall silently. This was my lot in life, and after tonight I wouldn't feel sorry for myself again. There was no time for that. It got us nowhere, and I hadn't been raised to be weak.

The rest of the week went by quickly. After dropping all my classes, I had quit my job and let our landlord know we would be out by the end of the month, which was Monday.

Momma had wanted me to tell Rock, but I wasn't going to. Not yet. He had a family to take care of. This was our battle, no one else's. I would tell Rock eventually, but not until we were moved and I was working. He would try to stop that. I wasn't going to let him. It was the only way. Friday I took Momma to the doctor, then drove fifteen more minutes to the big city of Mobile. It was so different from Sea Breeze, but I felt like I was hidden from everyone. No one knew me. It was easier this way.

I headed to Delilah's in the tightest dress I had and a pair of stiletto heels. This wasn't like Jugs. The clientele was higher class and had more money to spend. Which meant they had high standards for their girls. I was starting at the top, but I realized that I might not make the cut, so I had a list of other clubs to go try out if this one didn't work.

It was a twenty-four-hour establishment since many businessmen came here during their workday to relax, so I was instructed by the lady I spoke with on the phone to come to the back door and knock.

I did as I was told and the door opened up. A large man who was no doubt a bouncer looked me up and down and then stepped aside. "Dee's expecting you," he said without asking my name. I must have been the only afternoon appointment. That was a good sign.

"Thanks," I replied.

"This way," he said, and turned to walk down the hallway. I followed quickly behind him. Music from the club could be heard back here. The sexy beat to it made me nervous. I had never imagined that I would be doing this. Momma had always said she wanted better for me, so I had expected more too. Life had a funny way of proving you wrong.

"In here," he said, opening another door and standing back to let me enter. "Dee will be with you in a moment. You can have a seat," he told me before closing the door.

I looked around the room and realized it was a solid white

room with one red leather straight-backed chair. No windows and nothing on the walls. I noticed a speaker in the ceiling. It all seemed like an odd holding room.

The door opened and a woman who was older than my mother but looked well preserved stepped inside. She was wearing a tight royal-blue dress that made my cleavage look pitiful. Her heels were covered in spikes. Her long red hair was pulled to the side, and she had startling green eyes. If this was what they expected, I was out of my league.

"You're Jess?" she asked, looking at my body in a way no other woman ever had. She was literally studying me.

"Yes," I replied, thankful I hadn't stuttered.

"And you have ID to prove you're twenty?" she asked, lifting her gaze to mine.

I nodded and started to open my purse.

"Not now. I just want to make sure you have it," she said, holding out her hand. "I'm Delilah. Or better known around here as Dee." She dropped her gaze back to my boobs. "You have the body. You'll make a fucking killing. The men here will eat you up. A face like an angel with that body is all their fantasies. But I need you to pass the test. Can't get them all excited and then you suck at this," she said with a smile.

She turned and opened the door. A tall, attractive older man walked inside. His hair was that distinguished gray, and although he was wearing a dress shirt, it was obvious his body was well built. Kind brown eyes met mine and I managed to return his smile.

"This is Garrison. He owns half the place. We were married once, but we're better business partners. I find the women and he tests them. You've impressed me. Now you must impress him."

Garrison walked over to the red chair and sat down. "It's nice to meet you Jess," he said in a deep, smooth voice.

I wanted to reply, but I was so unsure of what test she meant that I couldn't find words. I looked back at Delilah. She waved a hand at Garrison. "The music will start up in a moment, and you have to give him a lap dance. Garrison won't touch you, just like the guests aren't allowed to touch you. Unless, of course, one asks for permission and pays you for it," she finished with a wink.

I wouldn't be letting anyone touch me. That wasn't part of the job description. I also hadn't been prepared for lap dances. That was up close and personal.

"Don't be nervous. It's just us. With that face and body, you're not gonna have to do much to make them happy. Listen to the music and forget the man. Move to the music and enjoy the way it feels. Do it because dancing feels good, not because someone is watching you. It isn't about them."

But it was about them, and I would be doing it in their laps. I was going to hyperventilate.

"Breathe, sweetheart. Don't panic on me. You can do this," he said encouragingly.

"I hadn't realized I had to do . . . I mean, dance so close," I finally said.

"If you've changed your mind I'll be disappointed, because I think you'll become a favorite here, but I'll let you leave. It's okay if you think this isn't for you."

My momma needed me to. I had to make enough money to get us through this. Then I could quit. I could get another job. This wasn't forever. No one was going to touch me. I just had to forget that they were looking at me naked. I couldn't focus on that.

"I can do it," I said, more for myself than for him.

He nodded. "Okay, then. Let's start with stripping. I need to see what we have under that little bit of fabric you have covering you."

Oh shit. He wanted me to strip for him and dance naked in his lap? My heart sped up again, and I twisted my hands nervously in front of me. There was no other way. This was the only job I could do and make this kind of money. My momma had done much worse for me.

I didn't make eye contact with him. Instead I listened to the beat of the song, and I focused on moving my body in ways that I knew men liked. That was something I knew how to do. I unzipped the dress slowly, then let it fall forward just enough to tease at its falling off. He saw naked females all the time. I could do this. It was just my boobs.

I lifted my hands in the air and shimmied until the dress worked its way down my body and then fell around my ankles on the floor. I hadn't been wearing a bra, and the tiny black panties I had on weren't going anywhere. Garrison leaned back in his chair, and his eyes looked appreciatively over my body. I blocked that out.

I had only seen a lap dance on television once, so I wasn't sure I knew exactly what to do. I figured I would dance over him without touching him.

Closing my eyes, I let my head fall back as I moved between his legs and danced. I didn't think about the fact that I was topless with a strange man in a room and I was trying to turn him on. I just did what felt good.

"Put your hands on the back of the chair and lean close without touching," Garrison said in a hoarse whisper.

I opened my eyes and did as he said. My chest was close to his face, but I didn't look at that. I continued to dance.

"Put your foot on my knee," he said.

I paused. "That's touching," I replied.

"The bottom of your shoe on my knee isn't actual touching," he replied, grinning at me.

I did as I was told, and his nostrils flared as he took a deep breath. "Okay, that's good," he said tightly.

From the tense look on his face I was afraid I had done

something wrong. "If I messed up, I can try again. It was my first time," I started to explain, and he shook his head and let out a relieved chuckle.

"You're hired, Jess. That was perfect. You'll have this place so packed that we won't have any damn seats left."

Garrison stood up and walked swiftly across the room and jerked open the door. "You can get dressed. I'll send Dee back in." He hurried out, and I reached for my dress and slipped it back on. When I started to zip it, Dee opened the door.

She was smiling triumphantly. "I'm impressed. It's been years since a girl affected Garrison on her tryout. Bravo. Let's go to my office and get your paperwork and your work schedule filled out."

I followed her out into the hall.

Loud moaning and banging filled the hallway as we walked down it. I glanced over at a door we passed, and I had no doubt in my mind someone was having sex. Did some of the girls do that, too? I wasn't okay with that. I was a look-not-touch only. I needed to make sure they understood that.

"I told you that you got him worked up. Good thing Farrah was here to help him burn off some steam," Dee said, opening a door for me to follow.

I glanced back at the room as a loud male groan echoed off the walls. "That's Garrison?" I asked, making sure I had heard her right.

"Yes. You had him sweating and shaking when he walked

out of that room. He grabbed the first girl he knew would fuck him and dragged her into his office. No worries, though—he only fucks the ones who want him. He won't touch you."

The sick knot I lived with these days was back. This was terrifying. My world was changing, and I realized my desire to feel safe was a childhood fantasy. This was my life.

JASON

Even if I never spoke to Jess again, I needed to get revenge. I wanted to hurt her as much as she'd hurt me. The more I thought about her pushing this off on me like I deserved it only made me angrier. It was like she had laid down a fucking ultimatum that I had failed by saying I was taking Jo to that stupid cotillion. I didn't like being controlled. My parents had been trying to control me my entire life. All I ever did was fight to be free. Jess had been one more person wanting control of me.

I had been so damn willing to give it to her too. In a way I had. I'd let her break me. Falling in love wasn't something I had ever wanted. The only thing I had on my side was the fact that I had never told her I loved her. She didn't know she'd hurt me as badly as she had. My pride was still somewhat intact. Not that it did me much good.

After planning on taking Jo back to my place for sex once the cotillion was over, I had failed miserably when the time actually came. I couldn't stand to touch her. Kissing her had been bad. It lacked more than I could possibly label. She had felt wrong in my arms. She hadn't fit right. Her curves didn't send my heart into a wild frenzy, and the idea of getting her underneath me did nothing for me.

I had taken her home and gone back to my apartment to drink myself to sleep. Jo called the next day and the next. By kissing her, I had led her to believe I was attracted to her. How the hell she thought that after the kiss we shared, I wasn't sure. Had she not been there for that kiss? It had been bland and boring. I focused on ignoring her at school and sending her calls to voice mail, but she wasn't giving up that easily.

Two weeks later Winston was standing outside the door to my apartment when I got home from class. Winston was one of Jax's bodyguards and had been with Jax since the beginning of his fame. I didn't even look at him when I went to the door. "Good afternoon, Mr. Jason," Winston said politely. It wasn't his fault my brother was in there, nor was it his fault my brother paid for the apartment. I nodded. "Hello, Winston," I replied, and stepped inside.

Jax was standing at the tall windows overlooking the small city with a soda in his hand. He turned to look at me and smirked. "You aren't answering my calls. What did you expect?" he said.

I threw my books on the table. "I don't know, maybe some fucking privacy," I replied, annoyed.

Jax let out a low whistle. "Your language has taken a downward spiral."

My brother's witty comments were only making me more pissed off that he was here without asking.

"I'm not in the mood to talk. To anyone," I snapped.

Jax nodded and walked over to sit on the bar stool closest to him. "Is it Mother? I heard her basically planning your wedding to Jo."

"She can forget that shit. Jo needs to sniff elsewhere."

"You took her to the cotillion," Jax said as he studied me for a reaction. I knew what he was doing. He had always tried to figure me out by reading my facial expressions. Most of the time he was accurate.

"Meant nothing. I did what I said I'd do, and now I'm done."

"You end it with Jess?" he asked, and I felt my entire body tense up at the sound of her name. I hadn't said it or heard it in three weeks. And I wasn't ready to hear it now.

"Don't," I said, walking away from him and across the room in case I started throwing things. She was already alive in my dreams at night. Haunting me. Driving me crazy. I didn't want to acknowledge her existence while I was awake.

"Don't what? Ask you about Jess?"

I fisted my hands at my sides and glared at the wall in front of me. He was trying to push my buttons. No reason to react. If he thought he'd gotten to me, he would chant her name until I lost it.

"That's over," I snarled.

"She end it?"

He wasn't going to let up.

"For once in your goddamn life, don't push me. Let this go."

He didn't reply, and I stood there prepared for him to say more. When he didn't, I forced my hands to open and relax. This reaction was ridiculous. I had to get control of this.

I heard Jax stand up and I turned to look at him. He put his glass on the counter, then met my glare and nodded. "I'll leave you to your brooding since it seems to be your thing. I got the answer I came for."

I didn't reply as he walked across the room and opened the door. He was really just going to leave. I started to say bye, but after that encounter it seemed empty.

Jax stopped and looked back at me. "You've never been hungry. The decisions you've had to make in your life haven't meant life or death. And you've never had to give up something because you had no other choice. Being my brother hasn't been easy. I get that. Having our mother obsess over your future sucks. But you haven't known real fear. It's been easy for you just like it has for me. When someone loves us enough, they'll lie to protect us. Don't forget that," he said before closing the door.

I stood there and let his words replay in my head. Did he think I didn't realize I had been given an easy ride in life? Was that his attempt at brotherly wisdom? I didn't need him telling me my problems were nothing compared to the rest of the world's. And why the hell was he talking about lying to protect someone you love? Who was lying? Him? Mother? Me? I shook my head and jerked the fridge door open, then closed it again.

I was restless. Jax's words were going to eat at me. He had meant something by them. Jax didn't just say shit like that for no reason. I picked up my phone and started to call Sadie. She was the only person in his head. She'd know what he was talking about. But then she'd tell him I'd called.

I scrolled through the names in my phone and my finger hovered over Amanda's name. She'd know about Jess.

No!

I wasn't going to ask about Jess. Hearing about her relationship with Krit was more than I could handle. My heart wasn't anywhere near being ready for that yet. I tossed my phone down and headed for the shower.

Chapter Twenty-Six

JESS

This was the third time this week that Krit had shown up during my shift, causing problems. He had literally dragged me away from one man I was doing a lap dance for while wrapping me up in his jacket. He had cursed a blue streak.

I had begged Delilah to let me handle him and not have him thrown out. She had understood when she found out he was a family friend who was having a hard time dealing with my new job. She had just warned me that it had better not happen again.

So now Krit was coming and paying for all my available times for lap dances and taking me to the back, where he continued to tell me he'd marry me and he could take care of my momma's medical bills. When that hadn't worked, he had pleaded with me to get Medicaid. I had explained that the care Momma would receive wasn't sufficient. Medicaid didn't cover everything she needed, and the medical bills would start piling up soon. I had to strip for several years to pay it off as it stood right now.

Once my shift was finally over, Krit walked me out and to my truck. "I can't fucking stand this anymore, love. You're gonna have to stop. I'm gonna get motherfucking arrested the next time I have to hear one of those horny fuckers talk about your tits and the things they want to do to you."

I liked to pretend those men weren't there and they didn't talk about me or think about me. Hearing Krit tell me only made me feel dirty. My skin was sensitive from my rubbing it raw when I scrubbed myself each night. Even though no one touched me, I could feel their eyes on me. It made me feel cheap and worthless. But I had paid all our bills and I had put down enough on Momma's surgery cost that they were scheduling it now.

"Krit, please. Just stop coming. I wish Rock had never told you. He knows why I'm doing this. He knows I have no other option. You knowing is only making it hard on me. You can come every damn night I work, but I can't stop. I need this money. So just, please, let it go."

Krit kicked my wheel and swore, then let out an angry yell. "This is bullshit! Where's that pretty boy at now? Huh? With all his fucking money? He wanted you, but he ran like hell when things got tough." He pointed at himself. "I'm not running!

Someone has got to give a damn, Jess. Someone has got to fucking give a damn, or you're gonna lose yourself."

I had already lost myself. I hated looking at myself in the mirror. I felt tainted. Knowing my momma had lived my entire life like this broke my heart even more. She had done it for me. This awful, disgusting feeling she had lived with for me. The jaded woman she had become made sense. Men couldn't touch her emotionally because she had cut them off. I understood that now. You had to do it to survive. If you let yourself focus on how they viewed you, it was too hard.

"This is my choice. I made it and I'll live with it. I won't let my momma die! Do you hear me?" I screamed, unable to control my emotions. "I won't let her die! So back the fuck off. I just need you to back off." I jerked the truck door open and climbed inside. I didn't look at Krit as I backed out of the parking lot. I made sure I was far enough away before I let the first tear fall.

Our apartment complex wasn't in the best area of town, but it was cheap. That was what mattered right now. Momma had a gun, and I was pretty damn sure I could use it if I needed to. I reached for my can of Mace as I opened the truck door and kept my finger on the trigger as I jogged up the stairs and to the door that belonged to us. Checking to make sure I was alone, I unlocked the door and hurried inside, then went back to locking the three locks that afforded us some security.

Once I was sure we were safe, I went quietly to the bathroom to get cleaned. Momma was always asleep when I got home, so when I walked inside with my mascara running down my face each night she didn't have to see it.

Turning the water on as hot as it would go, I stripped down and stepped into the small shower, letting the water wash me clean. Closing my eyes, I imagined the dirty that clung to me going down the drain with the water. It was the only way I could cope.

I stayed under the water, soaping myself over and over again, until the water ran cold. The iciness sometimes wasn't enough to send me away. There was a numbness that came with the freezing-cold water. Tonight I didn't stay for that part. I was exhausted mentally and physically. Delilah had mentioned that I had dark circles under my eyes tonight, and then she'd done some makeup magic.

My toes throbbed from the heels we had to wear all night, and I cringed as I walked quietly to the bedroom and crawled into bed. Momma was softly snoring beside me. We hadn't gotten a two-bedroom because this saved us money and because the house we had rented before also came with one of the beds we used—it wasn't ours. Only my bed belonged to us. We hadn't bought another bed when we could both sleep in this one. And once Momma was dealing with the chemo treatments, she would need me close to her at night.

I pulled the covers up to my chin and closed my eyes. It was my favorite part of the day. I could escape and dream now about things out of my reach.

JASON

I needed closure. That had to be it. I couldn't move the fuck on. I couldn't stop thinking about her, and I couldn't stop being so damn angry at everyone. I yelled at most people brave enough to talk to me.

Her truck hadn't been outside her house. No one's car had been there. The place had looked empty. I hadn't gotten out but had instead told Kane to take me to Live Bay. If she wasn't here, someone would be here who knew how I could find her. Before I'd left, I'd called her, but her cell was disconnected. Dwelling on why her number would be disconnected got me so worked up I couldn't focus on the real reason I was here. To end this with her. I needed to see her and tell her exactly what I thought of her, and then I could walk away.

Seeing her again and seeing she wasn't what I had built up in my head would help me deal with forgetting her. She was still sitting on a damn pedestal in my head, and the girl on the phone who had told me she'd slept with Krit didn't match the girl who had told me she loved me. The only way to prove to myself what she really was, was to see her.

I walked into Live Bay, and the jackass she was sleeping with was singing into the microphone. She'd be here. I scanned the crowd for someone I knew, but I didn't see anyone familiar and I didn't see Jess. I stepped through the crowd and looked back at the stage just as the eyeliner-wearing douche looked at me. He stopped singing and squinted his eyes against the stage lights as he stared at me.

I was ready for this. I wanted him to say something to me. I needed one good reason to knock the shit out of him. I took a step forward, and his eyes focused enough to realize it was me he was seeing. I saw one of the band members nudge him, trying to get his attention. He shook his head, not breaking his angry glare he had leveled at me.

He pointed at me. "You!" he roared, jumping off the stage and stalking toward me. I heard the rest of the band behind him as they started moving, but I couldn't look away. What was this guy's problem? He looked ready to murder me. I was the one who had the fucking right to be angry. Not him.

When he reached me, he drew back his fist, and it connected with my jaw in a vision-blurring punch. I staggered backward, unprepared for his swing, but managed to get myself together in time to duck his next swing and take one myself. My fist hit his face with a solid hit.

Two band members grabbed him from behind and the other one stood in front of me, holding up his hands. "Easy," he told me, and I cautiously dropped the fist I had drawn back to take another satisfactory punch. The blood on his lip wasn't enough. I wanted to see him on the fucking floor, unconscious. He'd taken her from me.

"I'm gonna kill him! He's a sorry motherfucker, and I want him dead!" Krit yelled as he fought against the hold the other guys had on him.

"Calm your ass down, Krit. Fighting with Jason ain't helping her. It ain't about him and you know it, so stop putting blame there and go calm the fuck off," Rock said as he stepped beside Krit. "Walk this off," Rock told him.

Krit swung his angry glare back to me. "He left her. Like the spoiled, arrogant piece of shit he is. Didn't even try to help her. She loves that sorry sonuvabitch!"

Rock stepped in front of Krit and said something low enough that I couldn't hear him. I wanted to know what he thought I had done to Jess, because he sure as hell didn't have his facts straight.

"Let him talk," I said. "I want to know what it is I did exactly, 'cause the way I'm looking at it, I was the one who got screwed over," I said to Rock's back, and everyone around us went quiet.

Rock slowly turned around, and his attention was completely focused on me now. "Excuse me?" he said. The warning edge to his voice just added to my confusion. What had Jess told them I had done?

"I didn't do anything to Jess. She slept with him and broke things off with me," I said, pointing at Krit.

"She didn't fucking sleep with me!" Krit roared, fighting to get loose again as they held him back. "She just wanted you! Trust me, I tried like hell, but she only wanted you and you ran, leaving her at the first sign of trouble. What's the deal? A stripper not good enough for you? Being forced to fucking strip to pay her momma's hospital bills too low for your uppity ass?"

"Enough!" Rock said, stopping Krit. "Get him the hell outta here before I shut him up myself."

I no longer cared that Rock was the size and build of a brick wall. I needed to know what the hell Krit was yelling about. "No!" I said, moving toward him. "I want to know what he's saying," I told no one in particular. "Who is stripping to pay her mother's hospital bills?" I stopped as the words coming out of my mouth clicked. "No," I said, shaking my head. They didn't mean . . . *"No!"* He was lying.

Krit looked at me incredulously. "You don't know," he said, almost too quietly. "She didn't fucking tell you." He shook his head and slung off the guys holding him. "Motherfucker!" he roared. "You don't even fucking know!"

I turned to look at Rock, still feeling the horror of what he was saying register in my brain. "What hospital bills?" I managed to ask through the gripping tightness in my throat.

"Her momma's. She's got cancer. They don't have insurance, and she's got to have a mastectomy. They had to move to a cheaper place, and Jess had to get a job that paid the bills and paid the large monthly payment she has to make to the hospital for her mother so she can get the surgery and get chemo."

My chest felt like someone had just dropped a load of fucking bricks on it. "When did she find out?"

"About four weeks ago."

"He doesn't even fucking know," Krit was still ranting. "She told me it wasn't his problem. I thought she was fucking protecting him, but she hadn't even told him."

I looked at him and her story all started to make sense. "She never slept with you four weeks ago." It wasn't a question. I knew the answer.

"Fuck, she wasn't even talking to me four weeks ago. She was too busy escaping town without telling anyone. I ain't had Jess since you took her away from me."

My blood pounded in my head, and I knew I was heaving, as my breathing was difficult. "Where is she?" I asked Rock.

"She's in Mobile at Delilah's," Krit answered instead. "Rock don't know shit. I'm the one who goes there and pays for all the damn lap dances so she doesn't have to give them to those horny-ass men."

The image of Jess's body being on display to a bunch of men was all it took. I turned and took off running.

Chapter Twenty-Seven

JESS

Krit hadn't been back since I had yelled at him outside. I needed to call him and apologize. He hadn't deserved that. And without him here deflecting all the lap dances, I was having to stomach my way through them more and more often.

It was almost my time for the stage. This was the easiest time of night. The lights blinded me, so I couldn't see the men watching. I was all alone up there and dancing for fun. I adjusted the top of the red velvet. My nipple was almost showing, it was cut so low. I would be taking it off soon anyway, but Dee liked us covered when we walked out onstage.

"You're up," the stage manager called, and I checked my lip-stick to make sure it was on correctly before heading up the stairs and to the curtains. The first night I had done this I had been so sick I was afraid I would throw up onstage. But then I'd walked out there and realized I couldn't see them.

The beat started, and I knew it was my cue. I pulled back the curtain and lifted my leg before slowly setting it outside, then let the rest fall back until I was standing there in my costume and stilettos. I heard the usual catcalls and cheers, but I tuned them out. The cool metal of the pole touched my hand as I started my routine and focused on the music.

A loud shout startled me, and then some other noise. I stopped dancing and squinted into the dark room. I could see a man moving through the crowd to the stage, but it was so dark all I could tell was that he was shoving people out of his way. I glanced around, looking for one of the bouncers before he made it to the stage. I had heard horror stories about men climbing onto the stage to get to a dancer. I wasn't sure I'd ever be able to get back up here again after that kind of experience.

I backed up, ready to run offstage, when the stage lights hit the man's face.

Jason.

That wasn't right. Why was Jason here? I watched as he jumped up onto the stage and stalked toward me with a determined look on his face.

He wrapped a coat around me.

"Off the stage, Jess. If you don't want me to take on every damn man in this club, you'll get off this stage for me." His voice was urgent. T.J., one of the club's bouncers, jumped up onstage and started toward Jason. I had to act fast. I pushed him behind me and shook my head at T.J.

"No. He's with me. It's okay. I'll deal with it," I told him, pushing Jason back as I walked backward.

"Garrison wants him out of here," T.J. informed me. I was sure Garrison did, but that wasn't happening. At least, not the way they thought it was.

"If Garrison wants me here, then he'll let me handle this," I replied.

T.J. flicked his gaze back over my shoulder toward Jason, then back at me. "I'll tell him. Hurry," he said.

I nodded and turned to Jason and pushed him backstage with me.

When we were out of view, I stared up at him, trying not to think about how clean he smelled. How unlike me. I started to back away, realizing he was touching me. I was dirty. He didn't need to touch me. His hands tightened on my arms. "You're getting your clothes and we're leaving."

I didn't know why he was here or how he knew where to find me, but I couldn't leave. I would lose my job. I wanted to leave with him. I wanted to look at him and hear him talk. But I couldn't. "I can't. They'll fire me."

"Good, because you're done here," he said, grabbing my hand. "Where is your dressing room?"

"I need this job. You don't understand. This isn't something I'm doing because I want to."

"You think I don't know that?" he interrupted me. "The only reason you're stripping in front of those men is because you're desperate. I've talked to Krit and Rock. I know everything that *you* should have told me." He shook his head. "I can't believe you lied to me. You . . ." He stopped and closed his eyes, then muttered a curse. "I'm gonna beat the shit outta Jax when I see him. He knew."

Jax? What the hell did Jax have to do with this?

"This isn't your problem. It's mine. I had a way to fix it, and I knew you wouldn't be able to handle me stripping, so I did what I had to," I explained.

"Because you were protecting me," he said, staring at me like I had done something noble instead of something degrading.

"If you weren't such a crowd-pleaser, I'd fire you," Dee said from behind me. "We finally get rid of the tattooed guy, and now this? Really? Can't you tell your boyfriends to stay the hell away when you're working?"

I started to explain, but Jason took me and pulled me behind him as if he was protecting me from Dee. "You won't have to deal with it anymore, because she won't be coming back," he said.

Dee cocked an eyebrow and a hip, then looked over his shoulder at me. "Is that so?"

I opened my mouth to say no.

"Yes, it is. Jess is done here," Jason said.

I had to do something. "No, Jason, stop," I said, struggling to get around him. "You can't come in here and do this. I have bills to pay, and this pays them. You can't just—"

"Do you love me, Jess?" he asked, interrupting me.

Why was he asking me this? He knew I loved him. I'd told him that already.

"Do you love me?" he repeated as I stared at him.

"You know I do," I finally replied.

"Say it," he said.

I didn't have time for this. I had said it once and he hadn't said it back. I wasn't saying it again. I had a job to save. "I don't see what that—"

"Say it, Jess," he pleaded, pulling me close to him. His voice had dropped to that sexy deep sound that always made me melt.

"I love you," I said, unable to tell him no.

"I love you more. And I won't let one more man see what belongs to me again. I will take care of it. Everything. Your mother will have the absolute best medical care available. I won't argue with you about it. That's how it's going to be. I'm taking care of you because you're the reason I wake up in the morning, and when you took that reason away from me I was miserable. Fucking miserable. I never want to feel like that again."

"You love me?" I repeated, still stuck on that part of everything he'd just said.

A grin tugged at his lips. "More than life," he said.

"Really?" I asked, needing to hear it again.

"Oh, for chrissake, he said it already. He loves you. Get your clothes and get going. I couldn't figure out why you didn't have a prince charming running after you to save the day." Dee's voice reminded me that we weren't alone. I turned to look at her, and she nodded toward the back door. "Go on. You never belonged here to begin with," she said, and turned to walk away.

"Let's go," Jason said in my ear.

"You can't just pay for my mother's medical bills. It isn't right," I argued. "You don't even have the money. Your mother does, and she hates me. She tried to pay me to break up with you."

"She what?" he asked.

Crap. I hadn't meant to say that. "She, uh . . . The day after you left me last time. She came by my house and offered me money to break up with you and disappear. I didn't take it and I told her no. Then I found out about Momma that night, so she got her wish anyway."

Jason took a deep breath and clenched his teeth. "She offered you money?" he repeated in disbelief.

I just nodded. She was really going to hate me now.

"Why didn't you take it? When you found out about your momma, why didn't you take it? Why did you do this?" he said, looking around him with distaste.

"I couldn't take money to break up with you. I love you. I couldn't do that," I said, thinking that this was self-explanatory.

He didn't say anything at first. He just held me against him. "Let's go," he finally whispered.

"I can't. Your mother won't pay my mother's bills," I reminded him.

"I wouldn't touch my mother's money. Besides, she's about to take a hit to her allowance. Jax owes me, and I have no doubt he's waiting for me to call him with this specific request."

I couldn't have him ask his brother for that kind of money. "No. I won't let you do that. I love that you want to help me, but I can't let you ask your brother to give you that kind of money."

Jason frowned. "Give me? Hell, Jax won't give me shit. He loans me stuff, but he won't be giving me anything. When I turn twenty-three, my grandfather's entire estate will become mine per his last will and testament. Jax is keeping tabs on what I'll owe him in a couple of years, I assure you. But I've got more money in the bank than that rock star brother of mine, and he knows it."

JASON

Jess was wrapped up in my coat and sitting quietly while I drove her truck. She hadn't said much since we'd left the club. Seeing her on that stage and hearing the men around me talking about her tits had all hit me at one time. I had acted on impulse, needing to protect her. Now I had her out of there, it was all starting to sink in, and I wanted to break something.

She should never have had to do that, but it had been her means of survival. It was all she knew to do, and she had been willing to do whatever she had to in order to help her momma. Everything but take money from my mother. Because she loved me.

I wished she had taken the money from my mother. I wouldn't even be mad about it right now. I would have been fucking relieved that she had had money to take care of her mother and that she was still safely in her home.

"Here," she said, breaking the silence, and I glanced at the run-down apartments to my left. It was just getting worse. I pulled into the parking lot, and the darkness surrounding the place from the burnt-out streetlights wasn't helping me deal with this. I turned off the truck and sat there, staring straight ahead.

"How long have you lived here?" I asked.

"A little over three weeks," she said softly.

"What time do you get home at night?"

She fidgeted with her hands in her lap. "About three," she finally said.

She was fine. Nothing had happened to her. She was alive. I kept reminding myself over and over again that she was okay.

"Jason?" Her voice sounded unsure.

I shifted my gaze to hers. "Yeah."

"I carry Mace with me when I go from the truck to the apartment, and Momma has a gun. There are three locks on the door," she said, trying to reassure me.

"Let me get your door," I told her, and opened the truck door. Kane had already parked the limo and was walking over to us. He was going to make sure we made it safely inside. Even Kane saw the danger here. It wasn't just me being over-protective.

"I'm getting them out of here tomorrow," I told him as I walked over to get her door.

"Good" was his single response.

I opened her door and helped her down. She pulled the coat tightly around her and let me lace my fingers through hers as she led me up the stairs and then to the far corner of the build-ing. She opened the door. I had prepared myself for the inside, but seeing it was still hard to deal with.

"I need to get a shower," she said, looking around unsure of what I was planning on doing. The small room with one sofa had a mini kitchen attached to it. Then two doors. One had to be the bedroom and the other the bathroom. They were sharing a room.

"Go take a shower. I'll be out here," I told her, nodding to the sofa.

"It takes me a while. I like to get ... clean," she said, the last word so soft I almost missed it. The meaning behind her words made my heart feel as if it had exploded. She thought she was dirty.

"Okay," I said, and when she turned to go to the bathroom, I followed behind her. She glanced back at me when she reached the door.

"What are you doing?"

"I'm going to bathe you," I told her, and didn't wait for her to say anything more. I stepped into the bathroom and found the light switch. The small room had a tiny shower in the corner.

"It's too small for both of us," she said.

"I don't need to get in to bathe you," I told her, and opened the shower curtain. "Take off your clothes, Jess. Let me do this."

She slipped my coat off her shoulders and hung it on the door. "Why?" she asked as she went to a button on her shirt.

"Why am I going to bathe you?" I asked her, reaching for her shirt and unbuttoning it and slipping it off her.

She nodded and let me take over the job of undressing her.

"Because I'm going to make sure you know by the time I'm finished just how perfect and beautiful you are. I intend to wash all those bad memories off of you with my hands. We're going to leave them here. We won't be taking that with us."

Her eyes filled with tears, and I stopped unzipping her skirt. "I love you," she said, then grinned through her tears.

"I love you more," I replied, and let her skirt fall to the floor.

"It's time you felt safe. I intend to make sure you feel that way every day of your life."

Her eyes widened and I tugged her panties down. She stepped out of them, and I took her hand and walked her to the shower before turning the warm water on. "Let me know if it's too hot," I told her as she stepped inside.

"I like it as hot as it gets."

I reached out and touched the smooth skin on her arm. "That would burn your skin," I said, stroking the soft flesh.

"It washes the dirty away," she said simply.

I reached for the soap. "I'll wash it away. No scalding water needed," I told her as I lathered my hands, then placed them on her shoulders and began massaging her body, slowly worshipping her with each touch.

Chapter Twenty-Eight

JESS

I opened my eyes to see my momma drinking a cup of coffee and staring down at me. She took a drink while I rubbed at my eyes and rolled back to find Jason no longer curled up against me on the sofa.

"Relax. Your white knight is outside on the phone dealing with our moving arrangements. He didn't want to wake you."

I sat up and looked out the small window. I could see Jason's back as he stood there, talking on the phone. "Moving?" I asked.

"Yep. Glad we didn't get around to unpacking most of the boxes, not that all that shit would've fit."

"Where are we moving?" I asked her.

"Not sure. He's been making all kinds of plans. I could only hear bits and pieces, but it sounds like they have the best doctors for my surgery and treatment in New York City. He's moving you to be with me there. Then when I'm finished and have a clean bill of health, he's making arrangements for me to have a nice gulf-front condo, and you'll be with him."

She had been listening to everything he said. "Not sure? Sounds like you know exactly what he's doing," I told her.

She shrugged. "He's right outside the window, and he talks loud. He also isn't a fan of this place. It makes him get all loud and angry when he mentions it."

I ran a hand through my hair, trying to smooth it before walking to the door.

"Stop fussing with your hair. The boy is so sunk it ain't even funny. I walked in here this morning to find him watching you sleep."

Smiling, I opened the door and stepped outside.

Jason turned his head to me. "Yeah, I want it done today. Let me know when it's handled. I have movers on their way now." He didn't say bye before ending his call and slipping the phone into his pocket and closing the distance between us. "Good morning, sleepyhead," he teased, then pressed a gentle kiss to my lips.

"Good morning," I said, wishing he would kiss me like I wasn't about to break. He had treated me so tenderly last night, and now this. The memory of last night was one I would never forget, but that was then. I wasn't fragile.

"We've got a lot to talk about, but right now why don't you go get dressed and I'll take you and your mother to breakfast."

Letting him handle everything was easy, but it wasn't right. Handing all my problems over to him wasn't what this relationship was about. "What about the movers?" I asked, not sure where to start.

"They're coming to pack your things and move them to Jax's place in Sea Breeze for now."

"We can't stay at Jax's place," I said, thinking about his mother showing back up again. There was a good chance my momma would scratch her eyes out.

"We're only staying tonight. We leave for New York in the morning, and your mother's surgery is scheduled for the next day, with the best surgeon money can buy. Her recovery and chemo will also be held there, and you're staying in the penthouse we stayed in when we were there together. It's reserved for Jax when he needs it. He's already got it booked for you and your mother. When she's ready, her things will be waiting for her in a two-bedroom gulf-front condo at the Turquoise Place. Complete with maid service."

"Jason, you can't."

"I can and I'm going to. I told you I was taking care of you. Let me do that."

"Buying my momma a condo is going a little overboard," I said.

"I have an ulterior motive," he said, bending his head so he could press a kiss to my neck. "If your momma is happy and secure, I can convince you to move in with me. I've got my own apartment in Boston and no roommates. I don't want to leave you for entire weeks at a time, and if I have you with me, I can focus on actually passing my classes."

This all sounded too perfect. "What happens when you get tired of me or you realize I'm not cut out for your future?"

"I'll never get tired of you. In fact, the more I'm around you the crazier I get about you. And what future of mine are you not cut out for?"

"I wasn't raised to be a politician's wife like Johanna," I said.

Jason chuckled and took a nip at my earlobe. "Thank God, because I'm not letting a politician near my woman. Can't trust the bastards."

I tilted my head so he had to look at me instead of kissing my ear. "I'm talking about you," I said.

He nodded. "Oh, right. More of my mother's talk, I assume. Well, let me assure you that I don't intend to ever be a politician. Not interested in it and never will be."

He didn't want to be a politician. I wasn't hindering his career. "Then my history as a stripper won't hurt you in the future?" I asked, hating to point out an obvious concern.

He laughed and ran his thumb over my bottom lip. "Stop worrying, Jess. The only thing that can hurt my future is if you don't agree to move in with me, because I can't concentrate without you near me."

I wanted this. All of it.

"Is this for real?" I asked him.

The door to the apartment opened. "I'm starving, and he said he was gonna feed me. Go get your clothes on and deal with the fact that you got that fairy tale you wanted," Momma said with a wink, and turned to walk back inside, then stopped and laughed before looking back at me. "Guess in the end it was Logan after all. And all this time I assumed it would be Jess who won Rory in the end. Huh. I was wrong. I'll be damned. I need to go rewatch that last season and see where I missed it."

When she closed the door behind her, I turned back to Jason. His frown was directed at me. "Who is Logan?"

I covered my mouth to muffle the laugh I couldn't hold back and shook my head.

Jason's frown wavered. He couldn't figure out why I thought this was so funny, which only made me laugh harder.

"Logan, Jess. Who is Logan?" he repeated.

I managed to control my laughter and wiped the tears from my eyes. "He is Rory Gilmore's wealthy boyfriend," I managed to get out over another giggle.

"Rory who?"

"Gilmore. My mother thinks all life's problems can be solved via *Gilmore Girls*," I said, and his confused expression was still there. "You do know what *Gilmore Girls* is, don't you?"

He shook his head.

"A television show. It ran for, like, seven seasons," I explained.

Jason looked back at the apartment door Momma had walked into. "I'm so confused."

I just laughed again and pressed a kiss to his lips.

JASON

Jess stood in my bedroom at Jax's beach house, looking out the window and smiling. I walked into the room and wrapped my arm around her. She loved me, and she trusted me to take care of her. I followed her gaze outside and saw her mother in a skimpy bikini lying out at the pool.

"She might be enjoying herself just a little too much," Jess said, the amusement in her voice clear.

"I can see where you got those excellent genes," I replied, and a small elbow jabbed me in the stomach. "Ow," I said, laughing.

"Don't go checking my momma out. I know she still looks good in a bikini," she said.

"She's hot for her age. That's all I'm saying. You by far have the more rocking body," I assured her, turning her around in my arms. "And I can't seem to stop touching it."

Jess looked up at me through her lashes. "You've been holding me. Not touching me," she said.

She continued to stare at me with that sexy pout, then stuck her tongue out and let it run over her bottom lip. "Sit down, Jason," she said, and shoved me back until the backs of my legs hit the chair behind me.

"Turn on your music," she said, handing me my iPhone.

"What are you doing?" I managed to ask as she bent forward and ran her hands up my thighs.

"Turn on the music. Something sexy," she said, standing back up so that her cleavage was right under my nose.

I couldn't take my eyes off her. I was afraid I would miss something. I glanced down until I found Nelly and clicked "Hot in Herre," then sent it to the speakers in my room before dropping my phone.

Jess grinned wickedly at my song choice and started moving her hips in ways that should be illegal as she slowly began removing her clothing. I wanted to help her and get her naked fast, but her eyes stayed locked on me as she danced, making it hard for me to move. I was fascinated. Nothing had ever been this sexy. Ever.

I could hear myself panting as each piece of clothing fell to the ground forgotten. When she wiggled out of her panties, I started to reach for her, but she held up her hand and shook her finger. "No, no," she said, and kicked open my legs. She moved between them and grabbed the back of the chair and began giving me a lap dance.

"You get to touch," she whispered in my ear as her hard nipples brushed against my chin.

"Does that make me special?" I asked, playing along.

"Very, very special," she said, pressing a kiss to my lips.

"Good, because I don't think I'm gonna last through the entire song," I told her.

"Then don't," she said, grinning at me and biting her bottom lip.

I reached up and cupped her face with my hands. "Give me that lip," I said, pulling it into my mouth and enjoying the plumpness of it before tasting her. She sank down onto my lap and gave up all pretense of dancing when she wrapped her arms around my neck.

I had never expected to fall in love, but then, I'd never imagined anyone like Jess. She was one beautiful contradiction. The idea of letting someone else own my heart wasn't appealing. It sounded weak and foolish. Something meant for the words of a song. I was wrong. When I thought about my future now, Jess was all that I could see, and that was all I needed. I couldn't ask for more.

Want to find out how Jax met Sadie?
Here's a sneak peek at

breathe

Prologue

SADIE

Life has always been a struggle for me. From what I could tell, it wasn't daisies for everyone else, either. But I never let go of the fantasy that one day I wouldn't feel so alone and isolated from the rest of the normal world. My dream was what kept me going many nights when I fought the desire to just disappear. It would be easier if I'd never been born.

I'm positive my mother sees things the same way. I know what you're thinking, and no, she never said those words, but my entrance into the world dramatically changed the course of her life.

My mother had been a beauty queen in the small Arkansas town where she'd grown up. Everyone said she would make it big someday. Maybe her beauty and charm somehow would have opened those doors if she hadn't met the man who helped give me life. The fact is, she ran off to become a star and fell in love with a very married man. A man who didn't acknowledge me or help her for fear of tarnishing his social standing in the big city of Nashville, Tennessee.

A one-room shack in the hills of Tennessee is where my mother and I spent the first part of my life. Until the day she up and decided life would be easier in Alabama. On the southern coast, my mother—who I now call Jessica—could find work. And the sunshine would be good for us, or so she said. I knew she needed an escape, or maybe just a place to start over. If anyone could be a magnet for losers, Jessica fit the profile. Unfortunately, she was about to bring another child into the unstable life she managed to lead, where she greatly relied on someone else—me—to handle things. If only she had let me make her decisions for her in the dating world, like she did with the rest of her life. But, alas, we were headed to southern Alabama, where the sun is supposed to shine bright and wash away all our worries. . . . Yeah, right.

Chapter One

JAX

This was it. Finally. The last stop on my tour. I shoved open the door to my private suite, and Kane, my bodyguard, closed it firmly behind me. The screaming on the other side of the door had only made my head hurt. This had been fun once. Now all I could think about was getting away from it. The girls. The relentless schedule. The lack of sleep and the pressure. I wanted to be someone else. Anywhere else.

The door opened and quickly closed behind me. I sank down onto the black leather sectional sofa and watched my younger brother, Jason, as he grinned at me with two beers in his hands.

"It's over," he announced. Only Jason understood my feelings lately. He'd been with me through this crazy ride. He saw my parents' need to push me and my need to push back. He was my best friend. My only friend, really. I gave up trying to figure out who liked me for my money and fame a long time ago. It was pointless.

Jason handed me a beer and sat down on the sofa. "You killed it out there. The place was insane. No one would ever guess you were looking forward to running off to Alabama in the morning to hide away all summer."

My agent, Marco, had told my parents about the private island on the Alabama coast. They were so ready to have somewhere other than our house in LA that they'd jumped at the idea.

Going back to my hometown—Austin, Texas—hadn't been something they wanted to do. Too many people knew who we were.

The security Sea Breeze offered had always allowed me the freedom I'd lost when the world had embraced me. For a few weeks every summer we were a family again. I was just another guy, and I could walk out to the water and enjoy it without cameras and fans. No autographs. Just peace. Tomorrow we were headed back there. It was our summer break. But this year I was staying the whole damn summer. I didn't care what my mother or my agent thought I should do. I was hiding out for three months, and they could all kiss Marco's ass. What had started as my mother's insistence that we spend the summers together in Alabama had become mine. I needed time with just them. I rarely saw them the rest of the year. It was the only house we had to call ours. I had my house in LA, and my parents and Jason had theirs.

"You're coming down, right?" I asked him.

Jason nodded. "Yeah. I'll be there, but not tomorrow. I need a few days. Mom and I had an argument about college. I want to give it a few days before I face her again. She's driving me crazy."

Our mother was a micromanager when it came to our lives. "Good idea. I'll talk to her. Maybe I can get her to back off."

Jason laid his head back on the leather. "Good luck. She's on a mission to make me miserable."

Lately I felt like she was doing the same to me. I no longer lived with her. I lived independently. I was the one who paid her bills. Why she thought she could still tell me what to do was beyond me. But she did. She always thought she knew what was best. I was done with that, and so was Jason. I'd talk to her, all right. She needed to remember who was actually in control here and back off.

"Take a few days. Enjoy yourself. Let me prep Mom for the fact that I'm not going to allow her to control your life. Then come south," I told him before taking a long drink of my beer.

SADIE

"Mom, are you going to work today?" I rolled my eyes at my very pregnant mother, who lay sprawled out on her bed in her panties and bra. Pregnancy made Jessica an even bigger drama queen than before having unsafe sex with another loser.

She moaned and covered her head with a pillow. "I feel awful, Sadie. You just go on without me."

I'd seen this coming a mile away before school even let out. The last day of school landed yesterday, but instead of being able to go out and be a normal teenager, I was expected to make the money for us. It was almost as if Jessica had planned on me working in her place all along.

"I can't just go to your workplace and take your position. Haven't you explained the situation to them? They won't be okay with your seventeen-year-old daughter doing your job."

She pulled the pillow from her face and tossed me a sulk she'd perfected years ago. "Sadie, I can't continue cleaning house with my stomach the size of a beach ball. I'm so hot and tired. I need you to help me. You can do it. You always figure stuff out."

I walked over to the air conditioner and turned it off. "If you'd stop running it at a continuous sixty-eight degrees, we might be able to get by on less money. Do you have any idea how much it costs to run a window unit all day long?" I knew she didn't know, nor did she care, but I still asked.

She grimaced and sat up. "Do you have any idea how hot I am with all this extra weight?" she shot back at me.

It took all my restraint to keep from reminding her that she got this way because she hadn't used a condom. I bought them for her and made sure her purse always contained several. I even reminded her before she went out on dates.

Remembering who the adult was in our relationship could be difficult at times. Most of the time it seemed to me our roles were reversed. Being the adult, however, did not mean she made smart decisions, because Jessica simply did not know how to be responsible.

"I know you're hot, but we can't spend every dime we make on the air conditioner," I reminded her.

She sighed and flopped back down on the bed. "Whatever," she grumbled.

I walked over to her purse and opened it up. "All right, I'm going to go to your job today, by myself, and I hope they allow me inside the gate. If this doesn't work, don't say I didn't warn you. All I am qualified for is minimum-wage jobs, which won't pay our bills. If you would come with me, I would have a better chance of landing this position." I knew as I spoke the words that I'd already been tuned out. At least she had managed to keep the job for two months.

"Sadie, you and I both know you can handle it by yourself."

I sighed in defeat and left her there. She would go back to sleep as soon as I left. I wanted to be mad at her, but seeing her so big made me pity her instead. She wasn't the best mom in the world, but she did belong to me. After I got my clothes on, I walked past her room and peeked through the door. She softly snored with the window unit once again cranked to sixty-eight degrees. I thought about turning it off, but changed my mind. The apartment already felt warm, and the day would only get hotter.

I stepped outside and got on my bike. It took me thirty minutes to get to the bridge. The bridge would take me from Sea Breeze, Alabama, onto the exclusive island that was connected to it. The island wasn't where the locals lived, but where the wealthy came for the summer. Jessica had managed to snag a job as a domestic servant at one of the houses that employed full staffs. The pay was twelve dollars an hour. I prayed I would be able to take over her position without a hitch.

I found the address on her employee card I'd retrieved from her purse. My chances of getting this job were slim. The farther I pedaled onto the island, the larger and more extravagant the houses became. The address of my mother's place of employment was coming up. She, of course, had to work at the most extravagant house on the block, not to mention the very last one before the beach. I pulled up to a large ornate iron gate and handed Jessica's ID card to the guy working admittance. He frowned and gazed down at me. I handed him my driver's license.

"I'm Jessica's White's daughter. She's sick, and I'm supposed to work for her today."

He continued to frown while he picked up a phone and

called someone. That wasn't a good thing, considering no one here knew I was coming in her place. For good. Two large men appeared and walked up to me. Both sported dark sunglasses and looked like they should be wearing football uniforms and playing on NFL teams instead of black suits.

"Miss White, can we see your bag, please," one of them said, rather than asked, while the other one took it off my shoulder.

I swallowed and fought the urge to shudder. They were big and intimidating and didn't appear to trust me. I wondered if I seemed dangerous to them, all five feet six inches of me. I glanced down at my skimpy white shorts and purple tank top and wondered if they'd considered the fact that it would be impossible to hide weapons in this outfit. I thought it somewhat strange that the two big guys were reluctant to let me in. Even if I happened to be a threat, I do believe either one of them could have taken me blindfolded with his hands tied behind his back. The image popped into my mind and made me want to laugh. I bit my bottom lip and waited to see if dangerous little me would be allowed entrance through the bigger-than-life iron gates.

"You're free to enter, Miss White. Please take the servants' entrance to the left of the stone wall and report to the kitchen, where you will be instructed how to proceed."

Who were these people who needed two men the size of Goliath to guard their entrance? I got back on my bike and rode through the now open gates. Once I made it around the corner, past lush palm trees and tropical gardens, I saw the house. It reminded me of houses on *MTV Cribs*. I never would've guessed houses like this even existed in Alabama. I'd been to Nashville once and seen houses similar in size, but nothing quite this spectacular.

I composed myself and pushed my bike around the corner, trying to not stop and stare at the massive size of everything. I leaned my bike against a wall, out of sight. The entrance for the servants was designed to impress. At least twelve feet tall, the door was adorned with a beautifully engraved letter *S*. Not just tall, the door was really heavy, causing me to use all my strength to pull it open. I peeked inside the large entry hall and stepped into a small area with three different arched doorways ahead of me to choose from. Since I'd never been here before, I didn't know where the kitchen might be located. I walked up to the first door on the right and looked through the opening. It appeared to be a large gathering room, but nothing fancy and no kitchen appliances, so I moved on to door number two, peeked inside, and found a large round table with people sitting around it. A large older lady stood in front of a stove unlike any I'd ever seen in a house. It was something you'd find in a restaurant.

This had to be the place. I stepped through the arched opening.

The lady standing noticed me and frowned. "Can I help you?" she asked in a sharp, authoritative tone, though she kind of reminded me of Aunt Bee from *The Andy Griffith Show*.

I smiled, and the heat rose, threatening to spike out the top of my head as I watched all the people in the room turn to face me. I hated attention and did whatever I could to draw little to myself. Even though it seemed to be getting harder the older I got. As much as possible, I tried to avoid situations that encouraged other people to speak to me. It's not that I'm a recluse; it's just the fact that I have a lot of responsibility. I figured out early in life that friendships would never work for me. I'm too busy taking care of my mom. So I've perfected the art of being uninteresting.

"Um, uh, yes, I was told to report to the kitchen for further instructions." I quietly cleared my voice and waited.

I didn't like the once-over the lady gave me, but since I was here, I had no choice but to stay.

"I know *I* sure didn't hire you. Who told you to come here?"

I hated all those eyes on me and wished Jessica hadn't been so stubborn. I needed her here, at least for today. Why did she always do these things to me?

"I'm Sadie White, Jessica White's daughter. She . . . uh . . . wasn't well today, so I am here to work for her. I'm . . . uh . . . supposed to be working with her this summer."

I wished I didn't sound so nervous, but the people stared. The lady up front frowned much like the way Aunt Bee looked when someone made her angry. It was tempting to turn and run.

"Jessica didn't ask about you helping her this summer, and I don't hire kids. It ain't a good idea with the family comin' down for the whole summer. Maybe during the fall when they leave we can give you a try."

My nervousness from being the center of attention immediately disappeared, and I panicked at the thought of our losing this income we so desperately needed. If my mom found out I couldn't work for her, she would quit. I pulled my grown-up voice out of the closet and decided I needed to show this lady I could do the job better than anyone else.

"I can understand your concern. However, if you would give me a chance, I can and will show you I'm an asset. I'll never be late to work and will always complete the jobs assigned to me. Please, just a chance."

The lady glanced down at someone at the table as if to get an opinion. She moved her eyes back up to me, and I could see I'd broken through her resolve. "I'm Ms. Mary, and I'm in charge of the household staff and I run the kitchen. You impress me and you have the job. Okay, Sadie White, your chance starts now. I'm gonna team you up with Fran here, who has been working in this home as long as I have. She'll instruct you and report back to me. I will have you an answer at the end of the day. Here is your trial, Miss White. I suggest you don't blow it."

I nodded and smiled over at Fran, who was now standing.

"Follow me," the tall, skinny redhead who appeared to be

at least sixty-five years old said before she turned and left the room.

I did as instructed without making eye contact with any of the others. I had a job to save.

Fran walked me down a hallway and past several doors. We stopped, opened one, and stepped inside. The room contained shelves of books from the floor to the ceiling. Large dark-brown leather chairs were scattered around the room. None faced any of the others or looked to be used for any type of visiting or socializing. The room was clearly set up to be a library. A place where people could come, find a book, and lose themselves in one of the large cushy chairs.

Fran swung her arm out in front of her, gesturing to the room with a bit of flair. It surprised me coming from an older lady. "This is Mrs. Stone's favorite spot. It's been closed off all year. You will dust the books and shelves, clean the leather with the special cleaner, and clean the windows. Vacuum the drapes; clean and wax the floors. This room must shine. Mrs. Stone likes things perfect in her sanctuary. I will come get you at lunchtime, and we will dine in the kitchen."

She walked to the door, and I heard her thank someone. She stepped back inside, pulling a cart full of cleaning supplies. "This will have everything you need. Be careful with all framed artwork and sculptures. I warn you, everything in this house is very valuable and must be treated with the utmost care. Now, I expect you to work hard and not waste any time with foolishness." The tight-faced Fran left the room.

I circled around, taking in the extravagance of my surroundings. The room wasn't really big; it just seemed full. I could clean this. I hadn't been asked to do anything impossible. I went for the dusting supplies and headed to the ladder connected to the bookshelves. I might as well start at the top, since dust falls.

I managed to get everything dusted and the windows cleaned before Fran returned to get me for lunch. I needed a break and some food. Her frowning face was a welcome sight. She moved her gaze around the room and nodded before leading me in silence back down the same path I'd taken this morning. The smell of fresh-baked bread hit me as we rounded the corner and stepped into the large, bright kitchen. Ms. Mary stood over the stove, pointing to a younger lady, who wore her hair in a bun covered with a hairnet just like Ms. Mary's.

"Smells good, Henrietta. I believe you've got it. We will test this batch out on the help today, and if everyone likes it, you can take over the bread baking for the family's meals." Ms. Mary turned, wiping her hands on her apron. "Ah, here is our new employee now. How are things going?"

Ms. Fran nodded and said, "Fine."

Either this lady didn't smile much or she just didn't like me.

"Sit, sit. We have much to get done before the family arrives."

I sat down after Fran did, and Ms. Mary set trays of food in front of us. I must have been doing something right since Fran directed her words in my direction. "All the help eat at this table. We all come at different shifts for lunch. You may choose what you want to eat."

I nodded and reached for the tray of sandwiches and took one. I took some fresh fruit from a platter.

"The drinks are over there on the bar. You may go choose from what's there or fix something yourself."

I went over and poured some lemonade. I ate in silence while I listened to Ms. Mary direct Henrietta as they baked bread. Neither Fran nor I made any attempt at conversation.

After we were done, I followed Fran to the sink, where we rinsed our plates and loaded them into the large dishwasher ourselves. Just as silent, we returned to the library. I was a little less nervous now and more interested in my surroundings. I noticed the portraits as we walked down the hallway. There were portraits of two very cute little boys. The farther I walked, the older they seemed to get. Toward the arched entrance that led to the hallway where the library was located, an oddly familiar face smiled down at me from a life-size painting. A face I'd seen many times on television and in magazines. Just last night during dinner he had been on television. Jessica watched *Entertainment Daily* during our meal. Teen rocker and heartthrob Jax Stone was one of their favorite topics. Last night he'd had on his arm a girl rumored to be in his new music video. Fran stopped behind me. I turned to her, and she seemed focused on the portrait.

"This is his summer home. He will be arriving with his parents and brother tomorrow. Can you handle this?"

I simply nodded, unable to form words from the shock of seeing Jax Stone's face on the wall.

Fran moved again, and I followed her into the library. "He's the reason teenagers are not hired. This is a private escape for him. When he was younger, his parents insisted he take a break each summer and spend time with them away from the bright lights of Hollywood. Now he's older and still comes here for the summer. He leaves now and then to go to different events, but for the most part, this is his getaway. He brings his family with him since they don't see each other much during the year." Fran paused dramatically and then continued. "If you can't handle it, you will be fired immediately. His privacy is of the utmost importance. It's why this is such a high-paying job."

I straightened and grabbed the bucket I'd been using. "I can handle anything. This job is more important to me than a teenage rock star."

Fran nodded, but from her frown, I could see she didn't believe me.

I focused more energy into my work. At the end of a long day, I listened while the quiet, frowning Fran reported to Ms. Mary. She believed I would be a good worker and I should be given a chance. I thanked her and Ms. Mary. I figured I should be able to save enough money for the fall, when my mom would have the baby and not work, and I would be back in school. I could do this.

Yes, Jax Stone was famous, had incredible steel-blue eyes, and happened to be one of the most beautiful creations known to man. I made myself admit that much. However, everyone knows beauty is only skin deep. I assumed the shallowness radiating off of him would be so revolting I wouldn't care that I cleaned his house and passed him in the halls.

Besides, guys were a species I knew nothing about. I never took the time to talk to one even when they did their best to talk to me. I've always had bigger problems in life, like making sure we ate and my mom remembered to pay our bills.

When I thought of all the money I'd wasted on the condoms I'd shoved into Jessica's hands and purse before she went out with the countless men who flocked to her, I really had a hard time not getting angry with her. Even in thrift-store clothing, she looked gorgeous. One of her many disgusting men told me I'd inherited the cursed looks. From her curly blond hair to her clear blue eyes and heavy black lashes, I somehow managed to get it all. However, I had the one thing I knew would save me from certain disaster: My personality came across as rather dull. It was something my mother loved to remind me of, yet instead of being upset by it, I held on to it for dear life. What she thought of as a character defect, I liked to think of as my lifeline. I didn't want to be like her. If having a dull personality kept me from following in her footsteps, then I would embrace it.

The apartment we lived in for almost five hundred a month sat underneath a huge old house. I walked in after my first day of work to find that Jessica wasn't inside. With only four rooms, she couldn't have gotten far.

"Mom?" I got no answer.

The sun was setting, so I stepped out onto what Jessica referred to as a patio. If you ask me, it was really more like a small piece of slab. She loved coming out here to look out over the water. She stood out in the yard with her increasing stomach on view for all to see, in a bikini I'd bought at a thrift store a few weeks ago. She turned and smiled. The facade of sickness from this morning no longer appeared on her face. Instead, she seemed to be glowing.

"Sadie, how did it go? Did ol' Ms. Mary give you a hard time? If she did, I sure hope you were nice. We need this job, and you can be so rude and unsociable."

I listened to her blabber on about my lack of social skills and waited until she finished before I spoke. "I got the job for the summer if I want it."

Jessica sighed dramatically in relief. "Wonderful. I really need to rest these next few months. The baby is taking so much out of me. You just don't understand how hard it is to be pregnant."

I wanted to remind her I'd tried to keep her from getting pregnant by sacrificing food money to buy her some stupid condoms, which didn't help at all! However, I nodded and walked inside with her.

"I'm starving, Sadie. Is there anything you can fix up real fast? I'm eating for two these days."

I'd already planned what we would eat for dinner before I got home. I knew Mom was helpless in the kitchen. I'd somehow survived the early years of my life on peanut butter and jelly sandwiches. Somewhere around the time I turned eight, I realized my mother needed help, and I began growing up quicker than normal children. The more I offered to take on, the more she gave me. By the time I turned eleven, I did it all.

With the noodles boiling and the meat sauce simmering, I went to my room. I slipped out of my work clothes and into a pair of thrift-store cutoff jean shorts, which happen to be the core of my wardrobe, and a T-shirt. My wardrobe was simple.

The timer for the noodles went off, letting me know the food needed to be checked. Jessica wasn't going to get up and help out anytime soon. I hurried back into the small kitchen, took out a spaghetti noodle on a fork, and slung it at the wall behind the stove. It stuck. It was ready.

"Really, Sadie, why you toss noodles on the wall is beyond me. Where did you get such an insane idea?"

I flipped my gaze up and over at Jessica. She was kicked back on the faded pastel couch, which had come with the apartment, in my bikini.

"I saw it on the television once when I was younger. It has stuck with me ever since. Besides, it works."

"It's disgusting, is what it is," Jessica mumbled from her spot on the couch.

She couldn't boil water if she wanted to, but I decided to bite my tongue and finish with dinner.

"It's ready, Mom," I said as I scooped a pile of spaghetti onto a plate, knowing she would ask me to bring her one.

"Bring me a plate, will ya, honey?"

I smirked. I was a step ahead of her. She rarely got up these days unless she absolutely had to. I slipped a fork and spoon onto the plate and took it to her. She didn't even sit up. Instead, she placed it on the shelf of a belly she'd developed, and ate. I placed a glass of sweet iced tea down beside her and went back to fix my own plate. I'd worked up an appetite today. I needed food.

ABBI GLINES is the *New York Times, USA Today,* and *Wall Street Journal* bestselling author of the Sea Breeze, Vincent Boys, Existence, and Rosemary Beach series. A devoted booklover, Abbi lives with her family in Alabama. She maintains a Twitter addiction at @AbbiGlines and can also be found at facebook.com/AbbiGlinesAuthor and AbbiGlines.com.

Jax Stone ♡ Sadie
breathe

Krit ♡ Blythe
bad for you

Jason Stone ♡ Jess
misbehaving

the
Sea Breeze
series
Abbi Glines

just for now
Preston ♡ Amanda

hold on tight
Dewayne ♡ Sienna

because of low
Marcus ♡ Willow

while it lasts

sometimes it lasts
Cage ♡ Eva

fallen too far

never too far

forever too far

rush too far
(book 1 from his POV)

Blaire ♡ Rush

twisted perfection

simple perfection

Woods ♡ Della

the
Rosemary Beach
series
Abbi Glines

Grant ♡ Harlow

take a chance

one more chance

Tripp ♡ Bethy

you were mine
(publishing Dec' 14)

when I'm gone
(publishing April' 15)